Adam's Apple

(Touch of Tantra #1)

by Liv Morris

Wendi,
Thanks for all the
wonderful support!
Liv
Morris
XOXO

Digital Edition: July 2013

Cover Design by Sarah Hansen of Okaycreations.net

Cover image: iStockphoto/Katarina Sokolova

Edited by Lauren Schmelz, Write Divas Editing

ISBN-13: 978-1490907154

Dedication

Dedicated to my sweet Nomad

Acknowledgements

A big thank you to my family for their constant encouragement. This book wouldn't have been possible without your support.

Humongous hugs to the most wonderful friends a gal could have. Thank you for cheering me on while I wrote this book. Kelly, Taylor, Michelle, TOM, Pammie, Becca, Dee, Jada, Marla, Kathryn, Lauren, Terry, Lesley and Betsy.

Prologue

April 23rd, 2005. Laurel Hill Cemetery, Philadelphia, PA.

The sky shines a crisp, azure blue, but my heart is a lifeless gray and quickly turning as black as the muddied dirt I'm holding in my hands. I squeeze my fingers so tightly into a fist that my hand begins to shake and bits of grit embed into my palms.

The task set before me is customary and very common among men. But the woman I mourn today was anything but common. She was brilliant, wise, and beautiful.

Now she's gone. . . Forever.

Sorrow will no longer consume her heart and soul. Instead it passes on to me.

I toss the black dirt into the dark and musty grave and fall to my knees. The eerie hollow sound of the clumps of dirt hitting the wood below is more than I can bear.

The tears I've been suppressing for days now fall freely down my face like a dam's flood after a breach. An unrestrained sorrow pours out of me, and the whirl of emotions I've hidden within myself is no longer concealed. My grief is freed as I realize all I love is now six feet below me, but it might as well be a million miles away. The distance will never be broached this side of heaven as she is God's angel now.

Returning to the hearse, I see a man's face in the distance. We make eye contact before he raises the tinted window of his black limo. His vehicle pulls away, disappearing into the morning's mist. Anger rises above my grief because he has no right to be anywhere near this solemn ceremony.

He's the bastard who slowly and silently destroyed the woman I'm leaving behind today in this cold and wet cemetery. She was my mother . . . My selfless life-giver, and I owe her everything.

Chapter 1

My legs feel as heavy as lead pipes, but somehow they carry me through the marbled lobby to the sidewalk outside of my office high rise. I find myself standing on grimy concrete with the New York City rain pelting me, staining my yellow silk tie. I am numb to nature's onslaught, as my thoughts remain at the conference table forty stories above—where the last meeting of the day still haunts me.

My head of corporate security had informed me that my trusted partner and friend, Simon Edwards, betrayed me by stabbing me in the back. My stomach almost retches as I think about his deceit. I've known him since our freshman year at MIT fourteen years ago. Through random selection, we'd shared a dorm room together. We weren't extremely close because we were polar opposites and different personality types. Especially when it came to dealing with people. Basically, I tolerated them and he didn't. But we formed a common respect for one another during our college years and beyond. Maybe it was our desire to make our mark in the business world, as we both had something to prove to the fathers we hated. It was likely the only thing we had in common.

After graduating college, four of us from MIT, including Simon, headed to New York City and formed Kings Capital, largely using the inheritance I received after my mother's death. It served as the company's seed money and positioned me as the company's head. Although Simon seldom made his way to the boardroom, his presence there was felt by us all. We'd relied on his genius mind to design a way around any obstacle or shortcoming we found in our software ventures. We capitalized on so many deals thanks to Simon. We had a saying among the board, "If Simon says so, we buy."

Never in a million years would I have thought he'd try to sell me out. When others said my dreams were impossible or if a wall was placed in my way, he was my go-to man. Now he was the wall. Simon was caught trying to sell me out by giving away corporate secrets to another company. My corporate secrets. Secrets stained with my own blood, sweat, and fears. Although I was assured our company secrets never touched any outsiders' hand, his act of betrayal has set my world's axis askew.

I wipe the rain off my face and see Eddie, my driver, standing beside my black Escalade, New York City's newest version of a limo. He holds an umbrella in one hand and the opened back door in another. I observe his rigid stance; not a muscle moves in his face as he remains at attention like a soldier awaiting his commander's arrival. I hurry toward him, anxious to get out of the rain and away from my building. Kings Capital has been the center of my life since it was started, but now I want to run from everything I've built.

As I'm nearing the car, I hear someone calling my name. A quick glance over my shoulder brings my assistant, Mrs. Carter, into view. I notice she's waving a piece of white paper as she runs toward me. I compare the two extremes of the people who work for me: one is stoically robotic, the other is embarrassingly chaotic.

"Mr. Kingsley, sir, I neglected to give you your ticket to the Swanson event!" Mrs. Carter rests her hand on her heaving chest, breathless. "Security is at a high level tonight since the Ethiopian ambassador is attending. No one will be allowed inside without this." I stare at the ticket in her hand; the black ink is starting to blur from the rain.

Mrs. Carter places the ticket in my outstretched hand. I watch beads of water from the rain roll down her plump cheeks. The rain washes away parts of her makeup, revealing bare reddish skin underneath.

"Thank you, Mrs. Carter." A crack of thunder rumbles around us, echoing off the towering buildings, causing us both to jump. "You'd better get back inside."

"I just want to say how sorry I am, Mr. Kingsley, about Mr. Edwards. I—" Pity is written all over her face, and I detest pity.

"Thank you, Mrs. Carter. I know your intentions are good, but do not bring this matter up again in my presence. If it needs to be discussed, I will let you know."

My harsh rebuke might as well have been a slap across her face. Mrs. Carter appears wounded, and her skin has now turned more the color of fire.

"Certainly, sir." She hangs her head briefly and then looks up at me with the same pity in her eyes. Perhaps even more than before. Dammit to hell. "Have a lovely evening at the benefit."

"My apologies for being short, Mrs. Carter. It's just been a hell of a day." My conscience tugs at me. Fuck, I've overreacted, given into my easily roused temper, and penalized her for a crime she didn't commit.

"I'll see you tomorrow morning," I speak more calmly, the angry tone in my voice now gone.

"Yes, sir. And I understand." I watch a timid smile stretch across her face. The rain has now fully removed any trace of makeup from her skin, and her pulled-back hair is soaking wet and plastered to her scalp. I should feel guilty for making her stand outside with me getting drenched, but the feeling doesn't come to me.

"Just remember, Mr. Kingsley. Karma is a wonderful thing." And with that quick statement she pivots on her sensible heels and runs back inside the building.

Karma. I have to laugh. I, of all people, know too well about karma and it's legend. However, I've chosen to operate under the old proverb of an eye for an eye. Karma requires no action and the hope of a chance. I rely on one thing in this world: my actions. I will leave nothing to chance and prefer playing the game of life with the strongest hand possible.

I turn toward my car and approach the open door.

"Good evening, Eddie." I greet my driver with a nod as I escape the pelting rain and ease into the backseat.

"Good evening, Sir." Eddie shuts the door behind me.

I immediately put on some rap music and turn the volume almost inhumanly high, hoping the noise will help drown out the stress of my day. Leaning back against the soft leather seat, I let the bass thump against me.

Eddie gets behind the wheel and mutes the volume of the music. I look at him annoyed. "Home, Mr. Kingsley, or do you have an engagement to attend?"

Normally, I confer with him on my agenda, but this afternoon's event with Simon has me off-kilter and I simply forgot. "I have a benefit at the Lincoln Center tonight. But take the long way so I can change into my tux."

"Yes, sir." Eddie pushes the mute button again, and the music blares from the speakers. I see him slyly smirk in the rearview mirror.

Eddie has been my driver since my company landed on the Fortune 500 list two years ago. It was shortly before I turned thirty. A magical year indeed. Heady and intoxicating. My first taste of obscene wealth and its rewards.

Since then I've fucked my way around this city, and poor Eddie has witnessed it all. I've burned through women like a wildfire roaring across a dry forest. Nothing has stood in my way. My passions have been all-consuming as I've indulged myself in all kinds of debauchery. I might think about settling down in a few years, maybe. But, for now, I'm content to sample the choice delights surrounding me. What single man in my shoes wouldn't say the same? Temptation is just too fucking tempting for me.

As Eddie prepares to pull away from the front of my building, I spot Simon being escorted out of the glass doors. A team of two security officers, one on each side of Simon, has their hands placed tightly above his elbows. I watch as they roughly release him once they have him fully outside. Simon stumbles but remains standing.

"Hold up, Eddie," I shout above the music before the SUV moves into the traffic. "Stop right here."

The SUV lurches to a stop and I brace myself against the back of the front seat. I shift slowly on the leather, wet from my rain-soaked clothes, until I'm totally facing Simon through my window. To my surprise he is approaching my vehicle and the look on his face is murderous. Never have I seen him show this much emotion. Never. Even when his fiancée left him a few weeks ago. It's unnerving.

Simon slowly approaches the Escalade and stares into the tinted glass of my windows. His eyes are wide and crazed, the veins in his forehead protruding. He appears ready to fight. Part of me wants to fling open the door and pummel his ass into the sidewalk. Pulverize him. Make him pay. I have about five inches on him and maybe forty pounds of muscle. He's no match for me. But something about his face, his eyes make me reconsider. I grip harder into the seatback, grounding myself into place.

Simon leans in closer, his nose almost touches the glass as he shouts something at me, but I can't hear him. His words are silent to me as I sit behind the car's dark wall of glass and listen to the loud music piped through the speakers and vibrating around me.

As I am getting ready to tell Eddie to pull away, Simon makes a move that conveys what his words could not. He places his finger beside his neck and drags it across from one side to the other. The universal symbol for you're dead. An eerie feeling runs through me, and I consider calling security to remove him from the sidewalk, but Simon turns away practically running from me.

Throughout Simon's angry display, Eddie is silently observing his behavior through the window. He's known Simon for as long as he's worked for me, so this stunt has to come as a shock. Glancing at Eddie in the front seat, I see a look of confusion mixed with concern on his face.

"It's been a hell of a day, Eddie." I take a deep breath and release my white-knuckled fingers from the seatback. An indent in the leather remains, a ghost outlining where my tension lay. "Get me the fuck out of here."

I'm tempted to tell Eddie to take me home and skip tonight's benefit, but I have committed to be there and make a major donation. I will likely be called by name and asked to stand and be acknowledged for my charity. An empty chair in my absence would be an affront to the organization. One that I'm actually quite fond of, which in this town is rare.

Resolved to keep pressing on, I remove the bag that's hanging from the hook behind my seat. Inside there is a black tux, brilliant white shirt, and shiny black shoes. I start to undress and as I do, Eddie, on cue, raises the divider between the seats. I laugh as he does. He's seen and heard just about everything in this backseat. Surely a flash of my briefs won't offend him. But he remains a gentleman as usual, even when I've given him no cause to believe that I am one.

As soon as I'm fully dressed, Eddie pulls up in front of the Lincoln Center, the location for tonight's benefit. I comb my fingers through my hair, trying to settle it back in place. It has a mind of it's own. Sex hair, I've been told.

Other than my white shirt, I'm adorned in black from the top of my head to the soles of my shoes. It's the color of success in New York City, and likely the color of most people's hearts attending tonight, too.

I'm scheduled to appear at two similar events this weekend, each one as stimulating as a prostate exam. Since my company made the Fortune 500 list, the invitations and requests from charities in this city have poured into my office. Poor Mrs. Carter practically needs an assistant to weed through them all. I think it's time to cut back on my attendance. I've frankly had my fill.

During the last two years, I've found the conversation at these affairs to be mundane and as boring as hell. The attendees address me speculatively, shocked by my success and youth. At thirty-two how I've succeeded is not the norm unless one's empire is built on family wealth and prestige. In a sick way my empire was built on family money—the hush money given to my mother when she fled this city thirty-two years ago. Funny thing about hush money, though, it's rarely kept quiet.

But tonight I'll have to endure all the disgusting verbal fawning. I can hear the people now, those shocked by my accomplishments.

"Hello, Mr. Kingsley. I've heard so much about you."

"Good evening, Mr. Kingsley. It's amazing how you've taken Wall Street by storm."

"Oh, Mr. Kingsley, what a striking man you are . . .blah . . .blah . . .blah."

The eyes on the nameless faces of my commentators have one thing in common: fear. Fear that I will dislike them, fear that I will crush them, and fear they will never obtain the wealth and power I have. It's pathetic how each dinner, gala, or benefit turns into a sycophant ball. A wicked dance where I'm placed in the center to be admired and envied. Displayed on some invisible pedestal until the sands shift beneath me and another up-and-coming man replaces me. Someone with more money, more power. The next bright and shining star. No one remains on top forever, and I have no illusions about my tenuous position among New York's power players.

Eddie opens the door and I exit with a quick nod to him. "Plan on company tonight. I need something fun to look forward to."

He nods back in a silent reply because he knows my routine and sexual appetites very well. It's a waiting game for him. He will receive my pick-up text and appear in five minutes at the curb. I'll let him know in my message if I'll have a friend at the end of the night. He will then prepare my arrival accordingly. Tonight, since I've alerted him early, he'll have some champagne ready when we enter the car, the backseat divider up, and seductive music playing in the background. Later, after I'm finished with the night's delight, he'll drop her off at her Upper East Side condo lovingly bought by her rich father who I've probably done business with.

Making my way to Lincoln Center's entrance, I pull the ticket Mrs. Carter gave me from my jacket's pocket. I see a line has formed in front of the building, and I dread having to stand with everyone outside. When I decide to bypass the line and proceed inside through the doublewide doors, a young woman with an official-looking badge pinned across her flat chest approaches me. Her blond hair falls haphazardly against her shoulders and she appears overwhelmed. I notice a little perspiration glisten on her forehead as she forces a smile at me. Sweating is so weak, I think to myself. I plant a smile on my face and prepare for her compliments, the inevitable suck-up that asks me to open my wallet and hand over its contents.

"Good evening." I decide to speak first.

"Good evening, Mr. Kingsley." She offers her hand to me in a formal greeting, and on reflex I respond in kind. "My name is Natalie Vincent. I'm the assistant to Ava Swanson, the executive director of The Swanson Foundation. It's an honor to have you attending our benefit tonight. We have special seating for you in the ballroom." She doesn't spew the usual false platitudes. How refreshing.

"This way." She tilts her head toward the direction she wants me to follow. She appears to be on a mission, and her high heels begin clicking with speed against the marble floors. Pulling my eyes away from her long, slender legs, I stop briefly to acknowledge some pompous men from whom I've legally stolen money. It's the Wall Street way, and the only place on Earth where stealing is applauded and rewarded.

I shake a few clammy hands and endure a couple slaps on my back, then hurriedly make my way back to Ms. Vincent.

She's halted her march toward the ballroom and stands waiting for me a few feet away. Her patience may be running thin as I watch her feet tap away until I'm back by her side. I have to smile to myself as I've never had a charity executive show such disregard to me. Me, the person who will likely be the biggest donor of the night.

"Excuse me," I say and add the best devilish grin I can produce. "I hate to leave a woman waiting." But I see her discreetly roll her eyes and huff as she turns in the direction she was headed. And I have to say I'm enjoying the view of her backside as she walks a few steps ahead of me.

Ms. Vincent and I enter the main dining area for tonight's event. I watch her stop at the head table and I start to tense. I despise sitting at the head table as it ensures that I am front and center. I prefer to blend in and watch others, not have all eyes fixed on me. Turning toward me, Ms. Vincent points out my seat and the identifying place card with Adam Kingsley written boldly across it.

"You will be sitting by the speaker, Sir Lawrence Scott. He's the organizer of The Hope House in Ethiopia. A wonderful outreach and a wonderful man."

"It should provide some stimulating conversation for the evening, I'm sure." I attempt to sound sincere but become distracted when I notice the elaborate diamond necklace lying on her pale chest. The clasp is moved to the front and ruins the piece's declaration of importance. After pulling my gaze away from her chest, she eyes me speculatively and continues.

"Stimulating might be a stretch, even for Sir Scott." She gestures toward a wall of open doors. "If you'll follow me, I'll show you the patron's reception area."

Once again, I'm trailing behind Ms. Vincent and wondering what's underneath the tight black dress she's wearing. My imagination conjures up lace encasing soft silk. If I found her more attractive, I might try to see if I'm right.

After entering the reception area off the main ballroom, Ms. Vincent departs, assuring me I will be speaking with her later. I head straight toward one of the several bars scattered throughout the large room and order my standard scotch, Glenlivet. If they have my favorite brand, I'm likely to contribute more money. Otherwise, my donation goes down considerably. After I successfully place my order, it appears The Swanson Foundation is in luck tonight.

Scanning the crowd as I wait for my drink, I see the usual suspects: balding men with pooching bellies holding on to their latest trophy wives or girlfriends. Some of the women meet my gaze with a knowing look as I've already been improperly introduced to certain parts of them when they were less attached.

I spot a former friend, Sarah Edmonds, I believe it is now. She has wonderful auburn hair that cascades against her alabaster skin, but her hideous laugh sounds like a hyena. I need to turn my gaze away from her quickly or she'll interpret my perusal as interest. I don't touch the merchandise once it's bought. And she most surely is bought. Poor fucker, Mr. Edmonds.

I take a couple more swigs of my scotch and let some of the better memories with the women I've known in the room come to mind. Between the scotch and brief sexual fantasies, I feel my body start to relax for the first time since this afternoon. I signal the bartender for a refill. I need a few more before subjecting myself to an evening next to Sir Lawrence. Fuck, this night needs to speed by.

In the far corner there's a stunning raven-haired beauty, and I shift my body slightly so I can watch her more closely. I've noticed her at a couple events the last month, and both times she has appeared alone. No one seems attached to her, which I find extremely odd as raw beauty like hers is uncommon in Manhattan. I wonder who she is and where she came from. No one suddenly appears on the New York social scene without some fanfare, especially at her age and her likelihood of being single. I bet she's family money, or a trust fund baby beautifully grown up.

I would guess she's older than I am, but I have never been close enough to see the details of her face and determine what her true age might be. Early thirties possibly. Her luminous skin gives her the glow of youth, so it's hard to tell. I enjoy watching the men around her as they hang onto every word she speaks out of her ruby lips.

Her congregation reminds me of a scene from Gone with the Wind when Scarlett O'Hara had all the naïve southern boys circled around her and eating out of the palm of her hand. I can almost hear this stunner mocking the men with a little fiddle dee dee thrown at them.

She ceremoniously extricates herself from the crowd of fawning suitors and moves toward the bar where I'm located. My heartbeat quickens at the thought of seeing her up close, maybe even sharing a word or two.

As she approaches me, I watch the sway of her hips and damn how they sway. Her tight dress accentuates her every move and I'm mesmerized, completely in her thrall. Her stature is petite, but curves grace her body seductively. Everything I see makes me thankful I'm a man. The sexy stilettos she's wearing belong in one of two places, over my shoulders or on the floor next to my bed.

Finally she looks my way and our eyes immediately connect, and at this moment I'm perfectly still. I can't break the intensity

I feel in this first interaction between us. Her blue eyes are surrounded by creamy skin and framed with her long, black hair. She is a fucking masterpiece. An artist's beauty.

The next thing I see on her lovely face is a knowing smile. She doesn't appear to be mocking me, at least that's my hope. And I decide right then that I need to know who this mystery woman is and where she came from.

I have an unspoken rule of never introducing myself at these shitty functions, but this woman I've got to meet. Now. I walk toward her, blocking her path to the bar and making it impossible for her to ignore me. She places her hands on her hips and looks up at me expectantly.

Feeling a bit on edge, I revert back to full-on business mode. What is it about this woman's beauty and expressions that make me feel uneasy? I stretch out my hand to her, but her hands remain solidly on her hips.

Well damn, this is interesting. There isn't a single wrinkle or line on her face, but the way she looks at me is intriguing, a confidence only acquired with time and experience. Everything about her fascinates me, and her sudden appearance on the social scene bewilders me. But most importantly right now, her body has totally aroused mine. This combination almost never happens with the women I meet at these things, so I start to speak.

"I'd like to introduce myself, I'm Adam Kings—"

She laughs before I can finish my name.

"Oh, I know who you are, pretty billionaire boy. Everyone in the room knows your name. Likely even the bartender I was on my way to visit knows you." She holds up an empty wine glass. "Do you know who I am, though?"

"I'm afraid you have me at a loss." Smirking, I draw my hand to my chest to feign feeling hurt and rejected. "And calling me 'pretty' and 'boy.' That stings."

"Please don't be offended. They're really meant as terms of endearment."

She moves closer to me, so close I see the full swell of her breasts as they disappear beneath the silk of her dark green dress. My cock responds to my perfect vantage point as I watch her mostly exposed chest move slowly and evenly. This intriguing yet nameless woman is an enticing tease, and I have to say I'm thoroughly enjoying myself for the first time tonight.

"Let me introduce myself. In polite company I go by Kathryn." I watch as she winks and runs her little tongue across her bottom lip. I swallow, hard.

"We have a name. That's a start." I find myself smiling at her. A full-blown grin, which contradicts my usual behavior. "And what do you do, Kathryn?"

"You want to know what I do?" She keeps her eyes trained on mine, and I swear I see a mischievous twinkle in them. "In my case that's a loaded question."

"Loaded question or not, I would still like to know," I say, hoping she'll reveal more of herself to me. "I've seen you before at other functions. It's like you just appeared out of thin air."

"Not quite thin air, but close. And it's funny; I've noticed you, as well." She moves even closer, and now we are nearly touching one another. "I wondered if we'd ever meet. You know I've been warned about you."

"Warned?" My question sounds hollow, unconvincing: I know what she's likely been told. Adam Kingsley is a player. A skirt-chaser. And I can't deny it, either.

"Yes, warned to keep my distance." I see a touch of amusement in her eyes, and now I'm sure she's mocking me. "I know we've just met, but I'm curious about something. Can I ask you a really personal question, Mr. Kingsley?"

"Sure, but you have to call me Adam." Honestly, I just want to hear her say my name. Watch her full lips mouth the sound.

"Let's stick to formalities, Mr. Kingsley. My question is actually a semi-professional one."

"A professional one?" I'm still left in the dark about her occupation, even her last name, yet she wants to ask me personal questions. Who is this ballsy woman?

"Yes, professional. I have a doctorate in psychology and coach couples in the intimacy department." The intimacy department? What the fuck does that mean?

"Well, Dr. Kathryn, I'm not sure how I can help with that subject. But okay, shoot away." I have a feeling I'm going to regret this.

"When I look around this room, I see women watching you and our exchange. Some looking sad, others looking envious. I'm curious to know how many of them you've slept with?" She stares at me with a serious look on her face. She doesn't blink or look away. It's then I realize she really wants me to answer her. Throw out a number. Fuck. I'm not sure how to respond or even count up the tally, so I decide to try a little humor.

"Somewhere between one and all of them?" She rolls her eyes to the side, not satisfied with my answer, but I'm not finished yet either.

"Honestly, I'd like to say you, just you." My voice is barely above a whisper. "That you're the only one I've fucked in this room." Kathryn appears a little surprised by my answer but then laughs, and I join her. I think she realizes I'm teasing her. But what I said might be partially true because no other woman in this room appeals to me like she does.

"They were right to warn me." Her mood shifts. Gone are her smiles. "Men like you will never understand what a woman really needs."

"Is that right? So you're an expert on me now. My judge and jury." I cross my arms over my chest as my temper starts to rise.

"Oh dear. I think I've touched a nerve," she says while throwing her head back and laughing at me. Quite frankly, I'm not amused. "Yes, Mr. Kingsley, I'm an expert of sorts."

"Care to explain?" My tone's short with her as I'm still a bit pissed.

"It would be my pleasure." She winks at me and I'm feeling conflicted. Do I really want to know what she's an expert at? Who am I kidding? Of course I do.

"I'm a specialist at taking boys like yourself and turning them into real men. I've never failed. Not once. At least that's what their wives and girlfriends say."

"So, what have you never failed at, in more specific terms?" I'm hoping she takes the bait and gives me the details of her exploits, as this woman confounds and frustrates me.

She brings her free hand up to my chest and runs her delicate fingers under the lapel of my Armani tux. My arms fall to my side as I feel her grasping my jacket and gently pulling my upper body down toward her, bringing our faces cheek to cheek. Her soft lips brush lightly against my ear.

"I take cocky, rich boys like you and teach them how to make love to women until they're barely able to mutter a word. Completely and utterly blissed. That's really what separates the men from the boys, Mr. Kingsley. Sex as an art form versus fucking for a release."

I find myself unable to respond, completely tongue-tied. Something I'm not used to experiencing. I always have a slick comeback. Always. I see fire in her eyes and notice her lips starting to move again, and good God, I realize she's not done with me yet.

"You see, Mr. Kingsley, when I said you were a pretty billionaire boy I meant every damn word. You're very pretty indeed, striking really, but still just a boy."

Chapter 2

Staring at Kathryn intensely, I can't miss the spark in her eyes as they challenge me. I have no words as my mind processes her declared opinion of me. It's a slight meant to sting and wound me, and I'm not sure why she feels the need to be so sharp and cutting.

But I'm silent and allow the silence to linger in hopes of staying in control. One thing I've learned in business: The first person to speak during an intense confrontation usually loses the deal. Capitulates. And I'd like to win at whatever game she's playing with me. So my silence plays into my hand, as she finally breaks it.

"Cat got your tongue?" The words she finally purrs at me are smooth and seductive. I twirl the melting ice around in my glass and eye the dripping condensation. I try to appear disinterested but I've never wanted to engage with a woman like I do with her. Oh what I'd love to do with my tongue. I sweep my eyes across her barely concealed breasts. They're full and real, which is quite to my liking.

Kathryn clears her throat, catching me appreciating her breasts, and I look up from her chest. Collecting myself, I respond. "Actually, I'm very selective about which pussy," I pause, "...cat gets my tongue." I watch her reaction and notice a wicked twinkle in her eye. She thinks I'm stepping into her trap, in reach of her claws. She is very mistaken.

"Rumors say otherwise. I think the worn leather in the backseat of your vehicle can attest to that." A smug look of satisfaction flashes across her face. A face remarkable in its beauty. I fight the urge to allow my fingers to pass along her cheekbones, feel her skin and touch her.

"You seem to know a lot about what happens in my backseat. Yes, there might be some mileage, but I've never had a complaint." I raise the watered scotch to my lips, tilt my head, and down the rest of the drink, swallowing my medicine. Leaning back against the bar, I sit the empty glass down with a thud, eye the bartender, and nod for another.

"No complaints?" She licks her cherry-stained lips. The color contrasts starkly against her flawless, pale skin. The combination stirs something deep within me. Dark. Licentious. I imagine her kneeling in front of me. Lips enclosed and sucking on my cock, but my thoughts are regretfully cut short.

"I hate to burst your bubble, but I'm acquainted with one of your backseat warmers. Her views of your sexual exploits are not flattering." I wonder who the hell she's been talking to, because I've never had a single complaint. Just the opposite, in fact.

"Were they looking for, what did you call it, an 'art form' type of fucking'?" As I speak I wonder if she truly knows one of my conquests, or if it's another attempt at catching me off guard. "I possess many forms of art. They sit on a shelf for display or hang unceremoniously on a wall. Illusions of beauty created by artists. Fucking is raw, animalistic, and sweat inducing. There is no beauty. Just selfish needs seeking to be met."

My words have a surprising effect on her. Instead of making her recoil, she draws closer to me, sneaking her hand up my arm. She brushes slowly, lingers slightly, until she guides her hand up my shoulder. Her feather-like touch contains an odd but powerful energy as my skin tingles beneath the layers of my clothes.

I feel the softness of her fingers caress the skin above my collar. I look down at her as she threads her fingers through the hair at my nape and brings my head toward her. Kathryn traces her lips across my jaw as she pulls me even closer.

"I wonder," she whispers in my ear, "Mr. Kingsley. Do the women you frolic with have a release? Do you make them come so hard they forget their name? Or did you leave them with nothing? Not even a parting gift or their dignity as you shuffle them out of your limo onto the sidewalk."

I draw back and stare into her eyes. She's pegged me like she's seen every one of my indiscretions, and she knows it.

Kathryn looks from my eyes to my lips and then leans again toward my ear. "The truth is all the money you possess can't make you a man." She brushes her lips against my ear and pulls away, gauging my reaction.

Deflecting the conversation away from her obviously incorrect observations, I say, "But it does make me irresistible." Teasing her and making light of her pointed questions is the only response I can think of. But my attempt doesn't ease the sting I feel from her unflattering accusations. "But not as irresistible as you. There isn't a man here who doesn't want to be with you. Single or attached. And I happen to be the lucky one who has your attention."

"Oh, you're very smooth, Mr. Kingsley." Kathryn doesn't address my comments any more than I addressed hers. We are dancing around each other in a circle of our words. A game of verbal foreplay.

"I imagine resisting you is impossible for many women here. They probably fall into your gravitational pull without even knowing. Completely succumbing to your charms. However, I've been rightly warned about you. I do wish you luck here tonight, though. Surely, there's some pretty young thing who is willing to serve you." She removes her hand from me, and surprisingly I miss the feel of her touch.

Wondering who warned her about me, I tap my chin and look her up and down. There is no way I'm going to let her see how affected I am by her remarks, and how they compound upon my already hellish day. It's exhausting, and I feel like a boxer who needs to go to his corner and tend to his wounds.

So I decide to play into her idea of my shallowness. I scan the room and spot a pleasant-looking brunette glancing my way. I return her gaze, smile, and nod. Kathryn watches the exchange, and I hear her laughter.

"Good luck, little boy." Her remark is laced with disdain, and she turns to the bar, placing her palms flat against the polished wood. She flags down the bartender and orders a new glass of white wine. She picks up the glass and starts to walk away without even a sideways glance back at me. Somehow her avoidance stings more than her sharp debate about my perversity.

"Wait a second, Kathryn. I endured being grilled on a rather intimate subject, surely you can tell me your last name."

I try to sound cool even though I feel a little desperate to know more about her. A fact I'm not happy with at all. However, my request isn't completely ignored as I watch her stop and look over her shoulder at me.

"My last name is Delcour." She replies in a very dismissive and cool tone. I don't like it one bit, but I can't for the life of me let her keep walking away.

"So you're French, then?" I ask, trying to keep the conversation alive.

"My late husband was. Good evening, Mr. Kingsley."

She turns away, and I'm surprised by her comment. She's left me speechless once again. Her late husband? It's just a little peek into who she is, possibly where she's from, but in the end it explains so little about her. And I want to know more. I need to know more.

I'm tempted to pull her back to me at the bar and resume our banter, but I refrain. Instead I watch her every movement as she leaves me.

She saunters across the carpeted floor, and every man she passes follows her with wide eyes. They're like me, taken aback by her beauty. Her path is like a promenade of sorts. Men appear to hold their breath until she passes them by, perhaps hoping she would dare to stop and speak to them. Disappointment shows on their faces as she passes. Now they contently gaze at the movement of her sweet, round ass. A tantalizing focal point that's tucked tightly into her little green dress, gathered lightly at the back to display the perfection of her curves.

At the edge of the room, Kathryn approaches a young man, possibly her next conquest to toy with or shamelessly torture. He's roughly my height, around six feet two inches. As she nears him, a welcoming smile graces his baby face and their arms link together. Whispering into his ear, she shifts him slightly to bring me into their view. I'm leaning against the bar and make eye contact with them both.

I raise my freshly poured scotch in their direction. A salute of acknowledgement. "To being a man," I mumble under my breath and laugh at the lunacy of her words. But there are two things I can't deny, the lusciousness of her body and a lingering disappointment since she's moved on to another man.

As Kathryn and her new toy walk toward the banquet's ballroom, I notice the rest of the attendees loosely scattered about the room following their lead. The main event must be starting shortly, so I need to plan my after-party. The day I've had requires one, and my audience with Kathryn Delcour has left my cock needy. Besides, knowing I have something to look forward to should make the evening ahead more tolerable. It's a pity Dr. Kathryn is preoccupied. Perhaps another time.

I need to find out more about her and get a better angle on who she is and what makes her tick. But mostly I need to define what she means by teaching sex as an art form. The scenarios in my head have me wondering. Dominatrix, perhaps? That's one kink I've not submitted to, literally. But there was something different in her touch. A phantom ghost of it remains from my arm to the back of my neck, it lingers.

I find the pleasant-looking brunette who held my gaze earlier. She's moved closer to where I'm standing, almost within hearing distance. I motion for her to join me. She walks over and I enjoy the view as she inches my way. I focus on her mouth; after all, that will be the host for tonight's party. It appears wide, red and, most importantly, willing.

Her perfumed scent hits me before her words do. "Mr. Kingsley, I've wanted to meet you for some time. My name is Lizzie. Lizzie Woodward. The Woodward's from the Navistar Fund."

I could care less who she is. "Please, skip the formalities and call me Adam." Moving almost flush against her, I stare down into her hazel eyes. Towering over her in size, I get to the point of my intentions. "I'd like to meet you after tonight's affair for a party of our own. Would that fit into your plans, Ms. Woods?"

"Woodward." She corrects me as I've mispronounced her name.

"Oh, yes, Ms. Woodward. My apologies. What do you think about my idea?" I give her a sexy smile, knowing the power it has to get the answers I want.

"I don't know if I'm brave enough to be alone with you," she replies innocently, winking at me.

"Feisty one, aren't you?"

Her smile communicates more than her words, and an approval of my request is reflected in her eyes. "I have been called lively."

"Well, Lively Lizzie, meet me at the coat check after the wealthy have released their wallets and eased their guilt." Confusion from my words traverses her face; not a very lively brain would be my guess. "I meant when the event's over, darling."

"Oh, at the coat check, right? I'll be there."

"See you then." I conclude my invitation with a swift exit.

After leaving her, I move through the crowd with ease. The seas part. Whispers follow behind my path. Several pathetic well-wishers try to get my attention, but I ignore their attempts, enjoying their scowls to my overt rejection.

Stepping away from the herd beginning to fill the empty tables, I make a quick phone call to the one person I trust. In New York City, trust is an expensive luxury, and Peters Investigative Services comes with a steep price. Peters operates as my personal ear to the ground. His skills often skate on the edges of the law. Which serve me well.

"Peters, I need a background."

"Anything, sir. What is the name?"

"Last name, Delcour, first name, Kathryn. Caucasian. Age likely early thirties. Widowed. She's attending tonight's dinner for The Swanson Foundation. Basic info tonight. Extensive details tomorrow morning."

"Got it. I'll get back to you."

I disconnect without a direct response and proceed to the head table, where I'm greeted by Kathryn's large blue eyes and ruby lips pinched into a disapproving grimace. Her brow furrows as I near.

Finding her at the head table seated next to Ava Swanson confuses me. Mrs. Swanson is the executive director of The Swanson Foundation. Her name graces everything connected with the group. After a quick glance to Kathryn's right, I see the young man who escorted her out of the reception.

Kathryn turns her head toward me as I stand to the side of her chair. Fortunately for me her sweet boy toy rises up from his chair and walks to the next table to greet a fellow patron. Kathryn stares up at me with big doe eyes, captivating. Smiling down at her, I speak. "We meet again, Mrs. Delcour."

"Small world. Or are you following me?" Her face relaxes into a smile. Surprisingly putting me at ease, too.

"Maybe a little bit of both." I trail my fingers along the top of her satin-covered chair and lightly graze across her bare shoulder. She shivers as my touch drifts past the last inch of her skin. I imagine her nipples taut and pebbling awaiting my touch. She continues to peek over her shoulder, our eyes meet, and I see an undeniable look of… lust. So a soft touch turns this vixen on? I hope to put this theory into practice more and prove whether I'm right.

I bend to whisper softly in her ear; my lips press gently against her earlobe. "A sweet, selfish release might do you good, Kathryn. Leave the 'art form' fucking to the idealists."

Observing her reaction, I watch her grab the edge of the table, clawing like a kitten into the white tablecloth. Avoiding me, she stiffens and faces frontward. I continue to nuzzle into her shiny, black curls as my nose becomes lost in them. The slight movement by her releases the scent of her perfume, and I detect a hint of spice, rich and exotic, like Shalimar. I take a long, deep breath as I remember the last time I smelled that fragrance. A childhood memory long forgotten.

I absorb her scent as she sits still and lets me. This time she is the one who remains silent. Unbendable. Looking forward as the crowded dining room fills with wealthy and shallow faces.

"Looks like the cat has your tongue this time." Chuckling, I pull away, expecting her to release the claws I know she has hidden away.

Instead, I see her breathe deeply, her breasts rise and fall as she digs down deep to bring forth her refined and polished breeding. A forced but still beautiful smile graces her lips.

"You're completely incorrigible, Mr. Kingsley. Shameless." Her scolding response sounds like something Scarlett would have spoken to Rhett as she picked up her skirts and turned in a huff.

A tap at my elbow pierces the invisible bubble around us. It's rather unfortunate since I was enjoying a moment of teasing Kathryn. Rising to a full stance, I discover Ms. Vincent at my side.

"Mr. Kingsley, may I have a word with you before we begin today's program?" I hold up a finger to indicate I'll be with her shortly; I have unfinished business with the beautiful woman in front of me. Ms. Vincent nods in agreement and walks away.

"Enjoy your evening, Kathryn." I say as I turn to leave her. I notice that the foundation's executive director, Ava Swanson, who's sitting next to Kathryn, has just finished conversing with one of the event staff and looks up at me in surprise.

"Good evening to you, Mrs. Swanson." I bow my head in acknowledgement to her.

Mrs. Swanson twists further around in her chair, a broad smile shining on her face. Her attire is stylish, a dark navy dress with a coordinating jacket, reflecting a slightly matronly appearance.

Mrs. Swanson offers me her hand to rise. "Good evening, Mr. Kingsley. Pleasure to see you. Thank you for joining us tonight."

"Think nothing of it, Mrs. Swanson, and, please, stay seated. You look lovely tonight." She displays a pleasant smile and settles back in her chair, smoothing out some imaginary wrinkles in her silk dress. Her diamond-encrusted hand sparkles, catching my attention for a moment. "Your foundation is a rare charity. It has integrity. And remember I've asked you to call me Adam."

"Thank you, Adam. Quite the charmer as always, aren't you?" I give her a little wink, and I watch a slight blush appear on the older woman's face. No doubt a stunning beauty in her day. She continues on. "It has been my aim since we started twenty years ago. I will be acknowledging your support in the program tonight. I hope you are comfortable with being in the spotlight?"

"I'd prefer it to be short and sweet." I notice an inquisitive look on Kathryn's face and a hidden fire in her eyes. A hellcat.

Mrs. Swanson glances at Kathryn and then looks back up at me. "Have you had a chance to meet my Kathryn?"

"Your Kathryn?" So Kathryn's Mrs. Swanson's daughter? How interesting. It does explain a few things to me, mostly why she's seated at the head table.

"Yes, my lovely daughter. She's finally came back home to New York City. She's been in Paris for years." Mrs. Swanson places her hand lovingly on Kathryn's arm. However, Kathryn's lips are pursed. She is fuming mad as her mother reveals details about her personal life, and I can't help my amusement by Kathryn's reaction.

"Lovely, indeed." I smirk and nod my head in response to Mrs. Swanson's comments concerning Kathryn. "Actually, Kathryn and I met in the reception area. I enjoyed our conversation, too."

"Yes, Adam was telling me about his favorite extracurricular activity. It keeps him rather busy." I smirk at her quip. Score one for the pussycat.

"I'm thrilled you two were able to meet. I've told Kathryn all about you and how you've helped the Foundation." Well surprisingly her mother approves of me, but I wonder what it would take to gain her daughter's favor. As Kathryn rolls her eyes at her mother's words, I decide it will likely take major convincing on my part, and I'm definitely up for the challenge.

"As I've said, your foundation puts every dollar it receives to good use. It's been my pleasure to support your endeavors in Africa." Mrs. Swanson beams up at me while her daughter scowls. The contrast between them makes me chuckle.

"See, Kathryn, I told you he's a wonderful man," Mrs. Swanson says facing her daughter, and then turns up to me. "You should take my daughter out to dinner, Adam. You do seem like her type. Besides she needs to get out of that apartment of hers."

Does Mrs. Swanson read the gossip columns in the New York City papers? Surely, she doesn't, they don't paint me in the best light. I'm no saint and definitely not a mother's dream for her daughter.

"And what is her type? I'm taking notes." I smile at the two beautiful faces in front of me.

"Dare I say a bit of a bad boy?" Mrs. Swanson giggles and winks at me. "But one with a good heart. Much like her late husband."

A look of sadness crosses Kathryn's face at the mention of her late husband. I wonder if she's a recent widow and the loss is still fresh.

"Please, Mother," Kathryn pleads, protesting her mother's candor.

"Well, I believe you're a bigger fan of me than your beautiful daughter. Maybe you could persuade her to join me for dinner." Kathryn huffs as she looks at me with daggers in her eyes, likely plotting my death.

"Well, if I was younger, I wouldn't need any persuading," Mrs. Swanson laughs, but Kathryn's anger is in full display as her face turns a bright red. I think Kathryn's had enough of this conversation, and Ms. Vincent's not a patient woman, so I decide to put an end to the fun… For now.

"Well, if you'll excuse me, ladies, I hate to keep Ms. Vincent waiting."

I know what the conversation will be with Ms. Vincent. My contribution tonight was left open-ended. Sometimes I vaguely hint how much I'm willing to contribute, never really revealing the amount. It leaves people guessing and kissing my ass, among other things.

Ms. Vincent turns toward my seat next to Sir Scott. As we pace the few feet to my chair, she begins to bring up the inevitable subject. How much will my check be? My thoughts on that subject have changed since I arrived. I planned on giving around five hundred thousand. Which is a very respectable personal contribution. But now Kathryn is sitting next to Mrs. Swanson, and obviously a close confidante, so I consider raising the amount to impress her. I'd like to see her reaction when they announce my obscene donation. I wonder if she'll join the others in their oohs and aahs? Something tells me adding another zero to the amount will not impress her, or at least she'll never let me know if it does. Now to drop the bomb on poor Ms. Vincent.

Chapter 3

"Let's cut to the chase, Ms. Vincent. I'm upping my donation considerably this year." I pause as she eyes me speculatively. "I'll be giving five million dollars tonight. I'd like the money to be used to build a state-of-the art medical clinic for the poor in Africa. From start to finish. Nothing spared. Mrs. Carter, my assistant, will wire the money tomorrow."

Ms. Vincent stares at me with her jaw slack. I almost snort at her expression. Flustered, she seems at a total loss for words or coherent thought.

"Are you okay?" The color in her face is gone. She's as pale as a ghost. I chuckle as I wait for her to regain her senses.

"Did I hear you right? Five million dollars?" Ms. Vincent is speaking barely above a whisper as if she's lost the wind from her lungs.

"I'm totally serious. I decided on the amount tonight, and from the look on your face, I'm beginning to think you would've preferred a fair warning."

"Mr. Kingsley, this is, uh, unexpected, but wonderful. Do you realize what we can do with support like this? Words can't express how grateful I am. Does Mrs. Swanson know?"

"No. She has no idea. I think I'll take my seat and let you tell her."

I pull out my chair and lower myself next to Sir Scott. I catch a distinct and assaulting smell of mothballs mixed with some cheap aftershave. Turning toward the cause of offensive odors, I take in the man who is Sir Scott, a tall and brown-headed Englishman in need of a nose and ear hair trimmer.

He stretches out his tweed-covered arm and shakes my hand. Interestingly, he didn't conform to the black tie dress code for tonight's event.

"Mr. Kingsley, it's so nice to finally meet you in person."

"Likewise, Sir Scott." I take small, shallow breaths to avoid a deep intake of air. Too much of his malodorous concoction would surely bring on a headache. And I don't want anything deferring my scheduled fun later with the alluring Lively Lizzie.

"Thanks to your contribution last year, we were able to fund a wonderful program to help single mothers start micro-businesses. It's remarkable to see what a little support can accomplish. Hopefully, you received the quarterly newsletters outlining what we're doing in Addis Ababa."

"Absolutely." I lie, but only a white lie to protect his pride and my ignorance.

I'm almost certain his newsletters arrive at Mrs. Carter's desk, never to be seen by me. He obviously has no idea what it takes to run a billion-dollar company. The tug and pull of forces around me keeps me from interacting with the mundane, like his little newsletter. I read the New York Times and a few select financial journals. I watch one television network, CNBC. Everything else is fluff and mind-numbing garbage. The only exception is my regular dalliance of porn.

Our conversation is miraculously cut short as the emcee for the night speaks into the microphone on the podium and welcomes everyone to the event. An African-American man is introduced to recite a special Ethiopian Jewish prayer. The man delivers the prayer without an introduction or conclusion. The prayer's words are enough.

Show and guide us, O Lord, to your light, that shines out from Your Torah,

That always gives light to Your faithful people,

To those who have faith and put their trust in You.

O Lord God of Israel, deliver us from our errors and blindness,

And from every teaching of sin that intoxicates

Every teaching of sin that intoxicates. Hmm. Interesting. As an earthly spectator, one could use this phrase as a perfect definition of our world. Intoxicated by the sins of lust and greed, to name a few. Dante's vision of hell, in full display everywhere. But in reality, this humble prayer and Dante's Inferno are simple interpretations, created by a man to judge another man or himself.

The pathetic reality of how Sir Scott's Hope House receives funds remains hidden. But I know how the righteous are financed to fulfill their good deeds as I scan the people occupying seats in front of me. They are the ones who fill the coffers of Hope House. But these men and women grab every opportunity to seize more money and sex. They disperse their gains to appease a fear that someone greater than them will hold them accountable one day.

Me, I'm accountable to no one, the one exception being the stockholders of my multinational company.

The menu for tonight is laced with foreign words: Madeira Braised Veal Osso Bucco and Drunken Pear en Croute. Our meal appears course by course. Forks clank and voices chatter. Glasses are drained and refilled. My mind switches to autopilot at these functions. Whether it's a formal sit-down, a stand and mingle, or a grand gala, I rely on my phone to keep my company. I try to discreetly keep tabs on my business affairs and communicate with my company's divisions around the world.

I respond to emails during dinner. Check with my company's security head, Walter Cox, concerning Simon. Simon took nothing with him when he was escorted out the door. I look over my calendar as Sir Scott is introduced and speaks to the crowd. His speech concludes as I look up from my phone.

Glancing over the program, I realize Mrs. Swanson is preparing to speak. She will be recognizing the major donors to The Swanson Foundation. Around the podium, I see the lovely Mrs. Delcour sitting poised and looking absolutely beautiful. She oozes class. I lick my lips and wish I had her taste on them. The thought awakens my sleeping cock; he'll have to settle for Lively's lips tonight. I can almost feel him weeping for Kathryn's lips instead.

Mrs. Swanson stands at the microphone and thanks Sir Scott for his presentation. Polite applause follows. She looks at me and winks as she smiles from ear to ear, obviously pleased with my contribution.

"The Swanson Foundation will celebrate its fourteenth anniversary this year. I established this work after my late husband Richard's untimely passing. In my years as the executive director, I have had many occasions to see the good in others. But tonight, I stand before you surprised by the charitable deeds of a brilliant young man here with us." Mrs. Swanson extends her arm in my direction with her palm straight up. "Adam Kingsley, would you please join me?"

Rising out of my chair, I stride the few feet to Mrs. Swanson's side and see a knowing smirk on Kathryn's face. It's as if she can see right through me and, as I guessed, she's less than impressed. Nevertheless, I prepare for the dog and pony show and place a plastic smile on my face as I turn to face the crowd.

"I'm working on Kathryn. Remember what I said." Mrs. Swanson whispers under her breath to me as I stand next to her. She's really wanting Kathryn and me together. Maybe she'll convince her after all.

"Mr. Kingsley is donating five million dollars to The Swanson Foundation. Words can't express my gratitude. His donation will allow Sir Scott's Hope House to build a modern medical facility in the heart of Ethiopia. It is the single largest contribution on record to our foundation. Mr. Kingsley, on behalf of the Hope House and all those you will be aiding, thank you from the bottom of our hearts."

This time the applause is raucous. The attention I'm receiving is something I always try to avoid. Peeking to my right, I see Kathryn is clapping but whispering into the ear of her boy toy. She's completely disinterested in the spectacle.

Mrs. Swanson quietly murmurs her thanks again and asks if I'd like to make a statement. I assure her that it will be brief.

As I step to the microphone, I see Lively sitting and clapping wildly a few tables away. Her enthusiasm softens the blow of Kathryn's disregard, but worries me, too. It seems over thc top. Fanatical, even. I hope this evening with her isn't one I will live to regret.

"Mrs. Swanson, thank you for your kind words. However, instead of focusing on myself, I'd prefer to encourage everyone here tonight to give generously. Please, dig deep and support one of the finest charities here in Manhattan. The Swanson Foundation shines alone in its reliability and veracity. Thank you."

The platform is turned over to the D-list celebrity emcee. He babbles on, attempts a less than stellar comedy stand-up, and then stumbles through an awkward dismissal. When he walks away from the podium, I see his brow covered in sweat, a strange display for a so-called professional.

Hoping to have another chance to speak to Kathryn before the night's end, I walk toward her chair and see her being escorted out by The Boy. At least they're heading where I am: the exit.

I shake a few hands, endure a couple of introductions, and rudely dismiss all attempts at conversation. I send a simple text to Eddie stating five minutes and company. I hurry toward the last spot I saw Kathryn as I try to keep her trail warm. I want to speak with her before Lively finds me.

Approaching the gilded hallways, I find Kathryn and head straight for her. She notices me as I approach and moves her hand to her hip. A smile and laugh greet me when I come to a halt in front of her.

"Bravo, Mr. Kingsley." Her gaze penetrates and burns me. It's a dangerous warmth that promises to smolder me. I find myself becoming a willing participant even though I know she's mocking me.

"You know why I gave that outrageous sum, don't you?" I search her face and observe a gleam in her eyes as she throws her head back. Her delicate throat beckons me, and I long to touch and possess her with my lips. I move closer, our bodies almost touching. She senses me drawing near, drops her head, and looks at me. Her mood becomes serious, all smiles and levity disappear.

"Of course I do. You're not that hard for me to read." I see The Boy approaching, dutifully carrying her fur coat. I realize we have only seconds before he's standing beside us.

Kathryn continues. "And for the record, I'm thankful for your gift, but not terribly impressed. There's more to life than money. Believe me, I know."

She turns to her side as the young nuisance descends on us. "Kathryn, here's your coat." The young man looks at me inquisitively, sizing me up. As they stand side by side, I notice something: a resemblance. There is something about them. They could almost be siblings. The color of their eyes leads me to this conclusion. A matching deep blue, trending toward violent.

"Thank you, John." He assists her with her coat. "I'd like to introduce you to Adam Kingsley. Mr. Kingsley, this is my brother, John Swanson." She finishes her introduction with a coy smile.

"Excuse me, but did you say 'your brother?'" Wait a second. He's her brother? Shit.

"Yes, I'm her brother. Our mother is Ava Swanson." He pushes his hand my way, expecting a handshake and I dutifully comply. "Pleasure to meet you. Let's just say that you've made my mother a very happy woman tonight. Thanks again for your donation. Your generosity was unexpected, a pleasant surprise to say the least."

A small hand grips my arm. I know who it is before I hear her greetings. Lively Lizzie has arrived.

"Finally. I've been looking all over for you," Lively says. I feel her snake her arm through mine. Connecting us and sealing my fate for the rest of the fucking evening.

"I'm right where I told you I'd be." I make a quick decision. The time I spend with Ms. Lively tonight will be short. Maybe more like a cab ride to her home.

To my surprise, I hear Kathryn speak. "Hi, Lizzie. You look lovely this evening." Fuck. I don't particularly care for Kathryn knowing my after-dinner hook-up by name. I glance at Kathryn and it appears she's enjoying my discomfort way too much. "Is Mr. Kingsley giving you a ride home?" I know what's behind her question. She's wondering if Lizzie's my fuck for the evening.

I butt in and decide to end this most uncomfortable conversation. "Yes, I'm giving her a ride home this evening." I grasp Lizzie's arm and turn to her. "My driver is waiting outside."

"Well, we don't want to keep anyone waiting, Mr. Kingsley." Kathryn stares impassively at me, giving nothing away in her expression.

"Well, it was nice to meet you, John. And good evening, Kathryn."

I need to leave, now. Grabbing at her hand, I pull a stunned Lively toward the building's exit. Something tickles at my temple. I wipe my forehead and cringe.

Goddamn it. Sweat!

I only sweat on two occasions: at the height of a good fuck or when pushing my body to its limit during a workout. What I find on my skin right now is totally unacceptable. Sweat from anxiety. But damn if that woman, Kathryn Delcour, didn't unnerve and drive me to it.

Once I have Lively outside the building, she struggles keeping up me with in her stiletto heels. I spot the black limo with Eddie standing at his post awaiting my arrival. He sees me, nods his greeting and opens the door; I pause to let Lively enter first. I hear her gasp, then utter the words "wow" and "oh, my God" over and over again. Clearly, the limo's interior impresses her.

Before I bow to enter the car, I need to find out some vital information from Lively.

"Where do you live?" I ask gruffly.

"77th and Lex. We can take the long way around Central Park," she replies coyly. Her suggestion is easy to decipher; she wants to fuck me.

I smirk back at her, because we aren't taking the long way anywhere. That's for damn sure.

Rising up from the car's door, I give Eddie Lively's name and direct him to drive her to the address she just gave me. I instruct Eddie to have the car at her building in roughly fifteen minutes. The entire Escalade was retrofitted for me to give it a limo feel. The middle seat area houses one captain chair that swivels its position. It's my usual seat, except when I'm entertaining a woman for the night. The backseat provides the best resting place and can even lay flat if required. I notice that Eddie has prepared for our party. Lights low, music rhythmic and seductive. Perfectly setting the mood.

Pouring two glasses of chilled champagne, I beckon her over to me.

"I have other business to attend to," she murmurs, refusing the champagne. I set it aside and lean against the buttery leather cushions. My eyes close as she tells me of her plans. Gently, I feel Eddie move the SUV as our journey begins.

She whispers in my ear that a generous man like me needs to be thanked properly for his selfless donation. With my head back and eyes still closed, Lively's fingers unbuckle, unbutton, and unzip.

She slides my suit pants and boxer briefs down as I slightly raise my hips. The bite of her fingernails drags back up my legs, sending chills through my body. A slight moan escapes my lips.

Kisses are scattered over my hipbones as she progresses down toward my hardening cock. Lively's mouth surrounds and sucks me in. A name and face flash before my closed eyes, and I bite my lip to avoid calling out the name. Kathryn.

Lively's hand wraps around my cock, moving in motion with her mouth. I rock my pelvis and push deeper into her willing mouth. She sucks me harder. A pace begins and finally ends, spectacularly. I'm completely spent, and I open my eyes to see Lively gloating and wiping her hand across her mouth.

After readjusting my pants, Lively settles onto my lap and kisses me. "That was quite the thank you," I reply.

"You're quite welcome. I've wanted to meet you for some time. And tonight when you spoke to me, I hoped for this. Us together, alone."

I feel the limo slow to a stop and the engine shuts off. I know without looking that we've arrived at her apartment.

"We've arrived at your building." After I speak, she looks astonished and squints through the darkened glass. Her mouth forms a little O as realization hits her that the "us together, alone" portion of the evening has drawn to a close.

"Okay, I guess this is my stop." Her tone reflects the disappointment I see in her eyes.

"Thanks for the thank you, Lively." I raise her hand to my lips and let my kiss linger as I gaze into her eyes. I feel that I need to do something to show some appreciation; after all, she did provide an intimate gift to me. Somewhere I hear the words Kathryn spoke from earlier about finding a pretty young thing to service me. I wipe the thought from my mind.

Gathering her coat and clutch, she scoots to the door Eddie has now opened, his timing precise as usual.

"Lizzie, a quick question before you leave." She stops her progression to the open door and turns to me as I stay reclined on the couch. "Any complaints about our time tonight?"

"Well." She hesitates, looking me over and taking in the excess she sees in my surroundings. "No, no complaints."

Smiling, I respond, "That's what I thought."

The door closes and I gloat after hearing Lively's comments. Kathryn was incorrect in her assessment of me. No complaints. But I picture her laughing in mocked amusement at me. Something tells me by posing this question to Lively, I've let Kathryn succeed in slinking under my tough exterior. Or maybe it's just the result of Simon's shocking betrayal. Making me sense an unusual apprehension in my mind.

Chapter 4

My phone vibrates in my pocket. Peters is calling with an update on the mysterious Kathryn Delcour, I hope. My knowledge of her is limited. And what I do know about her leaves me with more questions than answers.

She is Mrs. Swanson's daughter and probably the daughter of her late husband Richard.

Answering the phone, I hope to learn more. "Peters. What do you have so far?"

"She recently turned thirty-four." Two-year difference. Not an obstacle in my opinion.

"Daughter of the late Richard Swanson and Mrs. Ava Swanson." Nothing I didn't already assume.

"Kathryn has a brother, John. Age twenty-seven." So he's younger than I am, barely.

"Still more digging to do, but I did find something very interesting. Kathryn Delcour's family is directly connected to the Vanderbilts."

Wait, I remember her saying money can't buy you everything and then following it with, *"Believe me, I know."*

"So Peters, are you talking the New York City Vanderbilts?"

He answers my question quickly. "Yep. The old money ones."

"So she's a Vanderbilt." I quietly echo back to Peters as I digest Kathryn's an American aristocrat and part of a financial dynasty.

Truthfully this fact doesn't surprise me in the least. Instead it explains a great deal about this mystery woman. Her countenance has the polish of fine breeding, education, and a certain air of superiority, as if she knows a few of life's hidden secrets. Or perhaps just mine. An unnerving quality.

"I wonder if she celebrates Thanksgiving with Anderson Cooper," I say in jest. My laugh likely stuns Peters. We are all business and I never show any emotions other than anger or frustration when his results aren't sufficient to meet my need for information.

"Well, sir, I'll find out more details about her. Education, employment, and social contacts, if you'd like?"

"Everything. I want everything down to the last possible detail." I end the call. He knows what I want and will deliver. We've been down this road many times before. However, it's usually a business contact or financial enemy who he mines information on. I'm not sure where Kathryn stands yet. However, the one thing I know for sure… she is beautiful and alluring. She seems keen, unflappable, but I have no doubt she'll succumb to my charms given time.

The typical Manhattan woman and Kathryn have little in common. So I need to approach her differently than I do others. The women I usually dabble with are masochists at heart, wanting love, but willing to be with me at whatever cost because they believe I'm a man they can ensnare and possibly tame.

So far the beast inside me remains wild and undomesticated. However, I don't remember a woman inducing such a raw desire in me like Kathryn Delcour. And in just one meeting. Quite the accomplishment.

What happened with Lizzie tonight—quick unmemorable head—isn't how a woman like Kathryn operates. There is no need for desperate ploys. Her performance tonight made that abundantly clear.

The men I saw surrounding her were anxiously fawning to capture her attention, but she left them gawking without a hope for more. She is an enigma. All the more reason for Peters to produce a thorough and in-depth report on her. It's unlikely that I'll see behind her clever façade without some help. She's guarded and has been warned of my ways.

I stare out my car's window and watch the sidewalks pass by, trying to numb my mind and put thoughts of the day behind me. Eddie maneuvers the familiar streets lined with shops that cater to the wealthy. High-rise, coffee shop, restaurant, boutique. The pattern is repeated block after block.

We approach my building on Fifth Avenue. My penthouse occupies one of the top floors at The Pierre Hotel, a cavernous perfection with unmatched views of Manhattan's skyline and Central Park. The door to the SUV opens after we come to a stop in front of my building. I exit and say tomorrow's early morning instructions to Eddie, wishing him a pleasant evening. I thank him for his discretion. Something I've never done before. I don't stop to wonder why.

Another door opens as I approach my building's entrance. I've learned the wealthy here in New York City rarely open their own doors. We pay for others to provide that service. A rather odd thing I have become accustomed to.

The doorman stands regally as he greets me with a tip of his tall hat. I raise my chin, nod in his direction, and turn away. Once inside the lobby, I breeze past the concierge, whose head is bowed before a book, and make my way to the penthouse elevator hidden from the public's view. I enter the special access code, 1958: the year of my mother's birth.

I was born twenty-three years later in a sleepy little town outside of Philly. A pastoral community where my mother, Flora, gave me life but never fully lived her own. Damn, how I miss her.

For some reason, I think back to the Kathryn's scent tonight. If I close my eyes and inhale I can almost replay the moment I caught the sweet smell of her perfume. I'm certain it was Shalimar, what my mother wore. A therapist would have a field day with that one. The woman I want desperately to fuck has a scent that reminds me of my mother. The fact that it doesn't turn me off is what should be alarming, but I can't seem to control what has been set in motion. It's such a strange position to find myself in.

I stare at my odd smile reflected on the elevator's silver doors. Listening to the floors tick away, I ponder how I can have a second encounter with Kathryn. I don't want to wait until another drab event to see her. My fingers itch to touch her skin. My body awakens at the thought of her fingers' gentle touch as it whispered up my arm. I close my eyes at the memory.

Finally, the elevator arrives at the top floor. Few people have had the privilege of seeing what lies behind the mahogany doors standing in front of me. It's my sanctuary and escape from the world. Women are not allowed beyond the doors. The only exception is Rosa, my housekeeper.

Once I'm behind the doors, I proceed to my bedroom. I pass through the hall, a gallery of sorts. On the walls, I've hung masterful works of modern art, mostly in abstract form with bright colors that jump off the canvases. They are very good investments. In my bedroom, I walk into my closet, leaving the colors behind. My room's décor is calming and subdued, much like the clothes I wear. My wardrobe consists of typical Manhattan garb—black, dark gray, and a touch of light gray for variety. A bright tie for a splash of color. I remove my tux and place it in an empty hamper. Rosa will coordinate its cleaning tomorrow and return it to the limo, where it will wait to be donned again.

Skipping my normal nighttime routine of watching the opening of foreign markets, I approach my bed and examine the linen covers. The bed appears welcoming, but I move past it and walk toward the bedroom's wall of glass windows knowing that sleep will likely evade me tonight. My mind is too preoccupied to rest.

What a day. It started with lowest of lows with the news of Simon's deceit. His betrayal has gutted me. I still can't process what led him to try and ruin my company, the one he helped me build. His recent break-up with his fiancée left him devastated. I never met her, although Simon tried to get me to join them for a dinner on several occasions. I didn't socialize with Simon outside of work.

He was smitten by her from all accounts. I was thrilled for him, thinking at last he had found someone to love him. A woman who understood him, who would make a place in her life for him. He took a few days off work after the break-up. Personal days, Simon called them. Since he had never done this before, I should've known that trouble was lurking. But I thought time would help, and he isn't the kind of man who reaches out to others in any way at all. So I gave him space. All of the partners did. A horrible mistake, it would appear on our part.

When I saw him earlier today standing in the rain outside my SUV swiping his finger across his neck, there was pure hatred in his eyes. A murderous glare. Picturing it in my mind makes me recoil. Tomorrow, a meeting is scheduled with Tom and Patrick, my other partners at King Capital. We'll try to weed through all of this. Maybe they can help me connect the dots, figure out why Simon was led to sell me or us out. Simon's out-of-character behavior toward me makes me wonder if I was his target in all of this. The look in his eyes: revenge was there. A payback of some kind was aimed at me.

The evening drove the day away for a few hours at least. But my brain spins the night's events around in my head. The whirling stops when I envision Kathryn walking toward me at the bar. I relive the instant our eyes met and the smile that formed on her lips. My thoughts evoke something rare. Thankfulness. For once I feel grateful to have attended a boring fundraiser.

Standing before the wall of windows, I scan the neon skyline of New York City. Somewhere hidden and tucked away for the night are two forces my mind tangles with—Kathryn Delcour and Simon Edwards.

Onc is an intcnsc, bcautiful woman, full of mystcry and intrigue. The other is a traitorous friend, reeking of deceit.

I give up thinking for now and retreat from viewing the night's black landscape and slip between the cold sheets of my bed, alone as usual. A detail I've never had a problem with before today, before Kathryn.

****

I arise early, before the sun's direct rays light the sky, having had a surprisingly sweet night of sleep. A refreshing rarity for me, and my body feels rested, a nice reward and way to start the day.

Usually my dreams turn nightmarish, keeping me from sleeping more than a few hours at night. My physician advised me to try sleeping pills. But I hated their effect on me. My whole day would feel off, like my mind was disengaged. So needless to say, after several attempts I threw the pills away. I'd rather fight sleep then feel doped up.

But last night the usual terrors didn't invade my sleep, and I awoke without my heart pounding. Instead, I found myself fully erect as I remembered what I had dreamt about. Kathryn's full, red lips and long stocking-covered legs wrapped tightly around my waist as I held her sweet ass in my hands. My body pressed her against my bedroom's window while I fucked her hard. A thorough, rapturous pounding. An infinite view of the skyline was our backdrop. Her lust-filled eyes were my focus.

The erotic remembrance has me awakening with a smile on my face for the first time in years. I consider falling back to sleep, tempted to see if my mind will dream of her again. But instead, I tend to my erection in the shower and start my day.

A breakfast meeting downtown for an upcoming software venture brings me into the office later than I had expected. Mrs. Carter hunches over her desk shuffling through some papers as I make my way toward her. She's likely gathering the latest reports of my personal holdings. Her brows tighten together in worry. She's probably wondering if this morning's numbers are correct, and she's doing some fact checking before presenting me with the totals.

What she's yet to realize is that my trades were off, shot to hell, actually. The loss is novel, slightly frustrating, but oddly amusing. I should call in my chief investment officer to go over the numbers, but I don't really care. The loss of a few million is insignificant compared to meeting Kathryn Delcour.

"Good morning, Mrs. Carter." I hurry past her desk but stop when she stands. Probably on her way to get my coffee.

"Good morning, sir." She lays the papers down and greets me with a weak smile. Likely wondering if she should mention the numbers in front of her. There is no sense in engaging with her on this topic.

"No more coffee for me this morning. Had my fill at breakfast." I say to her, speaking over my shoulder after I've passed by. "I'll buzz you in a few minutes to go over my day. I'm making some changes to it." I close my door before she responds.

There is a scheduled meeting with Tom and Patrick at ten o'clock. During Sir Scott's speech last night, I called the meeting together. We need to discuss Simon and all the ramifications of his leaving Kings Capital. His loss will be felt deep and wide.

After settling at my desk, answering a few emails and reading through some reports, I push the intercom and buzz Ms. Carter.

"In my office. Please."

She walks in casually and takes the seat in front of my desk, hoping to look at ease, but I see the concern in her eyes. "Ready, Mr. Kingsley."

"I suppose you've seen the numbers this morning." My words are more statement than question.

"I was just reviewing the results of the trades. You're aware of their outcomes?" She's wringing her hands and fishing for knowledge, not wanting to reveal the loss to me.

"Of course. I made those pathetic trades. A rare loss for Kings Capital, and me, but we'll recover. After my meeting today at ten with Tom and Patrick, I'm booked with conference calls. Please have a lunch brought up around twelve thirty. Pick something from my usual list of lunch choices. Most of the afternoon will be spent on a call with investors. We're researching a possible new acquisition. Another social media start-up."

"Yes, sir." Mrs. Carter pounds away on her laptop as I give her instructions.

"Remind me of tonight's event. It's slipped my mind."

She appears shocked. I never ask her to refresh my memory. My mind is usually the one others rely on.

"There is a benefit tonight for the New York Public Library. A celebrity event, black tie. I'm sure it's on your schedule. I believe the event begins at seven."

"Okay, please inform Eddie that I'll be leaving at six thirty sharp. That will be all, Mrs. Carter." I spin my chair to face the windows behind me, effectively dismissing her. I hear her leave as quietly as she came.

A call comes in from my executive director, Tom Duffy. He's one of the three friends who came to New York City with me years ago. I've ignored five calls from him this morning, knowing he needs some time to calm down before we talk. This time I answer.

"Yes." My greeting's firm.

"What the hell happened this morning? Did you push the wrong fucking button?" he shouts into the phone. I consider ending the call but continue on.

"So I miscalculated a trade. Just proves I'm only human." I try to deflect the fact that I royally fucked up.

"All right, Adam. You realize that I've known you since our first days at MIT, and you've never blown anything like yesterday's trades." I hear him sighing into the phone. Finally, he starts to calm. "So tell me, please. What the fuck is going on?"

"Not sure, really. But I woke up this morning and there was nothing. You understand what I mean?"

"I was your roommate here in New York for three fucking years. How could I forget your damn dreams? So you didn't have one?"

"Nope. Well, I did have a dream but it was anything but a nightmare." I laugh.

"Okay, I'm heading upstairs to see you. Don't go anywhere." The call ends before I can comment, and I buzz my assistant.

"Mrs. Carter. Mr. Duffy's on his way here." I give her fair warning. I have a feeling his entrance will be nothing less than a whirlwind, or given his size, a mini-hurricane.

Leaning back in my chair, I tap my fingers on the desk's edge awaiting Tom's arrival, wondering how much I should really reveal. He remains the closest thing to a friend I have. Though he disapproves of my sexual lifestyle and prefers to keep our relationship revolved around the business, we share a longstanding history. But deep down I know he'll always have my back, much to his wife Lois' derision.

Our old college chant, "bros over hos," plays in my head as Tom barrels through the office doors.

"Wow. What took so long? Did you take the elevator?" He takes off his jacket and tosses it over the chair in front of my desk. This action signals one thing to me: He's planning to stay a while.

"Like hell. Elevators are for pussies," he says over his shoulder as he makes his way to the office suite's kitchen. He opens the Subzero and removes two water bottles, tossing one my way.

"I see you haven't lost your throwing arm." I catch the bottle and open it, drinking the cold liquid. Tom was quarterback for MIT's football team. Most people don't even realize they have a team, thinking we're all brains, no brawn.

"You know, I still hold the record for most passing yards at MIT." Tom fakes a throw and reacts as if a crowd cheers.

"Sometimes I forget there's a brain inside your oversized head." I roll my eyes as he takes a seat across from me.

"Speaking of brains, yours was obviously asleep when you worked those trades." He stops and pulls a long drink from his bottle. "But I'm curious. No nightmares, right?"

"No nightmares."

"What gives?"

"I attended a fundraiser last night. Same old boring shit, but I met this woman, Kathryn Delcour. She's the daughter of Ava Swanson. You know, she heads The Swanson Foundation. It's named after her late husband, Richard Swanson." I smile wickedly when I see the curious look on his face.

"So you took her for the infamous Adam Kingsley ride in your limo, I presume." Tom waggles his damn brows. It's hard to believe his I.Q is one sixty.

"No, Lizzie Woodward occupied the limo last night. This woman is older, just a couple years, but, damn, she's something else. And aggressive. Told me she teaches men how to fuck women into oblivion. Something about fucking being an 'art form'." I use my fingers to make quotes as I repeat Kathryn's words.

"Wonder why I've never heard of her. Other than the fact that I'm the most married thirty-two-year old in Manhattan and off the dating scene for years." Tom sighs.

"I'm wondering why, too. I've noticed her at a few fundraisers lately, but it's like she appeared out of thin air. So

Peters is gathering some background on her for me. Should know more by lunch."

"Gotta say Adam, she must have made quite the impression. No head or fucking and you still want to know about her?" He laughs. "So you think meeting her had something to do with your nightmares not happening?"

"I don't know. But I do remember the one dream I had last night, and she was in it." I stare out the window and reflect. "I held her pressed against the glass wall in my bedroom with her legs wrapped around me. The only thing she was wearing was a pair of black stockings…" My voice trails off.

"Shit. Don't stop, man." Tom throws his hands up signaling me to continue.

I take a moment to catch my breath, because reliving my dream's illicit feelings is something I try to avoid at work. When I cross the threshold of my building, my sex life doesn't enter with me. I leave it in my SUV, literally.

"You want all the details?" I'm surprised Tom wants me to share the dream with him. I usually don't tell him specifics about my sexual exploits. Maybe a dream makes it different.

"Hey, I said don't stop." He looks at me with desperate eyes, like a druggie begging for a fix.

"Okay," I decide to continue on the explicit version. "I fucked her hard. She moaned and clawed my back as I held on to her ass and pounded her pussy. It was hot, primal."

Silence ensues. Rare for Tom. Common for me.

"Wow. This woman's gotten to you, Adam. I've known you for fourteen years, and I've never heard you talk like this. So you're going to see her again, right?"

"Kathryn saw me leave with someone else last night and she seemed to know the girl, too. Besides, who knows when or if I'll see her again." I think about the if. It's unsettling and I know I'll make our paths cross. They have to. And it's not just my dick that wants to see her, or be in her for that matter, there's something more.

"Hell, who can resist you or your money? Although I'm not sure what the appeal is. Since you're a total fuck-and-dump kinda guy." Tom scoffs.

"True. My life may appear fucked up to you, but it's worked. Look around you. See where we're sitting." Tom begins to laugh.

"Good point. We're sitting here atop your building discussing your first night of good sleep since you graduated college, and how you fucked up a trade that cost this company millions of dollars. Hell, the media has been speculating about your move all morning. Sounds as if your life is peachy to me," Tom replies sarcastically while shaking his head at me.

"About that loss…" My computer screen flashes as a programmed trade executes. Technically, I've bet on the market's reaction to our company's losses. A legal type of insider trading where I am my own victim. A contrarian's move that has just made me a lofty dividend.

"What's up?" Tom moves behind me, peering over my shoulder at the screen.

"We're whole now. The loss was just covered and then some," I announce smugly with a proud grin plastered across my face.

"Goddamn it, Adam. You're a lucky son of a bitch." Tom slaps his hand on my shoulder.

"Luck has nothing to do with it. I just knew. My earlier bet might have been off, but my loss from yesterday created speculation in the chip market. I just exploited the capitulation from the fallout. Simple. What goes up must come down, and vice a versa, at least when I'm involved."

"Still, you're one lucky son of bitch." Tom laughs as he punches my bicep. "Oh, by the way. I'm a little early for our ten o'clock meeting. Your email said it was something about Simon. I've been hearing strange rumors this morning. But no one is confirming them. He's not in his office either. I know he's had some tough times lately, but I thought he was back to work. God knows this company needs him."

"I'd rather wait until Patrick arrives. Repeating myself and answering the same likely questions doesn't appeal to me."

"Okay, but now I'm freaking out. Before I was just worried." Tom needs details, I understand. He's not one to wait until Christmas to find out what he's getting under the tree. I predict he'll hound me until I spill.

"Here, let's get Patrick up here." I buzz Mrs. Carter. "Ask Patrick to come on up early for our ten o'clock meeting. Tell him it's urgent."

"Yes, sir," Mrs. Carter replies dutifully as always.

Tom stands from his seat and walks slowly to the window. He appears to be gazing out at nothing. His face void of expression. Deep in thought, something important is most definitely on his mind. I'm quietly waiting, not wanting to disturb or rush him. Finally he speaks, "Lois is pregnant, by the way."

"Congratulations, right?" Feeling guarded, I pause for a rcsponsc.

"Yeah, right." Tom's answer is flat, but full of meaning.

Tom and Lois have gone through hell trying to conceive during the last few years. When she suffered a miscarriage last year, I've never seen Tom so down. The loss put a strain on their marriage, too. I hope this pregnancy is successful, because I've never seen a couple want a child like they do.

"I wish you and Lois the best, Tom. How's she feeling?" I attempt to deflect Tom's anxious mood.

"She's feeling good now. The morning sickness was a bitch, but she's finally over it. We've been waiting to share the news until she was past the three month mark. She's fifteen weeks now."

I stand up and walk to him, putting a hand on his shoulder. We've been friends too long for me to sit there and not reach out to him. His concern is mine in some strange way. He's the closest thing on this earth I have to a brother.

"This week. Guy's night out. There's a new mid-town bar. We should check it out."

He turns to me and smiles. "Thanks, Adam, but I'm not sure that's a good idea. The last time you took me out for drinks, you ended up abandoning me at the bar. You left with two women, if I'm not mistaken. Rubbed my married ass into the ground with that move. Damn, they were hot as shit, too. Remember?"

"Distantly." I pause while my mind travels back to that night. The hotel room. The shiny surface of handcuffs. Ties attached to bedposts and long slender legs. "They were recent college graduates. Sorority sisters. Kinky fucking must've been their majors. They were practically pros. Who carries bondage shit around in their purse, anyway?"

"Man, the life you lead, Adam. Sometimes I envy you, other times I think you're a crazy motherfucker. One day, you'll fall for someone and it will be hard. Who knows, maybe this woman from last night? What was her name again?"

"Kathryn Delcour." Her name rolls off my tongue. Just the thought of her makes me smile and erases any trace of the kinky night from my mind.

"Wow, look at that smile. This woman I have got to meet."

"Don't hold your breath. I have a lot to learn about her. We just barely met."

"But you can't forget her, can you? She's gotten under your skin. Do you want to just fuck her or get to know her, too?" Tom scores big on his loaded questions and stares me down until I decide on an answer.

"Both." I answer honestly. Tom would see through my lies. He grins knowingly at me, shaking his head. "Where the hell is Patrick?"

"Nice subject change." Tom sneers.

"You liked that one?" I question back with a laugh and he joins me. I decide to buzz Mrs. Carter.

"Any word from Patrick?" I ask my assistant.

"Yes, Mr. Kingsley. He's just now exiting the elevator. I'll send him on in."

When Patrick pushes the doors to my office open, Tom and I are once again sitting in our seats.

"Hello, guys." Patrick enters the room and proceeds to my desk with a troubled scowl on his face. He can't be over five foot eight but has a commanding presence. He's tough as nails, and I will likely be leaning on him greatly now that Simon is gone. "I heard some crazy shit this morning about Simon. I hope you can help me out here, Adam.

"Take a seat, Patrick. This may take a while."

"Don't tell me it's true?" An angry fury washes over Patrick's face as he recognizes my silent confirmation. "Why the hell did you fire him? And without a word to Tom and me."

Resting my elbows on the desk, I place my hands on my forehead, slightly bowing my head. This conversation can't be avoided, so I raise my head and start at the beginning.

"Yesterday, our security head, Carl Young, intercepted an incoming email from Talcott Innovations. Carl set up a secret security system that scours data in our networks for key words. It even identifies emails from separate Internet sites like Gmail when someone logs on via our system. All our competitor's names are tagged with an alert. This system was so undercover that even Simon didn't know about it. And you know he is privy to everything." Patrick is shaking his head in disbelief while Tom has a confused look on his face.

"The email Carl found clearly confirms Simon was delivering something of great value to Talcott. He was going to leave Kings and take a high level position over there. He would pass on our Fireproof software to them, and in return they would thank him with a fat paycheck. Millions of banking customers could have been exposed if this software actually changed hands. Our entire company might've collapsed over the exposure."

"Why the fuck would Simon do this to us?" Tom has moved to the edge of his seat now.

Stunned disbelief registers on both Tom's and Patrick's faces. They are having as hard a time as I did believing that Simon would betray us and the company.

"He's been acting weird since his fiancée dumped him. I tried to get him to talk about it. But you know Simon, he keeps everything to himself. None of us has even met her. At times I wondered if she existed," Patrick says, attempting to make sense of Simon's behavior.

"I agree with you, Patrick. I'm angry as hell at Simon, but something doesn't add up here," I say, echoing their incomprehension. "Simon wasn't close with us. Nothing like we all are, but he's not close with anyone. We are likely the only friends he has."

"I've been at a loss, too," Tom chimes in. "Being so distraught over a woman that he turns on his only friends just doesn't seem like Simon's style. Not that he really had one, but this betrayal is something I would've never expected. Not in a million years."

"Carl emailed me last night with the rundown of Simon's departure from Kings." I continue explaining the situation to them. "Yesterday afternoon, Carl told Simon he was needed on the main floor. Simon dutifully followed. When they approached the main door, a lobby guard joined Carl. Simon was then told to hand over his company ID, corporate credit cards, and his Blackberry. Simon briefly protested but Carl presented a copy of the Talcott email. Simon offered no resistance at that point. I actually watched Simon leaving the building from my SUV as Carl escorted him out."

In my rundown I fail to mention Simon's approach to my vehicle, his rabid eyes filled with hate, and his finger that traced across his neck. When my mind repeats the scene from yesterday, it feels more like I'm watching a movie rather than replaying an actual experience in my own life. Tom's voice brings me out of the horrible vision.

"Where do we go from here? How are you planning on handling the public exposure with his departure? Our investors are gonna shit. Wall Street, too." Tom brings up the points we need to discuss. Nothing surrounding this whole debacle is going to be easy.

After almost two hours of debating and discussing the void created in our company with Simon's departure, we decide on the best direction with the media and attorneys. We all agree Patrick will step in and take Simon's place on an interim basis. Patrick will have his second in command take over his position as Chief Financial Officer.

When the meeting finally concludes, I'm exhausted. Tom and Patrick head to the door to exit my office. Their shoulders are weighted down, and there is a little drag in their steps. Simon's betrayal will take a long time for us to work through. Forgiving and forgetting aren't likely to happen any time soon. But we all want to know what led Simon to stab us in the back.

The door shuts behind Tom and Patrick as they exit my office, and I'm left alone. Solitude surrounds me.

Chapter 5

Mrs. Carter notifies me when Peters arrives. I close my laptop to give him my undivided attention. It's an appointment that occurs every day, rain or shine, here or via phone. I have tabs to keep up on and people to monitor. Today, however, my focus shifts to Kathryn Delcour.

I'm anxious to know what Peters has learned about her. Details are what I'm looking for. I wipe my sweaty hands across my trousers, stopping as I realize that for the second time in less than twenty-four hours, just the thought of Kathryn Delcour has made me sweat.

"Damn her," I angrily mutter as Peters walks in and takes his usual chair.

"Did you say something, sir?" Peters lifts his brow, looking at me quizzically.

"No, no. I'm fine." I'm quick to dismiss his question. "What do you have?"

"Which would you like first, Kathryn Delcour or the daily X report?" Peters motions with the two folders in his hand.

"Anything new on the X front?"

"Status quo. Let's say the wheels are grinding slow, but still exceedingly fine," he tells me with a hint of a smile on his mouth.

"Let's skip that update for now. Just give me the folder and I'll look it over later. I'm really interested in what you found on Kathryn Delcour."

Peters opens the folder marked Delcour, K. "I made two copies." He hands me some papers. Kathryn's information I presume.

"I conducted an intensive and thorough due-diligence report and also called in a special favor from our friends at Sprint." I smile remembering Peters' ability to skate the law.

I start at the top of the list.

SUBJECT: Kathryn Marie Delcour

DOB: February 15, 1979

AGE: 34

SPOUSE: Jean-Paul Delcour, June 21, 2009. Olympic silver medalist, deceased, Feb. 14, 2011. Death ruled accidental. Result of a skiing accident in the French Alps.

EDUCATION: Dalton School, 1998
Barnard College, 1998-1999
Sorbonne, Paris, France, 1999-2002
Université Paris Diderot, PhD in Psychology, 2008

ADDRESS: 997 Fifth Avenue #20A (Upper East Side)
New York, NY 10001
Sold for $6,499,000 on 10/13/2012

No mortgage lien
Yearly common charges: $19,229
3 bedroom/2 ½ baths

PREVIOUS ADDRESS: *732 Rue du Bastille, Paris, France (17th Arrondissement)

BUSINESS: The Spiritual Touch, LLC. New York, NY

WEBSITE: TheSpiritualTouch.com

Kathryn as a young widow is hard to reconcile in my mind. Her marriage to an Olympic athlete was short-lived, less than a couple years before he died. I imagine a tall and handsome man with her on his arm, both smiling. My fingers want to enter his name into my computer and search. Jealousy perhaps? Or maybe I'm just intrigued and want to learn more about the man who once held her heart.

Looking at her New York City address, I realize we live only a few blocks away from each other on Fifth Avenue. Surely, she used family money to purchase her apartment. How else could she afford such luxury?

But my reading stops when I reach the name of her business. I wonder what the hell type of business this woman operates.

"I need more details on this business of hers." I look directly at Peters. "Sounds like a seedy massage parlor's name to me."

"I thought the same thing and expected your response, so I did a little more digging. It's all in the report. Ms. Delcour is a certified Tantra teacher. According to her company's website, she left a successful practice as a psychologist in Paris after experiencing the…" Peters pauses to read from the papers in his hand, "'Freedom, sensuality, and healing power of Tantra,' whatever the fuck that is, sir. It seems she took up this practice after the death of her husband, a Giant Slalom silver medalist. She recently moved back to New York City, opened this business, and does whatever the hell Tantra teachers do."

"That's what she meant by teaching men to 'fuck women into oblivion.' Tantra is a sexual practice taken from the Far East, I believe, and teaches some new age type techniques. That sums up my limited knowledge." I sputter the last sentence then mumble, "I plan to find out more, though. And here I thought she might have been referring to her own personal lovers." Kathryn's comments being semi-professional make more sense. Now I want to learn more about Tantra as I'm completely intrigued.

"Peters, you mentioned calling in a favor from our cell phone company. I'm hoping it has something to do with GPS." I find myself on the edge of my seat, anxious to hear his response.

"Exactly. I have her cell phone's GPS tracking. I emailed you an app for it. Click on the link, then download it to your phone, and you should be good to go." He points to my phone lying next to me on the desk.

"How did you know I would want such an intrusion into her personal life?" I stare at Peters, unflinching.

"Call it a hunch, but other than your birth father, you've never asked for someone's background unless there's a business connection. And this request seemed personal. Am I right?"

"Spot on as usual, but that's what I pay you for—getting it right." Peters smiles, satisfied.

"I have what I need for now," I conclude while browsing over the documents from Peters. "But keep digging. I'd like to find out more about her switch to Paris for schooling. What made her leave New York City? Email me anything you find that adds to this report. That'll be all for today."

Peters takes my cue and leaves me rustling through the papers of Kathryn's report. She's become less of a mystery but remains a puzzle to me, so I carry on, hoping to learn more.

Her education reflects her pedigree: all elite schools. One year at Barnard and then finishing her studies in Paris is unusual. I hope Peters can find out more about her transfer. Having visited Paris many times, imagining her there isn't difficult. A beautiful young woman buried in her books while driving the young boys crazy.

I pull the first paper of the report back out of the pile and lay it on top, finding the web address for her business. I open my laptop and punch in the address, my fingers flying over the keyboard. On my screen pops her homepage with her picture sitting to the middle right of the page.

Fuck, she's smiling in a rather coy fashion, with a trace of seduction behind her eyes. Beautiful. She is simply breathtaking. My eyes can't even leave her face to read the words on the screen. I could really care less right now.

Acting on an impulse, which I never do, I set my mind on a course of action and get the wheels in motion. I'm going after her today, as in right now. I believe it's time to act on Mrs. Swanson's motherly advice and persuade the beautiful Kathryn to have dinner with me.

"Mrs. Carter. Cancel the rest of my meetings for today. Reschedule the conference call with the investors for tomorrow. Tell them I'm," I can't think of a good excuse, because I never cancel calls like this one. "Oh, hell, make up a believable excuse. And inform Tom Duffy that he and Lois will be attending tonight's fundraiser for the New York Public Library in my place." Lois lives for going to events where celebrities and New

York's elite mingle. A night out on the town might be a good thing for her, and Tom, as well.

"Yes, sir. Anything else?"

"Hold all my calls this afternoon. I don't want to be disturbed. Only notify me if something is code red urgent." I hear her affirmative reply and text Eddie to meet outside my building in twenty minutes.

I grab my Blackberry and open Peters' email containing the GPS tracking app for Kathryn's phone. The download appears to be working smoothly. I wait for the blue dot to display on the screen and grin wickedly when I see it appear.

I have a Fifth Avenue address to stalk.

****

The sunny weather's pleasant this afternoon with a light breeze blowing through my hair. I'm thankful it's not raining like yesterday as I lean against my shiny black Escalade illegally parked in front of 997 Fifth Avenue. I have removed my tie and loosened my collar, but my suit coat remains. I place my hands in my pockets after checking my watch and Kathryn's blue dot again.

I've been here for several hours now waiting for Ms. Delcour. Searching the Internet on my phone while I stand around, I start exploring the world of Tantra. It's some wild shit. The more I learn, the more I become confused. I switch to Kathryn's GPS app again and notice the dot has moved slightly but not from the address I'm staking out. Hopefully this slight change means she's finally leaving her apartment. I'm not sure how much longer Eddie can stay parked here. Traffic is becoming heavy as the rush hour nears.

I focus on the building's doorman. Any movement from him signals a resident's eminent exit from the building. He seems relaxed and jovial when he speaks to the residents as they come and go.

The doorman cracks his biggest smile yet and reaches for the door to let someone exit. I hold my breath. My heart begins to race because I know without a doubt who it is the second she appears in my line of sight. It's Kathryn with her face turned toward the doorman. She gracefully tosses back her head and laughs. I can vaguely hear her from where I stand.

She places her bag on her shoulder and starts to stride my way. I relish in the sight of her, observing her unnoticed for now. Tousled, wavy hair. Tight-assed jeans tucked in tall, black leather boots. Her hips have the sexy sway I noticed from last night. She looks up midstride and stops when she sees me.

Our eyes connect and she appears shocked or maybe confused. Rightly so, I would have never done this with any other woman. Judging from her wide blue eyes, she knows it, too. My appearance is unexpected, but after a quick moment she appears rather amused having processed I'm here for her. She lowers her head briefly before raising it again. Maybe she needed to look away and make sure she was really seeing me.

I feel my smile turning into that sexy smirk, my trademark expression when I'm attracted to a woman and on the prowl. I stuff my phone into my jacket pocket since I don't need to track Kathryn anymore. Instead I watch her approach as my presence becomes clear to her.

Goddamn, she's a sight to behold. Seeing her finally walking toward me was worth the long wait. My heart continues to race in anticipation as she draws closer.

Kathryn stops and stands in front of me. A sparkle in her eyes shines at me, and only one word describe the goddess in front of me: breathtaking.

She starts to speak, but I still her ruby lips by placing my index finger across them and mouth a simple and quieting word to her.

"Hush," I whisper. I remove my finger now that her lips have stilled.

"Good afternoon, Ms. Delcour. Lovely day isn't it? Glad you decided to leave the confines of your apartment. I was wondering if you had plans for dinner. Could I interest you in something to eat?" I pause and watch her beautiful face transform from shock to amusement. "Just following up on your mother's suggestion."

"Cut the 'good afternoon' crap. You really are something, Mr. Kingsley. Standing here waiting for me as if nothing seems out of place." She snarls out a laugh. "I'd ask how you found me, but at this point I have a feeling you know everything about me anyway. Probably even down to my bra size and favorite cologne." Smirking, she walks closer, almost touching me. A preferable position.

"That's easy. D cup. Shalimar, and you're a Tantra instructor." The bra size and perfume guesses don't faze her, but she appears surprised or maybe a bit uneasy when I mention Tantra.

"Oh my God, you do know everything." She knits her brow and shakes her head at me in disbelief.

"I confess to knowing a bit about you, but I still don't know the answer to my question: Dinner?" Raising my brow, I smile encouragingly at her. Usually this combination wins me the right answer, but with her everything is up in the air.

"Well, Mr. Kingsley, you're pretty sure of yourself, aren't you?" She laughs and I nod in agreement, knowing it's one of my innate traits. Insecurity isn't a feeling I experience, and the lack of it has served me well. "But don't you think it's a little early for dinner? It's New York City. No one eats dinner before seven."

In an attempt to distract me, she runs her fingers down my suit coat's lapel. This woman does have a thing for suit coats, and I make a note to remember this little detail. I notice a gold Cartier watch sitting on her thin wrist as her hand pulls away from me. It seems she prefers the finer things like I do.

"If I know your cup size, surely you can call me by my first name."

"I'll have to think about that request, Mr. Kingsley. One thing is for certain, though, I won't be going anywhere in that car with you." She points to the black metal I'm still leaning against, and disappointment hits me, hard. Rejection isn't something I'm used to hearing from the women I'm chasing. Then again, I can't remember the last time I chased a woman. Usually they're drawn to me like magnets.

"And why won't you go with me in my limo? I'll keep my hands to myself." I want to add "for the first few blocks," but think better of it.

"I doubt you have the ability to tell yourself or your hands no." Her doubts are probably right. She rolls her eyes at me when my devilish smile confirms them. "This is a belated question. But what are you really doing here? Well, besides stalking me."

"I took the afternoon off. The evening too for that matter. Canceled everything. I wanted to see if you would accompany me to dinner. I believe that question has already been asked."

"So let me get this straight, Mr. Kingsley, you have been standing outside my building in hopes that I'd walk out before you starved to death?" Her question is more of a tease. "I don't even want to know how you found out I was at my apartment. You know this is rather creepy, don't you?"

Telling her I can trace her cell phone via GPS technology would most likely have me spending a boring evening alone. Alone and wishing I'd kept my mouth shut.

So lying is the best option, or at least glossing over the truth. "As you said, it's New York City. Who eats dinner at home? Eventually I thought you'd surface. Looks like I was right." I wink and tap my temple with my index finger, trying to convince her of my divining powers. I smile as my line finally elicits a sweet little giggle from her. Distraction is my ally here.

I boldly encompass her small hand in mine, pulling her closer to me. So close that I'm now looking straight down into her eyes, and I see small violet flecks contrasting against the bright blue. A new discovery to this beautiful woman. The small bits of violet shine and get caught in the afternoon sun like a jewel's facets.

I decide to press her for an answer. I want her with me. No more delays. "Let me take you somewhere, anywhere. You can pick the place. Say yes?" My request is more a soft pleading as I hope to persuade and charm her.

"You really do have the seduction game down pat." Eyeing me speculatively, she pulls away. I prepare for defeat, even though I have no reference for a rejection like this. "I'll probably regret this, but I'll go with you on one condition."

"Okay. What's the condition?" I can't believe I'm listening to her demands. This is new territory for me. Relenting control in the mating game is something I never consciously do with a woman. But oddly, it's a total fucking turn-on. I feel my cock starting to press against the fabric of my pants, and a need to be deep inside her floods over me.

"You came to my turf and that's where we will stay. Capisce?" I smile and nod as I give into her stern demeanor. She has me. I wonder what schemes I would have resorted to if she had said no. Thankfully, I'll never know. My dignity remains somewhat intact.

"I was heading to meet a close friend at a coffee shop around the corner and I'm already running late." She sounds concerned and perhaps a little troubled I'm holding her up even more. "Feel free to follow me."

She scoots past me, laughing as she peers at me over her shoulder. "You coming?"

I open the door to the Escalade and tell Eddie to be on stand-by, knowing he and I are at the mercy of this gorgeous woman. Quickly walking up behind her, I hear the distinct sound of a mocking laugh. "I figured as much."

"I think I might just trail behind a bit and follow you. The view is, um, well, it's…" Words fail me as she stops, turns, and walks back toward me.

"You're something, Mr. Kingsley." She tosses her hair to the side, and I breathe in a faint whiff of Shalimar. "I'm not sure I want you walking behind me. It's unnerving. It's side by side for you. I need to see what you're doing at all times. Absolutely no hiding. Got it?"

"Another condition, I see." I chuckle, enjoying the playfulness between us. I can't remember feeling this carefree with another woman, or human being for that matter. I guess Tom's craziness is the closest thing, but it's all one-sided with him, and his humor and jabs are usually at my expense. And most importantly, he doesn't have the enticing curves this woman does. I find myself smiling, truly enjoying myself.

"With your history, my rules are something you might need to get used to. You're on a short leash, Mister." Surely she's teasing, but I need to stay on my best behavior. Knowing full well that I'll likely find myself in trouble with her again.

Eyes watch and the heads of strangers turn as we pass by. The men look at Kathryn, lustfully, and then see me walking by her side. Their looks of envy are reminiscent of last night's gala, and I wonder what happened to the "teach men how to fuck women into oblivion" Kathryn. The beauty is there, but her bite seems tempered. Perhaps it was the wine or the likelihood we would never see each other again. One thing's for sure, we will be drinking at dinner. Is it too early for shots? I silently pray it's not.

Dutifully, I walk with her down 81st toward Madison Avenue, past art galleries owing their patronage to the Met a block away. Occasionally sneaking a peek at her, she smiles at me each time. There's no missing the energy between us. It's electric and I swear if we touch…there would be a spark.

As we turn the corner onto Madison, a gust of wind hits our backs and catches her hair. Before I know what I'm doing, I pull the wayward hair from her face. My fingers brush her checks, and her breathing hitches with my touch. I comb the windblown strands back, my fingers dragging through her soft silk.

"Your hair is beautiful." My voice is low, but she hears me and smiles. A hint of a blush spreads across her cheeks. It's obvious I am affecting her physically, too, a heady feeling for me. And the only thought running through my mind is how I'd like to fuck her into oblivion.

"Thank you," she says. "Yours is, um… sexy. It's the first thing I noticed about you."

"Is that right?" I tease.

"Yes, other than the fact that you were the best-looking man in the room." She stops abruptly. "We're here."

I want to go back to her last comment, but the moment has passed. Our destination has appeared. We're standing on the sidewalk in front of a place called Nectar Coffee Shop. The café's façade consists of glass doors, all open and moved to the side al fresco style. I guide her under the awning as my hand snakes covertly to the small of her back, pressing lightly.

Hopefully, we can revisit what she thinks about me later. My focus stays on her words, "...you were the best-looking man in the room." A proud smile graces my lips, but it fades quickly as we approach a tall, dark and, well, some would qualify him as a handsome man. Fuck, this man must be the friend she was meeting. This discovery is highly troubling to me.

He's smiling brightly at her, and she returns it with one of her own. It's a totally different greeting than what she gave me outside of her building. An intimacy between them reflects on their faces as they look one to the other. A familiar togetherness.

I take a step or two back, unprepared for this. Peters didn't mention a boyfriend in his background report. I'm thrown off my game, not knowing what I was walking into. The man with a smile full of gleaming white teeth gives her that uppity phantom side-to-side kiss and embraces her, tightly. As he does, her petite frame folds into him and gets lost underneath his pumped-up biceps.

"Chéri." His accent, he's French. "Looking beautiful as always." A British accent I can tolerate, not his, not this. He pulls her away, leading her to a small table on the edge of the café, practically outside. Kathryn ignores me, and it seems Frenchie doesn't notice I'm standing here. Whether it's on purpose is not clear, but I follow them with the intention of finding out.

"Thanks, Jacques," she gushes while pulling back from his arms. "You're in a good mood. Already had your afternoon coffee fix, I see?"

As Kathryn engages with him, she acts as if I'm not there. She treats me in total disregard and walks away with Frenchie without even a backward glance. Being totally ignored grates on my pride, so I cut in. I started this fucking dance with her today and will continue to lead. But to be honest, I have played catch up with her since we've met. The best I can do is try to gain a little ground here instead of losing it to this other man. I step forward and take a place at her side.

"Kathryn, I assume this is your friend." I watch this man turn toward me. Finally acknowledging my presence. Game on, and I extend my hand for the customary gentleman's greeting. "Adam Kingsley." Territory marked.

Jacques, as Kathryn called him, clasps my hand firmly, almost to the point of pain. "Doctor Jacques LeBaron. Wait, you're that Wall Street mogul guy?" I nod, and I'll be damned if he doesn't start to laugh in a fucking French accent. But I see no humor in our introduction. What a fucking bastard. A heated craze courses through me as he continues his chuckling.

"Care to share the joke with Kathryn and me?" There's no hiding the anger in my voice. I don't even try to mask it.

"I'm sorry." Frenchie's hand covers his mouth as he stifles his fucking laugh. "My apologies. Are you here with Kathryn?"

"Yes, Mr. Kingsley's here with me. What's so funny, Jacques?" Kathryn appears to be as confused as I am.

After Frenchie learns I'm with Kathryn, he looks a little bewildered and cowers under my glare. My self-assurance in this awkward moment trumps him, and I feel victory. But then I notice him glancing to the side. A file is lying on the table he must've been reserving for Kathryn.

It's as clear as day. The letters and name pop out at me.

Woodward, L.

Lively's folder? Fuck. Why would Frenchie have a file related to last night's blowjob? He looks at me and quickly reaches over to cover the folder's name, and then begins to mutter in French, too low and slurred for me to translate.

"Kathryn, may I speak with you…alone?" Frenchie's brow scrunches together, and his eyes dart between Kathryn and me.

"Sure thing, Jacques. Just give me a second." Kathryn faces me, signaling sideways with her head that we need to move, so we shuffle a few feet away.

"This concerns my Tantra teaching. I need to speak to him alone for a second." She's looking up at me; a demure smile plays across those plump lips.

"Okay." My voice is tight, because I'm not okay with this entire situation. I want to know how Frenchie is involved in her teaching.

"Enough with the attitude." She rolls her eyes at me. "Jacques is a psychologist at Mount Sinai. He had a practice in Paris and we often worked together with clients. Occasionally he has a client who needs help in my area of expertise. He's the clinician, I'm more the practitioner."

"Yes, the 'how to fuck women into oblivion' thing you do." My words mock her.

"You remembered that." How could I fucking forget that declaration from her? And now instead of Frenchie, she is the one laughing at me. I am definitely catching a glimpse of the vamp I met last night. "Jacques wants to give me a file from a client he saw this morning. Apparently, she knows me and needs some help and direction with her love life. She specifically requested me. He gave me vague details earlier, but I agreed to look her file over. Can you give us a few minutes? Patient rights and all that."

"I'll wait outside. I need to make a call anyway." I reach in my suit jacket's inner pocket for my phone and move to the newsstands in front of the café.

A deep panic, something I rarely feel, grows within me as I process the meaning and implication of her words. Lizzie Woodward, last night's limo ride, is the patient Frenchie saw this morning. And possibly will be Kathryn's new student. With Frenchie nervously hiding her name from me, the conclusion is clear.

My name was brought up by the dear Ms. Lively this morning, and it's most likely written down somewhere in her file. Just waiting to be read by Kathryn, and something tells me that what Frenchie wrote down is anything but flattering. I'm royally fucked. My hopes of getting to know Kathryn are in tatters before I even get started.

Kathryn mentioned last night she knew about some of the women I'd been with. She implied they were less than satisfied with my performance. Some even going as far as to warn her about me. I recall when Kathryn greeted Lizzie outside the coatroom in the lobby. They knew each other before last night, and I fear they will be meeting together now.

I mistakenly thought their familiarity was social, but instead it's likely professional, patient, therapist or fucking Tantra teacher related.

I look back inside the café. Frenchie's talking animatedly while Kathryn regards me closely. I've quickly processed what this all means, and I have to laugh because I've managed to screw up what is likely my first attempt at pursuing a woman based on feelings apart from my cock. It's ironic how wicked fate has plotted against me. If I was a believer in Karma, I might have to wonder.

Maybe I should call Eddie. Cut my losses and have him pick me up. He's only around the corner and there's still time to make that fundraiser tonight. I'll have Mrs. Carter call Tom and tell him I've decided to go after all. I'll just leave out the reason why…or maybe I won't. It's simple really; I've likely fucked up my chances with Kathryn.

I refocus on my phone's screen, shielding it from the direct sunlight. The display shows one missed call from Peters. I can't wait to pin his ass against the wall for neglecting his work on Kathryn's background. I will not tolerate what happened today. Walking into a situation where I am left looking like an idiot is not acceptable.

Glancing up from my phone, I see Kathryn laughing at something Frenchie's said, likely at my expense. I can barely hear their conversation, though I know it's spoken in French. Her black hair swings to the side as she turns to face me. Her mouth produces a warm smile. It's for me. And it's paralyzing with the exception of one place that involuntarily responds to this beautiful woman's red lips and alluring eyes. She waves me forward to rejoin them and I respond. A moth to a flame.

But I need to make a quick decision. Buck up and endure what's ahead with Kathryn and Frenchie, or possibly find a person willing to help my belt get unbuckled at the Library gala? Which will it be?

I have a feeling I already know as I feel my feet moving in Kathryn's direction.

Chapter 6

As I'm reentering the café, Frenchie hastily stuffs the file of L. Woodward back into his attaché case. His angry movements betray him, and his rough shuffling of the papers make him appear on edge. After securing his case, he lowers his head and brushes past me. His only utterance is a gruff, "Good day."

My black oxfords spin me around to watch him exit the café. I hear a couple of frustrated words he's speaking in French.

"Mon dieu. Mon dieu. Quel idiot." Frenchie shakes his head, looking back to where Kathryn and I are left. I wonder what transpired between them. I watch Frenchie as he hails a cab and disappears into the congested traffic.

Kathryn moves closer to my side and gently touches my arm. I can't help but wonder what came over Frenchie. "I think he just called one of us a fool."

"Ignore him. He's just being overprotective of me. I don't think you're a personal favorite of his."

"He doesn't even know me. Or at least this was the first time we've met." At first his reaction confuses me, but I start to connect the dots. He's possibly had experiences with me through a patient. That's his frame of reference for me. Not a very flattering thought, either. But I decide to hide my conclusion to possibly hear the truth from Kathryn. "So tell me why I'm not high on his list?"

"I wish he'd stayed around to tell you himself, but he was afraid of violating privacy rights with the patient he saw this morning. And after seeing us together, he wouldn't even tell me who she was, although I do know it was a she." Kathryn raises her brow in a curious gesture.

There's no way in hell I'm going to confess to Kathryn the patient in question is someone who sucked me off last night. My hope of spending the evening with her would likely end immediately, and I just can't let that happen. Thankfully, Frenchie didn't expose me, any hopes I have with her tonight would've been lost. He abided by the privacy laws, although I wonder if he will keep silent about it forever. He seemed pretty upset Kathryn was staying with me.

"This new patient and my inability to take her on as a client is strange. Something changed when he saw you with me. I can't figure it out. Whatever it is, Jacques was upset and advised me not to be around you." Kathryn looks straight into my eyes, and I hope she can't see that I'm hiding a secret from her.

"So another warning from a friend about Adam Kingsley. He is a friend, right? Or is he more, perhaps?"

"He's been more to me. Off and on over the last couple years. Right now our status is off. But he does care for me, and basically he believes you are trouble. I told him I know you are. Big trouble, as a matter of fact. Dangerous, most likely."

She winks and once again runs her fingers under my suit coat's lapel. Her fingers press hard and move slowly down my chest. I swallow back a moan as her eyes take on a mischievous glint. The feisty Kathryn from last night's event has resurfaced. And God, how I love her feistiness. But I can't shake her words, the thought Frenchie has been more than a colleague. This leads me to one conclusion: They've slept or Tantra'd together. A rush of anger hits me at the thought of Frenchie having been with her. Kissed her, fucked her. There's only one label to stamp my feelings with: jealousy. But I squash them before she can see them on my face or in my eyes.

"Well, are you… trouble?" she purrs while looking wickedly at me.

"On the contrary. I think you're the one that's trouble for me. I skipped out of work early… unheard of. My assistant is holding all calls, which never happens. I'm forgoing a fundraiser tonight, making my partner go in my place." I continue on as if the thought of her and Frenchie isn't still bothering me.

"Oh, poor Kingsley. Missing out on some limo sex after the event for the night?" she says mockingly, sweetly. "So you don't make it a habit of showing up at a woman's doorstep on a bright sunny afternoon?"

"I can assure you I don't just show up on anyone's doorstep, no matter the weather or time of day. Today's adventure is a first for me, Kathryn. I couldn't seem to stop thinking about you." I want to take her hand, the one that just traced my jacket and now rests at her side, but I decide against it.

"You keep saying things like that to me, Kingsley, and I'm definitely going to be in trouble." She giggles, and I find myself loving the sound when she does. I dutifully follow her out the door of the café, hoping we can find some trouble together later. I'd like to erase the memory of Frenchie from her mind and body. But I'm not sure she'll let me have access to either one.

My phone buzzes as I see an incoming text from Eddie, inquiring whether I'll need him further this evening. Halting in my footsteps behind Kathryn, I ask her where we are headed.

“My driver is wanting to know if he’s needed. What should I tell him?” I’m holding my breath awaiting her answer.

"I thought you wanted to take me to dinner. Have you changed your mind?" She seems concerned as a slight frown frames her face.

"Dinner was my idea. Remember? Once I’ve made up my mind, it’s nearly impossible to change it. I’m going to release my driver for the night. I'm assuming you're still a no-go for my comfy Escalade, right?"

"That’s right, Kingsley.” She points her finger at me and moves it in a scolding fashion. I notice she dropped the Mister in front of my last name. I wonder if she’ll ever call me Adam, because I’d love to hear my name fall from her lips.

“No soft leather seats for me. We're on my turf tonight."

She scrunches her brow in a challenge. She's awaiting a comeback from me to try to persuade her into my backseat, but I cave to her demands. I'd prefer her warm company versus pissing her off by coming on too strong, for now, so there's no argument from me.

I dial Eddie on my phone to let him know his services aren’t needed.

"Call Mrs. Carter. Inform her I've released you for the evening and you'll be driving Tom Duffy to the Library Gala instead." I hang up before he confirms my orders as my focus rests on the smug face of Kathryn. She's so stunning, gorgeous, as her eyes shine back at me. I focus again on her mouth and fight back an overwhelming desire to claim it with my own. Lips on lips. Tongue to tongue. I push back my passions and realize she's won me for the night. Lock, stock, and barrel.

I mentally slash another mark in her column as she wins one more round between us. My column remains empty, but for once I don't give a fuck. I smile back at her, raising my hands, and shrugging my shoulders in defeat. As we walk toward some unknown destination, for me at least, I watch men gazing at her, even turning around to watch her retreat, and can't help but think I might actually be the winner this round, because she's with me, not them.

"Do you mind if I ask where we're going? Or are you wanting to surprise me?" I reach out to touch her hair as it blows in the wind. The texture reminds me of satin, soft and flowing, without anything trying to perfect it. All natural. "I've told you your hair's beautiful, haven't I?"

"I believe you did earlier." She giggles, almost in an embarrassed laugh. "But a woman can't hear compliments like that too often. Thank you, by the way. I have to say you've really surprised me today."

"How have I surprised you?"

"Every word I've heard associated with you: player, asshole and manwhore…" She lowers her head away from my gaze, shying from her own comments, perhaps.

"Ouch, that last one hurt." I fake a hit to the heart and hold my hand over my chest. Our exchange reminds me of our introduction last night when she tagged me as the pretty billionaire boy.

"Wait! Let me finish," she pleads, holding her hand up in protest. "Those words don't seem to apply to you right now. I'm pretty sure they did last night, though, but you're different with me today. Why?"

I realize we've stopped along the sidewalk during the discussion of my usual waywardness. She faces me, and I gently encircle her wrists and walk her to the front glass of the building behind us, a makeshift confessional. I release her hands before I answer.

"Why am I different?" I run my fingers through her hair again. I can't stop myself, and luckily she doesn't protest or pull away as my fingers twirl and twist through her long locks. Soberly, I gaze into her eyes as I speak. "I think who I am today has everything to do with you, and actually nothing to do with me."

I long to share my true thoughts, telling her that until I met her last night I've never felt anything more than a physical attraction toward another woman. This pull I feel toward her is something very different. I have no words to define it.

But since she knows all about my debauched reputation, telling her this, laying all my cards on the table, might feed into her notion that I'm a player who will say anything to get into her panties. Basically, a rehearsed line one might expect from a manwhore. So I decide to confess something else to her.

"It probably won't make any sense, but I woke up fully rested this morning." I sigh remembering the dreams that have plagued me since my mother Flora's death, and how they thankfully didn't surface last night. Instead, the nightmares were replaced by a beautiful and erotic dream of fucking Kathryn.

"A good night's sleep is what brought about this change? You've gotta be kidding me." Kathryn is skeptical of my response, and who can blame her? "Perhaps you should be waltzing down the street with Ms. Woodward instead."

"Ms. Woodward?" I'm disappointed, mostly in myself, to hear that name come up yet again. It seems to be haunting me today. "You're the one kidding me now."

I move in closer to her, but not too close. She seems leery of me, so I cautiously approach.

"I believe my unusually pleasant night of sleep was due to you and you alone. Now tell me where you're taking me for dinner." The subject change is needed, because Lizzie Woodward's name should be buried away and forgotten.

"My favorite place to eat is just a block from here." Kathryn starts to walk ahead of me but I'm quick to catch up. "It's probably not what you'd expect."

"I'm getting used to the unexpected with you." I smile down at her and am pleased when she returns it. "Can I hold your hand as we walk?"

"I suppose. But don't get any ideas, Kingsley," she replies quietly and extends her hand to meet mine. She feels soft, delicate, and warm as I wrap my fingers around hers. My entire body relaxes as I feel her touch.

"You want to hear something funny?" I say and she nods. "I thought John, was your escort or date last night. I was pleasantly surprised to find out he was your brother."

"Pleasantly surprised? How so?" Her question is clearly spoken in a challenging tone.

"If he was someone you were seeing, I doubt if I'd be here with you now." The thought of being unable to see her brings an odd, unfamiliar feeling to me. In reaction, I hold her hand a little tighter and purposely pull her into my side as we stride forward.

"John warned me of you last night after I introduced you to him. I don't think he would approve of us being together."

"He wouldn't approve of me, huh?" I say teasingly, but the number of people warning her about me is starting to add up.

"Can you blame him?" She answers me with a feisty question, but I enjoy the verbal sparring with her.

"No, I guess not. If you were my sister, I'd likely feel the same… protective." My frank confession surprises me, especially when I examine the truth of it. The picture it paints isn't very flattering, to say the least.

"Exactly, John helped me through the death of my husband a couple years ago, so he had his radar up with you last night. I'm not sure I should tell him about you and me, and our little date." She emphasizes the word "date." I smile as I admit to myself that I like the sound of the word, too. Actually, I can't remember the last time I was on a date like this one. No agenda. Carefree. A novelty.

"What about your mother? What would she think of our little date?" The brother may not be happy about us being together, but Mrs. Swanson seemed to have a better opinion of me last night.

"My mother would be thrilled." She looks up at me with a wicked gleam in her eyes, telling me she might agree with her mother. At least that's my hope.

She stops in front of a restaurant. "Well, we're here. Sant Ambroeus."

It's small with a green- and white-striped awning hanging across the glass front. "We just missed their famous afternoon tea. I'll probably shock them by stopping by now. I've never come in this early for dinner."

I open the door for her and follow her inside. An Italian-looking gentleman around sixty approaches us, smiling from ear to ear. He holds out his arms to her, and it's obvious they're well acquainted with one another.

"Bellissimo, Miss Kathryn." I watch the man greet her warmly as he places his hands on her upper arms and kisses each of her cheeks. I suppress my disappointment as I've yet to have my lips on her. It's a fact that sobers me, making me wonder what's become of the take 'em and leave 'em me.

"Maurice, I can't decide if it's the welcome I receive or your delicious food that brings me back to you." She pokes his side, playing with him, and he melts from her words. He's putty in her hands, just like I am.

"I'd like to think it's my welcome." Maurice flirts back, and I clear my throat to make my presence known, marking my territory once again. "Who do we have here?"

"Adam Kingsley, sir." I extend my hand to Maurice. His eyes appraise me warily. I can almost hear the questions he's likely forming in his head. Yes, the "Adam Kingsley," playboy extraordinaire. I wonder why this title never seemed to bother me before. Today it's pissing me the fuck off. He offers me his hand in return.

"Pleasure to meet you, Maurice." I stand firm, shaking his hand with purpose, as if I have nothing to hide. He drops my hand and regards me carefully.

"Mr. Kingsley, welcome to our restaurant as Miss Kathryn's guest." His tone makes me wonder how truly welcome I am here. "Please follow me. Your usual spot, my dear?"

"Yes, Maurice," Kathryn replies.

He seats us next to the window looking out onto Madison Avenue. The table is covered with starched, crisp, white linens. Menus are settled in front of us with an unlit candle placed in the middle of the table.

While scanning the menu and deeply breathing in the delicious aroma from the kitchen, I realize I'm famished, achingly starving, in fact. My unorthodox day of trying to capture some time with Kathryn, the beautiful woman across the table from me, caused me to skip my lunch. So the last thing I've eaten today was after my grueling morning workout. I had my usual egg whites and oatmeal.

"Since you're a regular here, order for me." I once again concede and allow her to make a decision for me. I hardly recognize myself but wonder if she has any clue what she's doing to me. She really has no frame of reference to gauge me by since we've only just met.

"So how often do you let people, or women in particular, order for you? I'd bet there aren't many people who make even the simplest choices for you. You appear to be an in charge kind of guy."

She understands me better than I think. It's written all over her face, and surprise is probably all over mine.

"That's right. I live my life in a somewhat controlled fashion, Kathryn. I'm a creature of habit, really. But it has definitely panned out well for me." I try to explain how I'm set in my ways without sounding like a control-freak. "At thirty-two years old, what I've achieved is beyond even my wildest dreams. I've called the shots and hit the financial bull's-eye, so to speak."

"I really don't give a shit about your money or how you made it." Her words are spoken tersely to me, confirming what I thought last night when I gave the obscene donation. A fat wallet doesn't impress her. "I'm just curious about you, the man. I'm trying to figure you out. Understand why you put up such a wall around yourself."

"It's more than a wall. It's a fortress." The confession slips from my mouth easily, but I wish almost instantly that I'd keep these thoughts to myself.

"So you pick up weak women, fuck them or let them blow you, and then never call them. You're such a catch, Kingsley." She likes to go straight in for the kill. And as usual she hits the mark.

"It's true, my usual pursuits seldom take more than a simple nod of my head." I look into her eyes before continuing. "However, I admit that things are different with you."

"And why is that the case with me?" she curls her lips into a coy smile loaded with a challenge behind it.

"I've not figured it out yet." I smile at her and reach across the table to touch her hand. She looks down at our fingers, then back up to my eyes. "But I'll let you know when I do."

"You really have quite the ego. So I'm just supposed to wait until you have a clue? Listen here, Kingsley, I'm not some puzzle that you can take out of a drawer because you find me fascinating in some unique way." She sighs and takes her hand away from mine, causing my heart rate to accelerate. Surely, she's kidding, but I see the stern look on her face. There's a seriousness about her that unnerves me.

As I'm ready to respond, Maurice comes unbidden to my rescue and brings us a complimentary bottle of wine. He opens it and defers to Kathryn for the first taste of approval. I watch her full lips surround the glass rim as she tips the stem up. Her movement is slow, precise, and completely sensual.

I can't peel my eyes away from her lips as they meet the deep red wine. Lips that I want to possess. Lips that I want encircling me. When she removes them from the glass and wipes her tongue across the lower part of her mouth, I feel my cock stir at this subtly erotic demonstration.

"Lovely, Maurice." She smiles and thanks him. As he pours my wine, Kathryn excuses herself from the table, tossing her napkin down by her wine glass as she stands. Her departure seems abrupt, and a sour mood reflects on her face.

Was it what I said? I was only teasing her, but she obviously found no humor in my glib remarks. Maurice's eyes appear concerned as he watches her. He likely notices the sudden change in her disposition, too.

"I'll be right back," she says, sounding curt. As she turns on her heels, I watch her head to the rear of the restaurant. Maurice is still standing next to me even after the wine is successfully poured. Oh boy, I think he has something to say as his eyes glower down at me.

"Mr. Kingsley, I've watched Miss Kathryn grow up from a little girl. Her parents brought her here to eat every weekend. She's always been my favorite." He glares at me over his spectacles. "She's never brought anyone in here besides her brother and a few girlfriends."

"Really?" This revelation surprises me. But he continues on as if I hadn't responded.

"My wife reads the Post's gossip columns to me, so I know all about you." I can't help but notice he's pointing the sharp, screwy end of the wine opener at me. I don't believe it's by accident. "I'm not sure what she's doing with the likes of you. But you better watch yourself with her. She's all class."

"She's in her own class." I take his assessment of Kathryn one step further.

"The minute you strode in here with Kathryn, your cards were marked with me. I may be an old man, but I have friends..." I detect a hint of a smile behind his eyes as his words trail off. It's as if his words are meant more in jest than as a warning. Being a smart man, I decide to turn on the Kingsley charm.

"I understand completely. There's something special about her, and I intend to treat her as such." I follow my words with a slight wink. "I do have my limits around such a beautiful woman. It may be hard to rein myself in."

He laughs and walks away saying, "Good luck with that." I chuckle but quit the instant I see Kathryn walking toward us, looking confused. Probably rightly wondering what transpired between Maurice and me. And quite frankly, I'm not sure what just happened. Did he warn me or in the end encourage me? I'm totally confused, too.

"Kingsley, what did Maurice say to you?" Her question is spoken in more of a challenge.

"I'm sure you can guess. He has fatherly feelings concerning you and issued me a warning as far as you're concerned." My eyes shoot toward the front entrance where Maurice is standing, appraising me still. "I assured him that my intentions with you were noble."

Kathryn huffs at my statement. It's a sound I don't like at all. "Maurice is no fool. I'm sure he found your comment amusing to say the least."

"He definitely isn't a fool, but he made it clear that I would be one if I treated you badly."

"So, what's it like to have such a stellar reputation?" She sits back in her chair and crosses her arms defiantly over her chest. "Is it hard having men afraid to have you around the women in their life, those they respect?"

I chuckle under my breath, "Okay, you've made your point with me." Raising my hands in the air, I surrender to her ribbing of me. Truthfully, I have no defense to speak of, and I need to also do something rare for me and apologize.

"And I'm sorry about the comment I made before Maurice brought us the wine."

She speculatively squints one eye and purses her lips. Not the response I was hoping for with my apology. "Hmmm. I'm curious. How many times have you apologized for your behavior on a date?"

Shit, her question pins me to the wall, and I don't see a way of escape. So I'll aim for honesty, hoping she'll give me a break.

"Zero, you're the first, Kathryn." A satisfied smile graces her face as she nods her head at me. "Please, can we change the subject?"

"All right. Tell me a little bit about where you grew up."

I flinch at her question, and I'm pretty sure she detects it with her keen psychologist's eye. I never discuss my hometown or upbringing with anyone. Only the guys who came with me from MIT to New York know a little bit about my past. But I wasn't one to bring up the specifics about her or my childhood. Thankfully, they never pushed for them, either.

"I prefer to leave my past where it belongs. In my past." My mouth suddenly feels dry as my mind remembers the sound of the first handful of dirt hitting the top of Flora's casket deep within the damp walls of her grave. Something in my gut twists and pulls. These dark memories bring back the pain of that day.

Kathryn's eyebrows rise as she likely perceives my distress. But she appears to be more curious than concerned. And I know she'll continue to prod and poke around at my open sores. My mother's death by her own hand; it's something I still can't speak about openly. Tom doesn't know the specifics about her death but saw how much it troubled me. He urged me to talk to a therapist about it years ago, but he dropped the subject after I scoffed at his recommendations.

"I'm disappointed you don't want to talk about your childhood, but not really that surprised." She sips her wine, her eyes never leaving mine as I try to digest the veal piccata she ordered for me. "I have something to confess to you. I searched you on the Internet today. It's silly, I know, but I was trying to figure you out. Find out more about you."

"Really? And what did you find? Were you able to figure me out? Find out what makes me tick?" I can't hide my teasing smile as I feel flattered and hopeful this beautiful creature across from me might feel the same odd connection that I do. The energy between us I felt last night seems even stronger today. The pull between us tinged with lust, definitely an intense sexual attraction, but there's something more around the edges that makes it different, deeper than just a physical rush for me to seek and discard.

"Your bios were fascinating but full of holes. The years before you entered MIT at eighteen are missing. Just basic facts, those that could be easily obtained from public records."

"Believe me, that's where the information came from, public records. It was most definitely not from me." The twist in my gut winds tighter as we return to what I consider to be forbidden territory.

Kathryn's tightened lips clearly display her frustration with me, but I'm not a man to be moved on this topic. "I'm sorry to push you. As I've said, I was just wanting to know about you. We can talk about what I did find out if you'd like."

She reaches across the table and soothingly rubs her fingers over my tightly closed fists. My hand instinctively opens and encompasses hers. I feel something strange as we hold hands and stare into each other's eyes. An unspoken conversation is occurring between us. And for the first time in my adult memory, instead of stopping someone's attempt at showing me compassion, I allow it to be reflected back at me. A caring sweetness travels from her to me and I don't want it to stop.

"Someday." Her fingers squeeze mine gently and my body relaxes, eases down from the tension. "Maybe someday you'll tell me everything. I promise to never bring it up again. Okay?"

"Thanks. I appreciate that." Maurice appears as we sit in silence, searching, gazing at each other. I think we're both trying to understand this thing between us.

"You finished, Miss Kathryn?" Maurice looks to her again, avoiding my mug.

"I think we are. The meal was wonderful as usual. Thank you." Her loving smile aimed at Maurice warms me. I might move heaven and earth to see it again or have it grace her lips for me.

"Miss Kathryn, Sofia wants to speak with you, alone, before you leave." Maurice hands me the bill as he finishes his request. I do not miss the emphasis on the word "alone." I look at Kathryn, who shrugs and rises from her chair. It appears Sofia is not to be ignored today. I don't have to guess what Sofia wants to discuss with Kathryn. Their conversation will likely be headlining me, the manwhore.

As she walks away, Maurice has not moved from his spot beside me. He's still holding our plates but makes no moves toward the kitchen.

"My wife, Sofia, doesn't like you, Mr. Kingsley. She feels you are bad for dear Miss Kathryn. She told me to tell you that she will be watching you, too. And believe me when I say this, you don't want her upset."

"Kathryn is lucky to have people who care so much about her." I smile up at him. If I were standing, I'd likely be eight inches taller than he is. My seated position works to his advantage. I take a business card out of my wallet along with several hundred dollars. "Please give this to your wife. The card has my personal number on it. Tell her to call me if she wants. She has carte blanche with me."

He looks befuddled. "I will tell her and I'd be ready for a call, Mr. Kingsley. She's not easily impressed by a few hundred dollars." In a huff, he stuffs the money into his apron pocket. I guess he is, though. I know it's not a bribe, but still I want to leave here on good terms, fatten the calf a little.

Kathryn follows Maurice's retreat to the kitchen. I see her in a heated conversation with Sofia. It's my reputation again. Before today, I never needed an excuse for my behavior with women, nor did I even want one. I was purely content with the person I was until twenty-four hours ago. Funny how things change.

It's time for me to meet Sofia, my distracter. As I rise and walk toward them, I hear Kathryn speaking in Italian to Sofia, and I wonder how many languages this woman speaks.

"Good evening, Sofia. I'm Adam Kingsley." I hold my hand out in welcome to her. I wait to see her reaction, and I watch as Kathryn nudges her arm and Sofia's hand reaches out to me.

"Mr. Kingsley." Her greeting is laced with contempt as she looks down her nose at me, and I realize that it's most likely a fair judgment on her part; after all, I read the gossip columns, too. I know what they write about me, and it's mostly true, although before I faced this woman in front of me, I usually would've laughed at their reports. But not today. The foreign shift within me is that great. It's puzzling to me. The sudden change was brought on by something I didn't initiate. It's like I'm its target, with no power to stop myself from succumbing to it.

"I had a lovely dinner with Kathryn. The veal was superb." Hoping to sound sincere, I decide to end my accolades. Nothing says fake more than heaping on tons of insincere praise. "Kathryn, are you ready to leave?"

I offer her my arm. "I'm ready, Mr. Kingsley. Goodbye, Sofia. I'll see you in a couple of days for sure." I open the door for her and gratefully lead her outside. I feel like I've been given a reprieve or stay by the governor when I inhale the cool early evening air.

"Well, I think I've survived the Italian Inquisition tonight." I place my hand at the small of her back, a possessive move. But I don't care. A man on the sidewalk eyes her up and down, but I glare at him and he hurries away. My body touching hers marks my territory like a hungry wolf. The thought makes me laugh.

"What's so funny?" She looks up at me with a sly smile.

"The man that just walked by looked too long at you and I didn't like it. Have you always had this kind of an effect on men? Wait, don't answer that, I don't really want to hear about other men in your life." Her sly smile turns to one of smug satisfaction.

As I get ready to speak, my phone sounds an alarm. I stop and search its screen. Rarely do I get this alert. A serious or grave problem is the only thing that warrants its action. Only four people have the ability to institute this "Def-con" alert: Tom, Mrs. Carter, Patrick, and of course Peters. The screen shows Tom is the one sending the warning.

I instantly stop and call him on my cell phone.

"Kingsley. Something crazy just happened at the Library Gala." His words rush together as if he can't get them out fast enough.

"This better be something besides a report of some overdue books."

"How does a threat on your life sound? Serious enough?"

Chapter 7

"What the hell are you talking about, Tom?" A threat?" I can't believe what he's saying to me.

"Yes, but it's really more than a threat." He pauses, and I'm getting frustrated. Answers aren't coming from him fast enough. "I hear traffic in the background. Are you out on the sidewalk or street?"

"Yes, but what does that have to do with this threat?" I question him angrily as I feel my temper starting to build. "Tell me what the fuck is going on."

Kathryn has been standing at my side during this conversation. She's biting her lip and anxiously wringing her hands. Her eyes look concerned, a likely result of my angry demeanor. My temper can flare at times. This heated exchange being a clear example.

I'd like to reach out to her, bring her into my arms, and soothe her. Just the thought of me soothing a woman makes me wonder who I am. But I'm not sure how she'd receive such a gesture from me. I feel like there is still so much ground to cover with her before I can get physical. I hope I have the patience to wait, as I've never been tested like this before. Adam Kingsley isn't known for being patient.

Tom's yelling pulls me back to our conversation. "You need to get inside and fast. Just do what I tell you, Adam. Get off the fucking street. Find a coffee shop. Hell, I don't care. Just get off the sidewalk."

"Have you gone crazy? Tell me what's going on. I'm not moving an inch until you do." I'm way past frustrated now. He had better start spilling the details to me.

"Damn, you stubborn asshole. It's Simon. He had a gun and fired it at me. Oh fuck, Adam. It's beyond belief, really. Get inside now and I'll tell you more. Fuck, you can probably even watch it on the news. Cameras are everywhere."

"Shit. Okay, okay." I look at Kathryn and then glance at the glass front of Sant Ambroeus. "Hold on, Tom."

I bring the phone down to my side. Kathryn appears confused, and I'm right there with her. I have no idea what the hell I'm going to say to her. Other than we need to get undercover. Completely crazy.

"I'm on the phone with my friend and business partner, Tom. He's saying a threat was made on my life. He wants us inside, out of open view. Something about our former partner shooting a gun at him." I point back to Sant Ambroeus's door. "Let's go back inside, and then I'll find out more."

Kathryn and I hastily walk back to the restaurant. Hopefully, my greeting from the owners will be better this time. I already have enough shit to deal with. Once inside, a confused Maurice approaches us.

"Mr. Kingsley. Is there a problem?"

"Yes, there seems to be problem, and I need your help." I hurriedly respond with my words running together. "Do you have a back room? Something with a TV?"

"We have an office in the back with a TV. Sofia likes her soaps." Maurice glances in Sofia's direction.

"Perfect." I slow down when I prepare to ask for an invasion into this man's private office. His feelings for me aren't stellar already, but I really have no other choice. "Can Kathryn and I use your office for a little while? Door open, of course."

"Certainly. Anything for Miss Kathryn." He motions us to follow him, and we beginning walking behind him. We make our way through the kitchen. The head chef looks up from his preparations and stops chopping an onion, almost dropping his knife. Once we've left the kitchen area, Maurice leads us down a short hall with his office situated at the end.

I give Kathryn a reassuring look as we enter the small room, but I don't think it's working. Her face has worry written all over it. There's no comforting it at present, either. I return my attention to Tom, who's been waiting on the line for me. Likely going crazy, too.

"Tom. We're inside now." I look around the office. A desk. A couple of chairs. A small television with antennas jutting out of the top on a filing cabinet. The office resembles something from the 1960s, like a scene from Mad Men. Kathryn stands close to me. A mere breath keeps us from touching. I'm focusing my eyes on hers. Their blue violet gleam reflects concern for me, and it's oddly comforting.

"What do you mean, we?" Tom asks.

"Kathryn Delcour is with me. We just finished dinner and are now in the back of the restaurant's office. I'm switching the phone to speaker so she can hear." I've given him more details on where I am and who I'm with than he's given to me on this supposed threat. "Now for fuck's sake tell me what's going on. From the beginning."

"While I was on hold waiting for you, Lois and I climbed into a police car. It's crazy. Completely fucked up." He's breathing fast.

"Right. From the top," I tell him.

I hear Tom swallow and take a deep breath. Trying to calm himself before he starts in. "Eddie picked Lois and I up around six thirty tonight for the event. Nothing seemed amiss at all.

The usual line-up of sedans and limos as guests were dropped off in front. One by one people exited their cars. Finally it was our turn at the curb. Eddie came around to open the door, and I was sitting on that side so I got out first." Tom stops and takes another deep breath, but I still don't know shit.

"Keep going, Tom. My patience is running thin." My tone carries a distinct reprimand to it.

"Right. Sorry. Just a little overwhelmed. Here's where the shit hits the fan. As I'm getting out, a gun goes off, and I feel a bullet whiz by my head. It was fucking unreal. Like in the movies. I look to my right and see Simon standing by the back tire. He's dressed in a black trench coat like some Matrix dude with a pistol in his hand. Pointing at me, Adam. God the look on his face was nothing but sheer hatred. The gun aimed right for me. Thankfully the bullet he fired embedded in the limo in front us. No one was hurt. I could've been shot in the head."

"But something happened when he saw it was me standing there. He appeared shocked and dropped the gun to his side. Lois had climbed out of the car by now and was standing behind me. She only saw the gun at this side. Thank God. But Adam, before he ran off, he said something that has scared the shit out of me." He stops and I hear him saying something to Lois. I think she's crying in the background.

"Don't stop now, Tom," I practically yell.

"Simon told me he thought it was you inside. He came to the event with a gun in hopes of shooting you. What he said, Adam, chilled me to the bone. He said, 'Tell Adam that bullet was for him."

Listening to Tom, one thing comes to my mind. Am I dreaming? A horrible, awful nightmare. I am at a loss for what to say back to Tom. Stunned, shocked. Nothing makes a bit of sense. Nothing.

"He's gone mad. Completely snapped," I say in disbelief.

I just can't figure out why I'm his target. I've been combing my mind since yesterday after I found out about Simon, but I keep coming up empty. I can't even remember the last unkind word we spoke to one another.

"How's Lois doing? I can hear her crying in the background. In her condition, this has to be even worse." Lois' sobbing doesn't seem to be subsiding at all.

"She's shaking like a leaf. If she doesn't calm down I may take her to the ER. I'm concerned about shock. But no one was hurt by Simon directly."

"So what happened after he ran off? Did he leave or were the police able to find his crazy ass?" The thought of Simon running free around this city hell-bent on killing me or someone else unsettles me to my core.

Kathryn is now seated in the one chair in the office. I'm sitting on the corner of the desk. But my eyes are solely on Kathryn, and hers are on mine.

"He ran away. Virtually disappeared. No one but Eddie, Lois, and me saw him with the gun. Since he's left-handed, the black arm of his trench coat and gun were right up against the black of the Escalade. He just blended in. Everyone was busy arriving. Waiting for the real celebrities to show up. Do you have any idea what might have triggered all of this with Simon? Besides the ex-fiancée."

"I've racked my brain. I can't think of a thing. "As far as I knew everything between us was on good terms. We hadn't talked outside of business in months, but you know that's not unusual for us. He asked me via email to join him and his fiancée Marta for dinner on several occasions. I didn't go. Had other commitments. But there's no way something like that would make him snap."

"I've been doing the same. Not a single thing comes to mind. It makes me think that when Marta broke the engagement off, he lost it, literally. He's a wanted man now. Which is unreal. The police are searching everywhere for him. They believe he took the subway from Bryant Park, and there are so many lines and options for him to take from there. No telling where he is now."

"It seems like all of this is a dream. Is Eddie doing okay? He's tough on the outside, but I bet this gave him quite the fright?"

"He's the one that ran and got the police after it all happened. The cops were stationed closer to the red carpet. Celebrity security, I guess. But Eddie was beside himself after he came back with the cops. I sent him on home. The police wanted the SUV left on the scene. They're sweeping it for prints."

"I should let you go. Lois needs you more than me. Call me later tonight after everything has settled down. Give her my best." I truly hope that Lois is all right. I feel partly to blame for this whole situation, even though I have no idea why Simon has me as his target.

"Will do, buddy. But please stay put at this restaurant until Peters gives you the okay to leave. It's all over the news. Camera crews are littering the streets. What a fucking field day the markets are going to have over all this."

"I don't even want to think about that right now, and you shouldn't either. Take care of your wife and the baby."

"You're right. I'll call you later."

Once the call ends, I look down at my phone's screen and see scores of missed calls and texts. I heard the numerous beeps signaling an incoming call while I was on the phone with Tom, but I ignored them. I needed to hear from Tom first. He witnessed it. Saw what happened. Thank God nothing worse than a threat to me occurred, but I'm chilled knowing Simon wanted to kill me.

"I need to make a few more calls. Can you bear with me?" I ask Kathryn. Her eyes are big, filled with surprise at what has transpired in my phone conversation with Tom. The shock she's feeling shows.

"Sure, please. I can't believe this, Kingsley. Who is this Simon?"

"It's a long story, but the short version is he's a man I've known since MIT. Four of us guys came to New York City from our graduating class and formed Kings Capital. He was one of those four guys. Tom was one of the others."

"So he just went off the deep end, then?" Kathryn's wide eyes and lips making a perfect 'O' reflect the bewilderment I feel, too.

"I guess so. I had to fire him yesterday afternoon. The day was a total clusterfuck with the exception of meeting you, of course." I swear this little comment gets a slight smile out of her. Even in all this tension. "But as bad as yesterday was, this stunt he pulled tonight is beyond belief. Guns, threats, and now he's a wanted man."

"I can't imagine," Kathryn replies. It's good to have someone to talk to about this whole thing. Unusual, but good.

"Let me make those calls real quick."

I pull up Peters' number first. He'll know what my next move should be. One thing's for sure, I can't stay holed up in this office with Kathryn all night. I need a plan of action, and Peters is the guy who specializes in that.

"Fuck, Adam," Peters yells into the phone. I've never heard him this animated before. "Where are you? I've been calling, texting, and alerting you via that crazy Def-Con1 warning on your phone."

"I know what's going on. Just got off the phone with Tom. He was the first call I took. And since he was an eyewitness, he was also the best one for me to speak with."

"Okay, you may know what happened, but I want to make sure Simon doesn't find you. That's all I'm focusing on right now. And you didn't answer my question. Where are you?"

"I had dinner with Kathryn Delcour, and we are sitting in a restaurant's back office on Madison in the Upper East Side."

"That's good. I was concerned you might be at your apartment. You need to stay away from there tonight. Too dangerous. Simon might be headed there next. It's you he wants to kill, apparently. Do you have any clue why?" Peters asks the golden question. One that Tom and I are clueless about.

"No idea whatsoever. Tom and I batted around the idea that when his fiancée dumped him he lost it. Other than that reason, it's anyone's guess." I am now pacing the tile floor in the tiny office. Taking two strides back and forth in front of the desk is all the room I have for walking off the tension.

"I've been after you for two years to get a damn bodyguard. No more fighting me on this. I placed a call to a buddy. He owes me a favor or two. He's got an ex-Army friend who will fit the bill as a bodyguard for you." Peters has everything figured out just like I knew he would. It's what I pay him to do. But hiring a bodyguard is something I've refused every time he's insisted on it.

"You know why I've held off on getting a bodyguard. Even the celebs here in NYC don't walk around with them." I despise the thought of having someone with me at all times. Watching over me. Silently judging me. Eddie is the closest person I have to security. He knows me, my habits, and keeps his opinions to himself. I've never once felt condemnation from him over my lifestyle choices. Having someone with me, guarding me 24/7, just seems too much.

"Those celebs you're talking about would be under lock and key by their agents and managers if someone was wanting them dead. Do you realize you're being protected from a potential killer? Simon, for some unknown reason, wants to end your life." Peters' sharp words cut me. Sadly, he's making sense. But I still don't like the idea.

"I just can't really believe he'd do it. The whole thing is crazy." I run my fingers through my hair, frustrated with this whole mess and its complications in my life.

"Crazy is the keyword. A bodyguard needs to protect you from crazy. And from what we've seen and gathered on Simon, he's acting mad. You can't take a chance and risk your life, Adam."

"Okay, I'm not going to fight you on this anymore. Simon's crazed. Wants me dead. So I'll say yes to the bodyguard, but it will not be a permanent situation in my life."

"Finally." There is no mistaking the relief in Peters' voice. "You're a stubborn ass sometimes, Adam. Your bodyguard's name is Jordan Hayes. He's already on his way up here from D.C. He's been working private security down there for a couple years. He should arrive and be ready to go by morning. He's also a native of Queens, so he knows the city."

"I'll trust you on this one." And it's true. I have no choice at this point. What are my other options?

"Now we need to figure out what to do with you for the evening as you aren't going back to your apartment. Hotels aren't an option. Too public. You said you're with that Kathryn woman you had me investigate, right?"

"Right." I reply wondering where he's going with this. I look over at Kathryn when Peters mentions her name. She's still biting her lip, and I see her brow scrunched together in concern. Likely wondering what the hell is going on.

"You need to stay at her place tonight. Simon will have no idea you're there. He doesn't know this woman or your connection to her, right? Ask her. Beg her if you have to. I'll wait while you do."

I pause and pull the phone away from my ear. My hand covers the receiver. I'd rather Peters not be privy to this conversation; I have no idea what I'm going to say or how Kathryn will react to what I'm about to ask her.

"Kathryn, my security guy, Peters, is on the phone. Says he doesn't want me going home with Simon loose on the streets. Checking into a hotel is out of the question, too. He wants me to stay at your apartment tonight. Are you comfortable with this?

"I don't know. It makes sense, I guess." Her head tilts, and her brow presses together in thought.

She's concerned with my request. Possibly wondering about the ramifications of me being with her. I don't want to put her in harms way, either. So I decide to ask Peters if he thinks it's a safe choice for both of us.

"Peters, how safe is it for me to be at Kathryn's tonight? I don't want her in any danger." My voice is firm. I will stay here in this fucking office if I have to and wait for the bodyguard if needed. But being in Kathryn's apartment for the evening sounds like the best plan. A tempting alternative, too. I'll be crossing her threshold sooner than I imagined.

"How far are you from her place? Upper East Side, right?" Peters asks.

"Just a couple of blocks. Not far at all. And yes, Upper East," I say.

"I don't like that your apartment is in the area. But I think you're okay. Have someone hail you a cab in front of the restaurant and then cab it over to her place. Even if it's only a couple blocks away, I don't want you on the sidewalk out in the open."

"Agreed. Anything else?"

"Yes, keep your eyes open. Simon was last seen wearing a black trench coat. Police are searching his apartment now. My guess is he's laying low somewhere. We should know more in the morning. I'm communicating with my NYPD contact. I'll update you hourly via email or call if there's something urgent."

"Sounds good." The call ends. But I have one more to make. Patrick. He's going to have to handle all the fallout for me. Tom's with Lois, who's understandably upset, and I have to hide out tonight. I press call as I give Kathryn a reassuring smile and mouth the words, "thank you."

"Adam. Have you heard the news?" Patrick says, animated, ready to jump out of his skin and through the phone. For him this is something extremely rare. He's even less likely to show emotions than I am.

"Yes. Spoke to Tom a few minutes ago. He filled me in on everything. Did you talk with him?"

"Just for a second. Lois was too upset, and I told him we'd talk later. Unreal. Fucking unreal." His assessment is right there with Tom's and mine.

"I still can't comprehend it. How does someone like Simon go from boring, software genius to hunted criminal?" I ask the question knowing there still isn't an answer. "I'm staying at a friend's apartment this evening. But I need you to handle our public exposure. Call the attorneys, PR, and try to get ahead of this story before it gets out of hand. Stress to the PR folks we are as confused as everyone else concerning Simon's behavior, and we're hoping he turns himself in and gets the help he needs. I don't want this to become anything more than a person who snapped. Got it? Keep it private. Just Simon acting alone."

"Sure. I'll get on the phone with them all now."

"Call or email me later after you've talked."

"Will do." Pocketing my phone, I hang my head and gather my thoughts before looking at Kathryn. I can feel her eyes on me.

Hesitantly, I lift my head and look over at her. "I guess we need to head to your place. Give Maurice back his office. My apologies for dragging you into this mess." I tilt my head and raise my brows, hoping she sees I'm sincere.

She's been sitting there patiently waiting with her hands in her lap, but her lovely face is marked with worry. If I were in her shoes, I'd likely have bolted and got the hell away from here. Who wants to be around a man who has a crazy gun-toting maniac intent on killing him? Truthfully, I don't want her in harm's way, but I don't want her leaving me, either. Silently we stare at each other. Neither one of us wanting to break our gaze.

"Are things always this intense on your first dates?" She says with a wink. And I have to laugh as she breaks the tension between us. "Not sure how you're going to top this one. Cops and would-be killers aren't something that pops up every day around here. It's usually rather boring in this part of town."

"I can think of several ways to top tonight," I say, adding a wink of my own.

"Oh, I have no doubt you can."

She rises out of her chair and in two small steps is standing in front of me. Her beautiful face looking up at me. Eyes kind and soft. And her lips. Damn those lips of hers. How I want to taste them.

She places her hands on my shirt beneath my jacket. I have no idea what she's doing, but I soon find out as she slips my suit coat down my arms. The formal uniform of my day lies next to us on the desk.

She runs her fingers up and down my forearms with the lightest trace. Her fingers caress and lightly massage. Soothingly they pass over my shirt-covered skin. The effect of her touch races through me, and I feel myself getting hard for her. I want to pull her against me and ravage her with everything I have.

But there's something different in her touch. A real caring feeling for me, and I can't remember the last time another human being comforted me this tenderly. Apart from my mother, no one ever has gotten this close. I close my eyes, tilt my head back, and let the foreign and intense feeling of her touch wash over me. I should be making plans to leave the restaurant right now, but everything can wait.

"God, Kathryn." I moan her name knowing she can hear the desperation I have for her in my voice.

"I specialize in touch," she says seductively. I know it's the whole Tantra thing she's talking about. "Are you all right?" Finally I open my eyes and see her staring back at me.

Her eyes appear darker than before, more violet than blue. There's no denying the want I see in them. She feels this thing between us, too. So I decide the time has come to act on this strange unnamed energy drawing us together.

"No, I'm not all right. But I know what will help. There's something I've been dying to do to you. And you know my restraint with women. Practically non-existent."

My actions are lightening quick. Giving her little time to think or react, I pull her to me. One of my arms wraps around her just above the hip. I bring my other hand to the back of her neck. My fingers weave through her silky hair. The scent of Shalimar floats all around us. This woman is so fucking intoxicating to me: a beautiful and alluring aphrodisiac. I feel her arms encircle me as her body leans into mine.

"I'm going to kiss you now, Kathryn." She doesn't protest. Instead she closes her eyes and tilts her head up closer to me. It's then I know I've won the right to claim her lips. And I do.

Our lips clash and press together. Tongues searching for more. There is no beauty in this kiss. Just two people needing to satisfy a hunger that's been building between us since we met.

My tongue delves farther into her mouth. I simply can't get enough. Wanting to feel every inch of her, I pull her body closer to mine and press her into my rock-hard erection.

When I place my hands on the side of her breasts, she abruptly pulls away from me. Both of us are breathing heavy, trying to catch our breaths. She's left me standing there empty-handed and panting with need. The need I have for her is like nothing I've ever experienced with another woman. It's consuming.

"Kingsley. I'm sorry. I don't know what it is with you. But I don't go around randomly kissing men."

"Randomly?" Why is she telling me this? Is she denying what we just experienced? "There's something between us, Kathryn. Can't you feel it?"

"Lust," she replies. "Just pure lust. Nothing more."

"Believe me, some of the best sex comes from pure lust. It's what heats passion. Makes us burn."

"You mentioned it last night. Fucking for a release, right? That's not enough for me." She steps away from me.

"You kissed me back. There's no doubt in my mind."

"You're right, I did." Her voice is barely above a whisper.

Chapter 8

Kathryn admits she wanted that kiss as much as I did. It's not a great admission, but I'll take it. There's no denying there's lust between us. But it's more than a basic lust that's satisfied with a single fuck and then burns out. It's more consuming for me. Definitely a first. The need to be buried inside her, fucking her within an inch of her life is all I can think about even in the midst of all the shit going on tonight. She's magnetic to me. I can't help but be pulled toward her.

A force is pushing me beyond my normal control. A force I've never felt with any other woman. A force that makes me wonder who the hell I am.

I take a deep breath and say, "You can't deny it. You feel it too, don't you?"

She looks away from me briefly before answering my question. "Okay, maybe. Just a little. But I know about your conquests. I've seen you in action strutting around like a matador. Sure, your charms are enticing and deadly to women, but your treatment of them is debasing and self-centered." She is proud of her punches, and I don't want her to see they landed where she hopes.

"I am not one to turn down opportunities when they are presented to me. I never have to pursue the women I'm with. Never. They want me, and I simply have given them something they asked for. With both parties satisfied in the end."

"You really are something else. I'd love to speak with the women you've been with and ask them how satisfied they truly were with a quick bang or the one-sided head they gave you. I bet their names, faces, and bodies all blend together. Nothing meaningful about them stands out to you"

I can see the slight flare of her nostrils. Her reaction to my philandering is quite passionate. She thinks it's anger, but I think it's something else entirely: an attraction she's trying to fight.

"Why are you so concerned with my past pursuits? You seem very upset about my behavior, especially since there's nothing more than lust between us. Or are you trying to fight what I think you really want: Me. You want me inside you, satisfying the desires I know you feel when you're with me." These words are my counterpunch, and I see they hit their target. Dead center in the bull's-eye. Her eyes are wild with anger. Hot and intense. I have to smile at her little display. It won't take much to have that anger of hers clawing at my back while I fuck her senseless.

"God, what is wrong with you? I've never met a man with such an ego. It's why I've called you a boy. But you aren't a boy anymore, Kingsley. It's time you realized there is so much more to life than living for the next fuck or mega business deal. You need to grow up."

What can I say to her assessment? No I don't need to grow up?

I am at a loss with nothing to say. A familiar situation with this woman. Her words have a way of silencing me in thought.

Do I really know how these women felt after being with me? They wanted my cock, and I gladly gave it to them. But that was it. No one received anything more from me. All my relationships have been skin deep.

One fuck turning into the next. One beautiful face replaced by another. One seemingly perfect body no different than the last.

Her words are like a mirror reflecting my actions back at me. I've never stopped and analyzed what I've been doing. I've been too busy enjoying the wave I've been riding. It's who I am, no matter how hedonistic it may seem.

This whole exchange with Kathryn pisses me off. Calling me a boy, self-centered, and a debaser of women. It confirms why I don't do relationships. Life is so much easier and simpler when I don't have to answer to someone. Even if it's the most beautiful woman I've ever known.

"I think you're wrong," I tell her. "Those women willingly gave themselves to me. I bet they'd be more than happy to have another round, too."

A sudden movement by the door of the office catches my attention. Maurice stands there shaking his head. Our argument probably carried beyond these four walls. Every thought he had of me before today was confirmed.

"Miss Kathryn, is everything okay? I heard you two arguing. Do you want me to make this man leave?" Maurice peers at me loathingly, and there is no mistaking the disgust in his voice. He appears to stand a little taller than I remember. It's obvious I don't intimidate him in the least.

"My apologies, Maurice, for invading your office and subjecting you to our disagreement," Kathryn is quick to reply. Attempting to be the peacemaker. "Mr. Kingsley just heard some troubling news, and that's why we needed your help."

"As long as I know you're all right. That's what matters." Maurice speaks and glances at me, not hiding the distress he feels. "What else can I do?"

"My apologies too, Maurice. And I have one more favor to ask of you." He's looking at me out of the corner of his eye. He's skeptical, but he's not rejecting my request either, so I continue. "Kathryn and I need to leave via a cab. Would you mind hailing one for us while we wait by your front door?"

Maurice eyes me speculatively. There is definitely a warning in his glare. Basically, don't you dare fuck with her, buddy. I read the signal loud and clear.

"I will help you for Miss Kathryn's sake." Finished speaking to me, Maurice turns toward Kathryn with a worried look in his eye. "I hope you know what you're doing leaving with this… this… man."

After spitting out his last word, Maurice turns directly toward me, staring me down, squinting. "I'd rather see Miss Kathryn with a common man who loves and respects her, and treats her like she deserves. Not a rich and famous user like you. All the money in the world can't make you worthy of her."

I wanted to tell him Kathryn is the kind of woman no man will ever be worthy enough to have. But I keep my mouth shut. Maurice won't believe anything I say at this point anyway. Instead, I nod his way and bow my head.

Maurice spoke his piece, and I don't want to provoke him further. Right now all I want to do is to get the hell out of his restaurant and go back to Kathryn's apartment. Although she may be having second thoughts about having me there, especially after our argument and Maurice's warning. His warning being one of many.

"I understand you want to protect me, Maurice. You're the sweetest man in the world. I want you to know that." She hugs him and gives him a quick, chaste kiss on the cheek.

Maurice becomes putty in her hands, and I have to laugh. She says I have the disarming charm? I think it works both ways, dear Kathryn. The difference between us is knowledge and awareness. She doesn't have a clue what she does to men, when she releases her charms unknowingly and naturally. Unlike mine, which are generally calculating and result driven.

"Since you're father passed away so young, I feel things need to be said to this man. Believe me, your father would have agreed. I've never seen another man dote on his daughter like he did you. You were the apple of his eye." Kathryn's eyes water with the mention of her father.

Maurice hit his mark. Attacked me and upset her. I'll be black and blue by the time we make it to the apartment, if I'm still invited. In an odd way, I feel as if he's more a threat to me right now than Simon. He's definitely wounding my big ego, as Kathryn called it.

However, his jabs stick to me and aren't easily dismissed. The mention of her late father hits me strangely. Maybe it has to do with my own mother's death. Unfortunately, I know the heartbreak surrounding such a loss. I was my mother's world, too, even in her own death.

I can imagine her father walking into this restaurant with Kathryn. A pretty raven-haired young girl with a promising life ahead of her. From Peters' report, I know he passed away when she would've been around nineteen. Not too much younger than when I lost my mother at twenty-two.

One thing is for sure, her father would be so proud of her today. Any parent would be. She's a smart, not-to–be-tangled-with woman and her beauty stands alone.

Thankfully, I believe Maurice is done berating me for now. We start to make our way out of the office. The kitchen is busier than it was before, so no one even looks our way as we pass.

Once we enter the restaurant's dining room, I see almost every table is full with customers. Eating, chatting, and paying us no mind. We are being ignored, which works into my game plan of laying low until the bodyguard arrives tomorrow, or until the police find Simon.

We stop at the front door and watch Maurice walk outside to the curb. Holding his hand in the air, he signals a cab to pull over and stop.

"He means well, Kingsley," Kathryn quietly says.

"I know he does. He cares for you deeply. He overheard me talking to you, and it probably fueled all the rumors he's heard about me."

She turns her head to me as a serious expression spreads across her face. That look she gets when she's about to lay it on me. So I stand straighter and square my shoulders in preparation.

"Are they rumors, Adam? Or the truth?"

Again, I'm left speechless after she corners me with my player reputation. I'm not used to defending what I've viewed as just a single guy's carefree lifestyle.

But I can't avoid her loaded questions: Are they rumors or the truth? Deep down, I know she has me and I can't deny all the gossip is most likely the ugly truth. This time I don't have a funny comeback to give her. Humor can't help me here. Woman by woman, I've dug my own hole.

I'm not ready to tell her what I'm thinking, though. Being this exposed and introspective isn't who I am or what I share with others. Since yesterday afternoon my whole world has tilted on its axis. Nothing seems right tonight, with the exception of being with her in this moment.

Maurice waves for us to come outside when a cab finally stops for him. I open the door for Kathryn and usher her onto the sidewalk. Maurice has the door open and waiting for us. Kathryn scoots in first, and I try to follow but feel a hand grabbing my arm, stopping me. It's Maurice with one more thing to say to me. Oh great, looks like this won't be an easy escape from him.

"Mr. Kingsley, promise this old man that you'll be good to her." He has a desperate look about him, like he's begging me to answer, "yes."

And before I can really think about the ramifications or another more appropriate response for a rakish man like me, I say, "Yes."

The smile that appears on his face could light up Brooklyn. He's ecstatic I've given him the answer he wanted, and I'm left wondering why I just agreed to his request.

Can I even live up to what I just promised? I know I have my work cut out for me. Even I'm not fool enough to think I'm good. The real Adam is far from it.

Maurice joyfully shakes my hand and thanks me for my promise. I in turn thank him for helping us tonight. For opening his office and letting us camp out there until I knew what was going on and which direction to take.

I bid him goodbye with a quick handshake and climb into the cab next to Kathryn. She's not on the far side of the seat, out of my reach, where I expect her to be. Instead she's in the middle, closer to me. As I settle into my seat, I find myself sitting right next to her, leg to leg. She has a knowing smile on her face. I believe I know why. She overheard my exchange with Maurice.

"Promising an old man you'll be good. What's gotten into you, Kingsley? Have you fallen off your high and mighty horse?" She leans her head back and laughs at her cute remarks.

"I get a distinct feeling everyone is out to get me tonight. Simon with a gun and Maurice with his words." I sound pitiful, even to myself.

I feel her fingers weaving through mine as she presses our hands together. There is a distinct warmth and togetherness in her simple act of reaching out to me.

"What do you say we both promise to be good to each other tonight?" Kathryn asks while curling her lips into a smile.

"I suppose I could manage to be good for at least one night. How hard can it be? But can you be good to me?" I say the last words in a way that clearly gives the word "good" a double meaning.

I feel her arm moving, and while still holding my hand she elbows me. A direct hit to the ribs.

"Damn, why did you do that?" I flinch from the pain.

"Because you're impossible. A woman can be good to you Kingsley without having to spread her legs."

I mutter something under my breath about strong-headed women and hope she doesn't make out what I'm saying. There's only so much my ribs can take for the night.

"So does the cabbie know where we're going?" I realize I climbed in and didn't offer directions to the driver.

"I gave him my address while you were lying to Maurice." I stare at her in disbelief after that comment.

"Lying?"

"Oh, so it isn't a lie, you plan on living up to that promise?" And she's got me.

"Uncle," I say, raising the white flag in surrender. Something I never do.

Chapter 9

The cab ride to her building is quiet. Our driver repeatedly changes lanes and speeds down the city blocks trying to make all the green lights. Pretty much the usual fare for a cab ride, and why I'm thankful for having Eddie.

Neither one of us utters a single word. My surrender to her witty entrapment of me still hangs in the air. I'm an MIT genius for fuck's sake, but she's been winning all the arguments with me. Hands down kicking my ass. Who would've thought my mental match would be a sexy-as-hell vixen wearing red lipstick and Shalimar? Both of which are driving me crazy right now.

I'm not sure she has any idea what she has won, as I willingly gave into her. And truthfully I'm not sure, either. We are still holding hands with the promise of nothing more. Normally in this situation, I'd be looking for the next willing woman. Holding hands was great in middle school, but I have needs that want to be addressed. Yet here I sit with her. Hand in hand like we're at a church picnic.

Additionally, the only good behavior I've promised a woman relates to sex. Giving her a down-and-dirty fuck, an expert tonguing to her clit, or maybe a little something kinky and naughty. Nothing good has ever happened from restraining myself sexually.

Everything appears to be upside down in my life right now. Simon has lost his fucking mind. I resemble Tom more than myself. Which is frightening as hell because Tom's been pussy-whipped for years. I've even seen him carrying Lois' purse for her, and a man toting a Chanel bag isn't right.

Funny thing, though, I find myself enjoying every damn minute I've had with her. Even when we were arguing in Maurice's office. Our anger was more like a warm-up of verbal foreplay. It's the only glimpse I've had at her passion. And one thing's for sure, this woman has it in spades. I just have to convince her to share some of it with me.

As we make our way down Fifth Avenue, I recall standing and waiting for her outside her building. I stared at the entrance and doorman for hours. Watching as scores of people came and went. I can't believe how long I waited for her. An important conference call was delayed. Now with Simon's situation it will likely be days before I can reschedule.

I lightly rub circles over her soft skin. I glance up and give her a smile, which she blazingly returns to me. Something happens when she does. Even though I'm a stubborn man, I have to admit what I've realized tonight. This woman might be worth my being good. At least I'm willing to try.

"We're almost there," she whispers, breaking the silence between us. The cab is sitting at a red light, but I see her building's green awning up ahead.

"Back where we started today. I did get my wish, though. Do you want to know what it was?"

"Something tells me it doesn't matter what I want. You're going to tell me anyway."

"Are you sure we haven't met before? Maybe in another lifetime? You have an uncanny knowledge of what I'm going to say. It's unnerving."

"It's the psychologist in me. Human nature. There's really nothing new under the sun. You're not as special as you think you are." Her sarcastic remarks actually turn me on. I enjoy her feistiness. Maybe it's the challenge.

"Ouch. Now back to my wish, you sharp-tongued goddess." She laughs at my wisecrack. But I realize she's rather talented at getting me off subject. I make a mental note of this sneaky trait of hers.

"Okay. I'll play along. What did you wish for?" she asks with a curious look in her eyes.

"Exactly what we are about to do. An invitation to your apartment. A ride up your elevator." I tease her by wiggling my brow at the word ride. "A peek at where you live, along with a tour of your bedroom, perhaps." I end with my patented devilish smile.

"You mean an invitation to ruffle up my sheets," she says, mockingly. I can't see her face as she's turned away from me, but I'd bet money she's rolling her eyes.

"You have a way of crushing my hopes, don't you?" She laughs at me again. I enjoy our teasing, although I'd enjoy her more under me on her sheets. Some habits die hard.

We pull up to her building, and the doorman comes to the cab and opens the door for us. I pay the cabbie and exit after her. She stands close by waiting for me. I instinctively grab her hand and start to run quickly to the entrance, bringing her with me.

Leaving the doorman behind us, I open the glass door and we hustle inside. I breathe a sigh of relief once we are in the lobby area. It's classic in design. Marble floors, elegant lighting, and rich colors of wood greet us.

"Show me to your elevator, woman," I say playfully.

"This way, Mister." She teases right back and leads me to the hallway behind the concierge desk.

She pushes the up arrow and the doors open instantly, like they were awaiting our arrival. I follow behind her as we step inside. She lights up the number twenty, and we feel the cage start to climb.

Kathryn leans against the shiny wood side of the elevator wall and gazes up at me. I move in closer to her. The nearness of her body and scent wreak havoc on me and my ability to rein myself in like I promised. I don't want to push this woman too far, but I've never had to control myself like this, either.

Totally new territory for me. And my cock doesn't like it one bit. When a woman gets me aroused like this, waiting is something I don't have to do. Usually by now my cock would be buried inside of her.

Restraint was never required, at least not until now. One thing for sure: The confines of this tight space are pressing me to the edge of my control with her. My thoughts turn to kissing her again and pushing her roughly against the wall while my lips devour her. I'm lost in my fantasies when she begins to speak.

"Our running into the building like two silly people was stupid and probably drew more attention to us. We kind of stuck out."

"True, but I liked holding your hand." I reach out for her hand again. She willingly lets mine encase hers. I walk a step forward. Now our bodies are almost touching, my eyes looking down into hers. God, how her lovely eyes do crazy things to me. I place one hand on her back while the other one cups her chin. I tilt her head upward with my fingers, and bring our faces even closer together.

This time I don't ask for a kiss. There's no need. Her eyes are full of desire, and her lips are parted in anticipation. I know the tell-tale signs when a woman is saying, kiss me. Leaning down I take her mouth with mine.

Her lips part and my tongue meets hers. This simple contact ignites me. Fuels my desire. I've never felt this hard, this desperate, with just a kiss. What happens when I can't have more from her? The thought makes me nearly delirious.

I hold her tighter to me. Her body yielding, melting, and molding into mine. Bending into me she holds me around my waist. It feels so good to be in her arms. She tightens her arms around me, drawing us even closer.

She has to feel my cock pressing hard into her stomach. There's no mistaking how much I want this woman. Now she knows. But like before at the restaurant, she pulls her lips away from mine and breaks the kiss. I am feeling on fire, and by the flush on her face and darkened eyes, I know she's feeling the same thing. Even if she's not willing to admit it.

Her breathing is heavy, matching mine. She stares up into my eyes. The elevator is the only movement or sound around us as we near her floor.

"I want you, Kathryn," I whisper to her, nibbling on her ear between breaths. She lets out a slight moan. "I've never wanted to fuck a woman like this before. Spread you wide and take you."

"What are you doing to me, Kingsley? I don't do things like this."

"That makes two of us."

"This is all you do," she replies sarcastically.

"You're wrong. I never have to wait or ask with a woman. They give and I take." I draw her to me and hold her tight. Pressing her small body to me. My face buries in her black hair. I close my eyes and just breathe. She smells like heaven, but having to hold myself back is hell.

"But I'm willing to play by your rules." I release her and feel the elevator's carriage come to a stop. The doors part, and I take her hand in mine.

"Lead the way. I'll be good. I promised, remember?" I need to somehow cool things down a bit. I'm torturing myself, and possibly her as well, by pushing for more too quickly. But when I get hard for her, it's impossible to think straight.

"I have no doubt in my mind you'll be anything but good," she says with a laugh. Once again this woman knows me so well.

She exits the elevator and I follow her down a long carpeted hallway. There are very few apartments on her floor. I remember from the information Peters dug up that her apartment is rather big by New York City standards.

When we reach the hallway's end, she unlocks the door to her right and opens it. "Home, sweet, home."

I walk into her foyer. Marble lies under my feet. A table sits against a wall with an ornate silver-framed mirror placed above it. A flush chandelier hangs over my head.

Moving forward into the open space in front of me, I find myself in the living room. The décor is unmistakably French. Beautiful and stylish. I'd expect nothing less. Classically elegant, but still comfortable. A perfect reflection of Kathryn.

But what catches my eye is the view from her large glass window. Central Park. It's a view almost as magnetic as Kathryn.

I find myself walking toward the windows. Once I'm in front of them, I gaze out at the park. Night has fallen and only a few lights appear through the trees. Such a contrast against the normal Manhattan skyline of lights and high-rises. It's peaceful. Untouched by man's need to build bigger and higher.

"Beautiful view. Believe it or not, I share a very similar one just a few blocks away. Nothing like it. Especially in a city like this."

"I agree." Kathryn concurs after joining me to stare out the window. "You only live a few blocks away?"

"My penthouse is at The Pierre."

"The hotel?"

"There are a few floors in the hotel where people actually live. Mostly penthouses. I enjoy the hotel's service. Makes life more convenient at times."

Turning toward me, Kathryn leans against the glass. "I'm sure. I've been inside the lobby. It's very grand."

"I'd love to show it to you someday. You would be the first woman, besides my housekeeper, to enter as my guest." I'm not sure why I just confessed this to her.

"First woman? Where do you take all of them? Or do you just use the back seat for all your fun?" I swear there's a hint of anger in her voice. Could it possibly be jealousy? Part of me hopes it is because then I'd know she has feelings for me. What else would make her jealous other than wishing she were one of the women?

"Various places." I want to end my explanation with these two words. She doesn't need to know that I have an ongoing hotel room waiting a few stories below me at The Pierre. I can imagine the disgust in her eyes if I told her this little fact.

"I don't want to talk about other women when I'm with you. But I can assure you that you'll be my first."

"For some reason that isn't very comforting, but in your case I guess I should be flattered. I bet there are likely very few firsts left with you." She moves away from the glass. Her words, as always, cut through my bullshit and go right to the truth.

"Touché." I concede. My phone vibrates in my pocket. I know this little bubble we are in is about to be invaded with news about Simon. Amazingly, I keep forgetting about him. She's that good at distracting me. Or maybe what I feel for her is distracting me? Who knows?

"Excuse me, Kathryn, while I take this call." I pull the phone out and see it's Peters.

"Any news?" I say with no formal greeting.

"Yes. Simon hasn't been apprehended but his credit card was used a short time ago at a gas station in East Orange, New Jersey. Does he know anyone there to your knowledge?"

"I have no idea. He's from Buffalo, originally. You know my relationship with Simon. It isn't that close."

"He could be heading to Buffalo or Canada for that matter. The route through East Orange would take him there. The police have confirmed his Mercedes is not parked at his building's apartment garage. So they've issued an all-points bulletin for the car. I'm still not convinced he's left the city and need to see the video surveillance camera at the gas station to be convinced. He's a shrewd man. Why would he use a card to announce his whereabouts? Seems like an idiot move."

"I'll let you worry about the details. That's what I pay you to do. Remind me to give you a big bonus for this." Peters is really overpaid as it is, but he's the best and I don't want anyone luring him away.

"Right, I'll remind you of that." He's laughing to himself because he knows I'll remember without him having to mention it. "How did everything go getting to Ms. Delcour's apartment? You're there now, right?"

"Everything is fine. Brilliant idea, me staying here." On many levels, I'd like to add but refrain. "Simon has no idea that I met Kathryn last night, either."

"I think you're safe for now. I've told my police contact that you are unavailable until tomorrow morning. They want to speak with you, but I said they would have to call and discuss a formal interview with your attorney. Speaking of, have you heard from MacDonald?"

"Not yet. Patrick is handling all of that for me tonight. I am sure I'll be hearing from him later. Keep me updated."

"Will do." Peters ends the call and I pivot away from the window to find Kathryn standing in the middle of her living room by a large coffee table stacked with books and magazines. There are books and picture frames everywhere. Large to small ones dotting the room. Leaves it with a welcoming feeling. I'd love to browse through them and get a glimpse into her life.

"Sorry for the interruption, but good news. Simon may have left the city. Something about a credit card of his being used in New Jersey.

"What a relief. I hope they catch him, Kingsley. This has to be hard on you. A life-long friend and partner. I can't imagine."

"To say it's been crazy is an understatement. But what troubles me the most is why? What made him snap like this, and in such a spectacular way?"

"Who knows? Sometimes people have troubles that boil over and become too much for them to handle."

"Maybe so. But I want to thank you."

"Thank me? For what? You liked that grilling at the restaurant, didn't you?" She giggles, and it's the sweetest sound

I've ever heard. Musical, joyful. I can't help but laugh with her. It's contagious.

"Yes, Maurice's grilling." I shake my head trying to remove the memory. "Not my favorite part of the evening. But I need to thank you for being the best kind of distraction tonight. There are times I've even forgotten about this whole Simon debacle. Like when we were kissing. He was the furthest thing from my mind."

"I could tell." She raises her brows, and a smile dances across her lips. She's wickedly stunning and quite the minx. I'm sure her words and expression reference my hard-on pressing against her stomach in the elevator.

"And you're very welcome, too. Every girl loves to hear that she's been a great distraction." She rolls her eyes at me. But the way she said this makes my compliment sound horrible. Was it?

I'm so out of my element here. Fucking women never required work or having to say the right words. It was as easy as breathing but boring when compared to being around her. I'll just have to watch my words, which may prove to be an impossible task.

"Let me show you the rest of my apartment." She turns slowly away from me, tossing her long hair over her shoulders. I love the way it bounces, picks up the light, and shines with the motion.

I imagine the long waves of her hair lying across my pillow in wild disarray. Her smile and arms welcoming me. I stop myself before I go farther down this fantasy road, as it will only get me in trouble tonight. So I clear the thoughts out of my head and follow her lead down the hall. It's a position I don't mind being in as the view walking behind her is divine. Her small, tight ass and swaying hips. Oh, what a man could do with that ass.

"The kitchen is down that hall." She points in the opposite direction we are headed. "But first I'll show you where you will be sleeping for the night. And just to make it clear, it's not my bedroom."

Her rebuff is firm. But who knows, perhaps she'll change her mind. It doesn't hurt to have hope.

We turn down another hallway. The walls are painted a unique shade of gray with glossy white molding that pops out in contrast.

She stops in front of a door and walks inside. "This is your room. There is a bath connected to it. My brother stays here with me sometimes. Like he did last night after the benefit for my mother's foundation. He's a med student at Harvard and only makes it into the city for special events. I think you're about his size. You'll find some of his pajamas in the top draw of the black dresser."

The room is surprisingly masculine and modern. Almost sterile in contrast to the large living room. However, the one common theme in her decorating seems to be books. Hundreds of them line a built-in shelf that covers an entire wall of the room.

"Thank you. Yes, the brother who I thought was one of your trainees."

"My trainee?" I realize she has no idea what I'm talking about. I need to explain.

"Last night, when you spoke using the phrase 'turn boys into men.' Well, when you left me at the bar and I saw your brother greet and escort you to the ballroom, I naturally thought he was in training. You know. To be a man."

"Oh, well that explains a lot." She laughs. "I wondered about the look on your face when I introduced him. You appeared shocked."

"Shocked, but mostly disappointed," I say.

"Disappointed that he was my brother?" Her head tilts, and she has that adorable confused look on her face. Adorable? I'm using girlie words used to describe cute photos of kittens. What the fuck has gotten into me? I quickly clear my head and get back to answering her question.

"No. Not that John was your brother. I was disappointed because I thought he was your lover. I would have tried harder with you last night had I known otherwise."

"Tried harder for what? Getting into my panties for the night?" She moves a little closer to me. Again it's like there are magnets pulling us together. It seems impossible for us to stay too far apart.

"Yes, I'll admit it. After I met you last night, I didn't just want in your panties, I wanted to camp out for the night. Make you want to invite me back." I add a little wink of my eye and a smirk. But I am only half kidding her, and my words aren't far from the truth. "But you already suspected this, right?"

"You're incorrigible. I don't even know how to answer you back. I think we'll just continue on with our tour." She walks past me to head out of the room and lightly punches me on the bicep.

"Hey!" I say in protest even though I barely felt a thing. A stern look in her eyes lets me know she's on to me. I can't pull any punches past the woman.

Our tour continues, and we enter the next room. She doesn't even have to tell me it's her bedroom because it has Kathryn written everywhere I look. A beautiful, mahogany poster bed centers the room. The posts have to be more than six feet tall. Grand and quite the statement.

"This is my room. Just remember clothing isn't optional in here." She's such a killer of my wet dreams.

"So is this where all the Tantra action occurs?" I place my hand on one of the bedposts and give it a little shake, checking for stability. It doesn't budge. Quality.

"You don't know shit about tantric sex, do you?" She knows the answer already, I'm sure, but likely wants to hear it from me first.

"Clueless. I've heard bits and pieces about it. I know your definition, though, 'Sex as an art form.'"

"For the record, nothing Tantra happens in my bedroom. This room is associated with sleeping, and nothing about Tantra makes one want to sleep." She has a dreamy, lost-in-pleasure appearance. It's an unfamiliar expression on her face to me. I wonder if this is how she looks when she practices Tantra. I hope to God I find out. At this point I'm willing to sign up for anything.

"I'll show you where the Tantra action does occur. Follow me." This room I have to see. But funny thing, I've never left a woman's bedroom without having fucked her in it first. Sadly, another first for me where Kathryn's concerned.

We pass back by my room. The room where I'll likely be lying awake most of the night thinking about her sleeping a few feet away. Once past it, she stops in front of a doublewide door. Two brass handles mark the center where they meet.

"Welcome to my office." Her eyes have a glint of mischief as she twists on of the brass handles and waits for me to enter the room.

What greets me looks like anything but an office. I know my face shows the shock of what I'm seeing. I feel as if I've been transported to an ancient desert king's tent. The type used for housing a harem. It's from another world. Another time.

The walls are covered with silken-like tapestries in dark, rich tones. Gold threading glimmers throughout. Pillows lie scattered across the room with a large one situated in the middle. It looks more like a soft pallet. Beneath the pillows, the floor is covered with oriental-style rugs. They are dark, too, and flow into the wall coverings. The floor and walls harmonize to a point where there is hardly a distinction between the two.

The silk-covered walls circle around the room. Their dark hues blending to create a sultry illusion, and no corners showing gives the space a tent-like feeling. Even the ceiling has fabric draped, hanging above me in waves. I can almost feel the sand of the desert under my feet.

"Where's Aladdin?" I ask her sarcastically before my mind has time to think. Stupid me. Kathryn's face turns red, and her angry eyes peer at me. I think she's about ready to unleash on my ass.

"Aladdin?" she spouts at me. Her voice tight and controlled but her eyes are anything but as she shakes her head and huffs. I've really ticked her off this time. Insulted her most likely. "I knew I shouldn't have shown you this room. You're making fun of it at my expense."

"Kathryn, please. I apologize. I shouldn't have said that to you." I'm groveling and might even fall to my knees in supplication to gain her forgiveness. Me, Adam Kingsley. When I sneeze the markets react. Alerts are sent out to Wall Street. But this woman's feelings make me buckle. I'm amazed at myself and perplexed by her. No one has ever had this kind of power over me.

She crosses her arms over her ample breast and looks at me speculatively. "I guess it was to be expected. You don't really have a frame of reference for Tantra and what it entails to practice it. And you do have asshole tendencies, too."

What can I say to that? After twenty-four hours she has me totally pegged. No escaping from her now.

But one thing is for certain, I'm beyond curious now and would gladly become her eager pupil. Time to repair the damage.

"It was a horrible choice of words. But I do feel like I'm back in time. It feels like I've just ridden across the desert on my camel to find this oasis. It's uniquely beautiful." I want to add, just like you, as I try to get back in her good graces. I never meant to hurt her or belittle what she practices, and truly the room is beautiful, captivating even.

A loud buzzing sound radiates throughout her apartment. Uncharacteristically, I jump at the sound. Between getting lost in my thoughts with her and Simon's actions tonight, I'm slightly on edge.

"That's my doorman calling up." I sense the same startled feeling from her that I felt. We are both a little unnerved. "Let me see what he wants. Tour over for you, Mister."

She shuts the door behind us as we leave the room. I wanted to explore it more, but I'll settle for another time. Maybe I'll sneak in after she's asleep, God knows I'm not getting anything tonight. That unfortunately applies to sex, too.

In her main hallway, Kathryn picks up a phone's receiver to communicate with her doorman. I can't hear what he's saying to her but I can tell from her expression she's surprised. I immediately begin to worry. What if Simon is here? It seems impossible but I wouldn't put anything past him at this point.

"What is it, Kathryn?" Impatient, I press her for details.

"Hold on, Carl." She removes the receiver from her ear and gives me the "you've got to be kidding me" look. "Kingsley, calm down. It's just a client of mine. I forgot about an appointment I had for tonight. You showing up unannounced at my apartment this afternoon. The commotion surrounding Simon. It slipped my mind."

"Appointment?" Something tells me I'm not going to like where this may be going. I know her business is called The Spiritual Touch, and I can just imagine what kind of sessions make up her so-called appointments. My hands form into fists at the thought of her and another man in the harem tent.

"Yes, an appointment. He's a client I've been working with for a couple of months." Her eyes have a conciliatory look to them as if she's trying to gain my favor. "I feel bad I forgot and don't want to cancel. Are you okay with him coming up here? It will only be for about forty-five minutes, tops."

I want to tell her, fuck no, I'm not okay with this arrangement, but I partially understand where she's coming from. I'm a businessman and have to respect her business, even if the thought of her working with a client behind closed doors drives me crazy.

"Forty-five minutes, right?" She nods. "I can survive for that long, I guess."

But I know it's a lie. I'm as jealous as hell because I want to be the man spending time with her intimately. I have to ask her what this will entail. She's likely to blow up at me, but I have to know the truth.

"What happens with your clients? Will your appointment also include having sex?" If looks could kill, I'd be buried and rotting away right now. Livid might be a great way to describe the look on her face.

"Oh my God. You are simply unbelievable. I'm not some high dollar call girl. I teach tantric sex. T.E.A.C.H. Capisce?" Yes, she's as mad as hell. She's a firecracker that exploded right in front of me with her eyes throwing daggers at me.

"Well, then, tell me what goes on. I have no idea what you do in that office of yours." I move toward her. We're about a foot apart. The intensity I feel between us stirs. I have to blink quickly to break our connection or I'm likely to pull her to me and attack her lips again.

"To get you to shut the hell up, I'll tell you what will be going on. But I need to give my doorman permission to let my client come up here first. You will behave."

I sigh and know that I'll comply with what she wants. "I'll behave." I cross my heart with my right hand, and like a child cross my left hand's fingers behind by back.

"All right, Carl. Give me five minutes before you let Mr. James come up the elevator." Kathryn turns her shoulder away from me and speaks low into the phone. "No, everything's all right."

I have no idea what her doorman asked of her, but I bet it has to do with the conversation he overheard while she was speaking with me.

After she places the phone's receiver back in its holder, she spins around to face me. And boy, oh boy, she's as pissed as hell.

Chapter 10

Kathryn moves closer to me and I want to cower from her approach. Her eyes reflect an angry fervor, and I'm wondering if this will be her worst berating of me yet.

She's steaming mad with eyes trained on me. The passion she's showing makes her sexy as hell. I can't look away from her beautiful face as she stands in front of me. What a sight to behold. All fire and no ice.

"For starters. I am a certified Tantra instructor. Secondly, no one takes their clothes off when I'm teaching. It's a lesson, not the actual act. My hope is they will learn from me and then try it out on their partner when they're home." She points a finger in a scolding manner as she gives me the details of her Tantra instruction.

"My client tonight is a young man around your age. He's been with his girlfriend for about two years, and there are certain issues between them. That's where I'm needed, and that's all the information I'm sharing. I've likely said too much as it is." She stands before me with her hands on her hips as she concludes her little speech.

Okay, that wasn't too bad. She told me what I wanted to know. Nobody will be taking their clothes off in her harem tent.

I'm not sure exactly what they will be doing, but for my own physical safety, I didn't push her further.

Kathryn starts straightening the already perfectly placed pillows on the couch. Picking them up to punch and fluff them before replacing them on the couch. She blows a stray hair out of her eyes as she mutters under her breath; I make out a few choice words. Mostly calling me an asshole repeatedly. I back off a little and give her some space.

I wonder where she wants me to be when this man comes up for his sex training. I'd like to be in the room videotaping the session or taking notes, to be honest. However, there's not a snowball's chance in hell of that happening.

"Um, where do you want me to hang out while your doing, um, what you do?" I try to ask in a helpful tone. I don't want to hide away in another part of her apartment; I need to check this guy out.

"Just stay in the living room area, I guess. Use the time to catch up on emails or make calls. I don't know, but just don't watch TV. The sound really travels around the apartment, and I can't have distractions during my sessions." She picks a couple books up off the side table by the couch and walks over to me. "Here, read these. They will explain a little bit about Tantra. And don't just look at the pictures. Really read them. Okay?"

"Okay." A look of satisfaction crosses her face as I willingly take the books from her hand. Truthfully, I'm anxious to learn about Tantra, because I'm at a total loss. It also can't hurt to learn about what's important to her, what she believes in enough to teach others. A better understanding of this would get me closer to her mind, and to this beautiful woman who's seized my attention from the start.

"Would you care for something to drink?" Her question is saccharine sweet. The smile that spreads across her flawless face tells me that pleasantries are back, and I'm relieved.

"Yes, please. A glass of water would be great." My throat's parched. It's probably all the sexual frustration I've been experiencing with her and the tension surrounding Simon. My body feels like it's run a marathon tonight. Kathryn leaves the room and goes down the hallway toward the kitchen.

I nervously pace her living room with her books in my hands. Waiting for her trainee to show up at the door is complete torture. I want to grab hold of her newly straightened pillows on the couch and start punching them, too. A raging bout would be the only thing to relieve the anxiety I feel for this man intruding on our time together.

But I have to be honest with myself; I have no claims on her. We've held hands. I kissed her, twice. And unbelievably, she's graciously letting me stay as her guest knowing a gun-welding maniac is after me.

I have no right to demand this man stays away. But one thing's for sure. He better be ugly as sin with horrible body odor and nose hair, or I'm going to go nuts at the thought of her behind closed doors with him.

Kathryn returns from the kitchen with a tall glass of ice water for me. I take it from her hands with a grateful smile.

"Thanks," I say sincerely. Her doorbell chimes the second after I speak. We stand still and look at each other, our eyes silently saying, "This is it."

Her "appointment" has arrived. My stomach feels tight and cramped, even my palms are starting to sweat. Such a rare thing, but I don't like the thought of meeting this guy at all.

"Excuse me, Kingsley. My client is here." I swear there is a touch of nervousness in her voice. "Please make yourself at home."

Kathryn stands at the door for a second or two before opening it. Almost like she's bracing herself. I find this behavior very interesting and it helps confirm I'm not the only one feeling uncomfortable with this situation. She turns the knob and I prepare for the man of the hour, or the next forty-five minutes, to enter.

When this man, Eric, steps over her threshold, well, I don't like what I see one fucking bit. The guy is a tall, athletically built young man, maybe around twenty-four. His hair is a sun-bleached blond, and I bet it's as fake as a porn star's boobs.

He looks as if he drove in straight from the Hamptons in his shiny BMW convertible. Preppy, reeking of old money, and model-handsome if I had to describe him.

Fuckity fuck. I don't like this guy one damn bit.

After he's inside the foyer, he greets Kathryn with a big bear hug and a kiss on the cheek. It's not one of those feigned New York City embraces. It's a real one, and the fact she responds in kind to him makes me dislike him even more.

"Kathryn, you look lovely as always." He's pulled back from her but still holds onto her arms, assessing and giving her a way-too-long once-over. I swear he's definitely checking her out. I'm sure he finds her as perfect as I do. Fucking blonde beach boy asshole.

"Thanks, Eric. You're too sweet." Sweet? No, Kathryn, he's here to be taught about sex from you. He's likely one horny fuck. God knows I am.

I step into the open, drawing attention to myself. He moves forward a bit to match my movements. At least he's dropped his fucking hands off her. I glance over to Kathryn; she's biting her lip, likely nervous I'm going to misbehave I bet. Well, I can do charming, too. Watch this, Eric.

"Good evening." I extend my hand to a surprised-looking Eric, recognition apparent in his eyes. Everyone in Manhattan knows Adam Kingsley, this asshole isn't an exception. It's time to show this punk my take-no-prisoners nature.

"Adam Kingsley." My voice is commanding and my handshake firm, perhaps bordering on a bit painful.

"Wow, the Adam Kingsley. He really does exist." He shakes my hand more avidly. Blondie is impressed, a look of almost adoration showing in his eyes. For once I'm not disgusted with someone fawning over me. I might even be enjoying it.

"In the flesh," I respond matter-of-factly.

"I'm Eric James. Wow, it's incredible meeting you. You're kind of a hero to us young guys." Eric shakes his head, correcting himself. "Sorry, let me back up. I work at Goldman's in the distressed assets department. To be honest with you, you're more of a legend. I can't believe I'm meeting you."

I shift my gaze to see Kathryn, who's shaking her head while she laughs at our exchange. There's no way to impress this woman, it seems to me.

Humbly, I put my hand over my heart. "Hero, legend . . . that is a big stretch, but thanks."

Blondie looks at the books in my left hand and glances back up at me. "Are you here for a Tantra lesson, too?" Kathryn clears her throat after Blondie asks the question, likely wanting to change the subject.

"Now that you two have met," she acts quickly by patting her patient's back, "we better get started, Eric."

Kathryn is all professional. It's time for her and this guy to get down to business. I'd be lying if I said I was okay with it.

I'm as jealous as hell that this blonde kid from Goldman's is getting to spend time with her alone.

"Sure thing, Kathryn. Nice to meet you, Mr. Kingsley," Eric says turning back to me once again. The admiration in his eyes is still there, and I wonder if he can see the jealousy in mine.

"Same to you." My response more terse then I would've liked. Kathryn's look of disapproval plows right into me. Surely I should've learned by now to rein myself in with her.

"Have a nice…" Shit I'm stumped. Trying to remedy my smart mouth, and now I'm stuck. What do I call their time together? A Romp? Pillow time? Finally landing on my feet, I say, "Um, session." I don't even want to look at Kathryn, but my eyes find her anyway. She's sporting a knowing smirk; a damn sexy one, in fact.

"Eric, why don't you head into my office and change? I'll do the same and join you in a couple of minutes." Kathryn instructs him with a wave of her hand toward her office, or harem tent.

Change into what? I want to ask but hold my tongue. I have never watched my words so much in my life. But I will learn to control my mouth around her, even if it kills me.

Eric heads back toward the harem tent, but Kathryn doesn't follow. Instead, she turns in my direction.

"Try to be good while I'm busy. Forty-five minutes isn't too much to ask, right?" I don't think she believes I can sit here and not cause trouble. Smart woman.

"Yes, yes. I've already promised, remember? Besides, I have some reading to do." I hold up and shake the Tantra books in my hands and take a seat in her oversized armchair. "Not to mention countless emails that likely need my attention. I'll keep myself entertained."

"I'm holding you to that promise." She ends with a wink at me, and that delicious smile that makes me want to get up from the chair and kiss her breathless. I grip the armrest to keep me planted in place.

God, how the fuck am I going to survive this, but I return her smile and give a quick salute with my hand. Then she is gone. Vanishing down the hall. Off to Tantra.

I hear doors opening and closing in the distance. Then there's nothing coming from the hallway leading down to her office. Just silence. My mind keeps traveling back to the room, the pillows, and what they might be doing in there.

To get my mind off these rather tormenting thoughts, I decide to open the Tantra books on my lap. What the hell? If I can't be in there to join them, I'll just have to settle for second best: educating myself on the subject.

I'm an intelligent man; this shouldn't be too hard. I also know my way around a woman's body, so who knows, maybe I can show her a thing or two. But that's getting a little ahead of myself. We haven't gone beyond a kiss.

All the emails requiring attention can wait a few minutes. I can't concentrate on work right now, anyway. Not knowing what Kathryn's up to, what she's teaching him, is very disconcerting. I pick up one of the Tantra books and thumb through the pages. A thought crosses my mind: Hopefully, Kathryn might teach me Tantra at some point. Getting lost thinking about anything involving Kathryn is easy, but I can't forget more pressing matters, either.

All this Simon business can go to hell, too. There's not a thing I can do right now to make it right or better. Just wait for his next move, or until authorities catch up to him. I'm resolved to focus on the things at hand where I might have a little more control or payback for my efforts.

The first book's title is simple enough, Tantra Sex: The Loving Touch. I can handle this if it's just about touching. Been there, done that for the last eighteen years. I was fourteen when I felt my first nipple. I came in my pants after about five minutes of kissing the girl while groping her breast. But damn, no man can forget his first boob, first pussy, and especially his first fuck.

I remember the coy way, as a teenager, I had to fool around with her in hopes of touching her tit. Lightly rubbing her back. Letting my hands wander closer to the sides of her breast with each pass I made.

In some ways, this adolescent scenario reflects my evening with Kathryn. God knows she pulled away from me in Maurice's office as my hands grazed the side of her breasts.

Thank fuck I didn't try to go further. Can't say it didn't cross my mind, though.

Back to the book, I find the table of contents. I'm shocked at the odd titles of the chapters. One section pops out at me above the others; "The Power of Touch" on page twenty-eight. Seems like the best place to start, so I locate the page and begin.

As I read the start to this chapter, the words seem to hit me. "Touch, the most powerful force in our world". That statement has me scoffing at such a bold claim. Seriously, the most powerful? But I continue reading, trying to hold off my judgments.

The author explains the essentials of touch. How every human being needs it to survive. A basic need no different than food, water, and shelter. Infants who are withheld from human touch develop a condition known as "failure to thrive." The lack of being held, cuddled, and the denial of human social contact contributes to this possibly deadly condition.

A charity event I attended for orphans talked about this very thing a few months ago. They gathered armies of volunteers in their African community to come and hold the babies, speak to them, and caress their faces. Giving the infants a mother's touch.

The impact of their speech at the event hit me hard. I thought of my own late mother, Flora. She was always there for me. Never a morning went by when she didn't give me a hug and a kiss goodbye before I ran through our patchy yard to catch the school bus.

When I returned home at the end of the day, she was always waiting for me with open arms. Not a second of my life passed by where I didn't feel cherished. Her loving touch was her gift to me. The gentle way she pushed my unruly hair out of my eyes, and holding and comforting me when I hurt myself falling off my bicycle or attempted some crazy skateboard maneuver.

It's dangerous to let my mind reminisce about my mother like I'm doing now. The memories are way too painful and raw, but for once I don't stop the thoughts as I sit here in Kathryn's overstuffed chair. Instead I choose to get lost in them. Maybe it's the threat from Simon that makes me give into the feelings, but I do miss my mother and would give every last cent I've earned to have her back on earth with me.

Her gentleness. Her unconditional love. Long-buried feelings begin to bubble up inside of me. The ones I've carefully suppressed since I walked away from her graveside when I was twenty-two. I should stop the dangerous path I'm heading down, but my eyes automatically close and I drift away when I see my mother in my mind's eye. Her loving smile with eyes full of acceptance and kindness.

An odd feeling in my throat starts to well up. There's a tightening in my gut when I picture my mother alive and well.

The deep sadness hits me out of nowhere. I am having trouble swallowing and my eyes are becoming damp with tears I haven't shed in ten years. I quickly open my eyes and jump to my feet while rubbing my hands across my face, hoping it helps me snap out of wherever my mind just took me. This shit needs to get shut down immediately.

Holy fuck, what is the matter with me tonight? I never drop my guard and let those memories invade during waking hours. Being tormented with them at night is hard enough, but never during the day. Fucking Tantra and its touch bullshit.

On shaky legs, I walk to the large glass window where I once again discover the vast darkness of Central Park. Feeling feverish, I lean my forehead against the cool glass, not caring if I smudge Kathryn's window.

I think I've had enough Tantra reading for tonight, so I grab my phone out of my discarded suit coat lying over the arm of the couch. As I expected, there are calls, emails, and missed texts. But before it gets too late, there is a very important call I need to make.

I find the number for my housekeeper, Rosa. She never watches television, so she's likely not heard about the incident with Simon at the library gala tonight. If she comes to work for me at the regularly scheduled time tomorrow morning, I'm concerned she'll be in harm's way.

"Hello," she answers.

"Good evening, Rosa. It's Adam. My apologies for calling so late, but I wanted to let you know that you can have the day off tomorrow. As a matter of fact, take the entire weekend off. With pay, of course."

"I don't understand, Mr. Kingsley. Is there something I've done? Am I being fired?" Rosa speaks fast and in a near panic.

"Oh, good God. No, no. You're not being fired. An issue has come up for me personally and things need to get sorted out. Hopefully everything will be back to normal by Monday. I should know more this weekend." Hopefully my words are enough to convince Rosa that all is well.

"You had me worried, Mr. Kingsley. This is unlike you. I hope everything is okay." Her concern isn't hard to mistake. She's always been motherly to me.

"Everything will be fine. Unless you hear from me, plan on returning to the penthouse Monday morning at six a.m."

Somehow I'm sure she'll find out about Simon nearly shooting Tom. It's likely her older son will tell her. But right now, I'm too drained to go into the explanation and then address her concerns and questions.

"Good evening, Rosa."

"Night, Mr. Kingsley. And I hope everything is okay."

"Thanks, Rosa. I'm sure it will be."

Turning my attention back to my emails, I open one marked "urgent" from Patrick. As I expected, he's already handling the situation for me and Kings.

The attorneys were immediately brought on board to help with the crisis Simon caused. Minimizing financial and legal fallout with our investors seems to be the ruling theme in the back-and-forth email thread between Patrick and Ken MacDonald, our head counsel at Kings Capital.

Ken believes we are safe from anything major exploding in our faces, but he's paid too much to assume. I craft a quick email telling him such. I want him assessing every angle, any remote possibility of something coming to bite us in the ass. Or his ass will be on the line. I don't come right out and tell him this, but the tone and words I use imply the ugly result of an oversight on his part.

Being prepared and anticipating what might lie ahead is the hallmark of my company's success. Now it's time to test what we've practiced during the last nine years.

Next up in my inbox is an email from our corporate communications officer, Meg Daniels. She is taking care of any public damage control. Her office has already sent out press releases detailing our stance on the Simon events of the day.

The media will likely put together the earlier announcement of his dismissal and the assault against Tom. One will lead to the other. But Meg never addresses this fact. She treats them as two separate occurrences. Smart move on her part.

Anything implied and not factual isn't a matter for Kings to discuss. The facts are stated and to the point. The only words portraying emotion are at the conclusion where Meg mentions the hope of Simon's quick capture by the authorities.

The press releases were sent to all the major media outlets, and as always I'm blind copied in them. Communications of this magnitude always include me in the email. As the company CEO, I need to know the talking points we are using with the media. A united front makes a company appear strong in times of uncertainty. God knows that's what we're going through now. Uncertain and unsure: two words rarely used in my vocabulary.

After replying to a few emails from Peters, I pocket my phone and glance around the room. Kathryn has countless photos displayed on the tables and shelves. Everywhere I turn, they're decorating the furniture and bookshelves.

Curiosity gets the better of me, and I reach for the closest picture frame. It's a photo of Kathryn and her brother, John. Likely from about ten years ago, she looks young and her brother looks like he's in his teens.

The building in the background catches my eye. No one can mistake the iconic landmark of the Eiffel Tower standing tall behind them. A clear blue sky surrounds them all. Obviously this photo was taken when she was studying in Paris. I find myself smiling back at the photo in my hands. What draws me to this picture is the complete joy on her face. Kathryn radiates pure happiness.

Everything else in the photo remains in the shadow of her beauty. Even her brother gets lost in her brilliance.

Looking at them standing arm in arm under the Eiffel Tower, I see there is no way to mistake the closeness between them. It's clearly evident. The same tenderness for each other was apparent on their faces when I watched them from a distance at the bar last night. It's easy to understand how I misinterpreted their relationship.

I can't believe Kathryn and I met only twenty-four hours ago. The unexpected happenings of the last two days have disturbed my normally planned and concisely controlled existence. My life's busy schedule allows me very little flexibility. Overseeing a company the size and scope of Kings Capital affords me little time for spontaneity.

Leaving, or more accurately, abandoning work like I did today to basically stalk Kathryn is unheard of for me. It's been one hell of a day. One minute I'm trying to control my desires for this woman and behave in a gentlemanly manner. Totally uncharted waters for me. Then I'm faced with a friend and business partner who wants to put a bullet in my head. I'm fatigued from all the highs and lows. But it's unlikely I'll be able to sleep much tonight. My mind will not be turning off anytime soon.

Sighing, I replace the frame on the table. A large shelf lines the far wall and I stroll past the pictures there.

The white enameled wood of the shelves adjoins the wall of windows where I stop and look at all the snapshots. Mostly childhood photos of Kathryn and her brother, but a couple of pictures of Kathryn and her father stand out.

As lovely a woman as Kathryn's mother Ava is, Kathryn inherited her distinct pale coloring and raven hair from her father, Richard. He had the appearance of an old world aristocrat. But his eyes had a kindness to them, which softened the edges to his face.

In one picture, Richard holds Kathryn on his lap while he reads to her from a storybook. The moment caught by the camera is intimate. Caring. The love Richard has for her as he looks up for the camera's shot exemplifies a completely devoted father.

Though Richard passed away too young, Kathryn's fortunate to have cherished memories of her time with him. Something special to hold on to.

I wasn't as lucky in this regard, never knowing my father as a child. Actually using the term, father, is a gross overstatement. I believe the words "sperm donor" would be closer to the truth.

I sure as fuck don't want to take another trip down memory lane thinking of my father, so I continue viewing the photographs along the shelves. A few of them are when Kathryn was a young woman, perhaps during her college days. Kathryn with friends on vacations. Boating on a yacht. A recently taken one of Kathryn and her mother, Ava.

But I stop on one picture in particular. I have my fingers wrapped around the frame before I even stop to think. It's a wedding photo of Kathryn and her late husband, Jean-Paul, I believe was his name. He was tall with a surprisingly dark complexion. The picture only shows his side profile, but he has the appearance of being an attractive man, and one who was head-over-heels in love.

Together, they are a stunning couple. Simply breathtaking. I can't deny it. They shine together. Kathryn's creamy ivory, strapless dress cascades around her. The tops of her breasts on parade. Very tempting. Jean-Paul is sharply clothed in a traditional formal black tuxedo. His presence is commanding and domineering. A man with purpose as he claims this beautiful woman for his own.

But the most striking part of this photo is the love and commitment I can see between the two of them. Their bodies are facing one another, with their arms gently wrapped around each other's waists. It's an intimate moment but of a different kind, not in a sexual way at all. Their faces appear to be caught in a laugh. One filled with pure joy.

The love between the two of them seems so foreign to me. Having such an intense connection with a lover is something I can't even fathom. I never loved any woman like this. Hell, other than my mother, I've never loved a woman at all.

Plain and simple. Their love reflects back at me and leaves me lacking.

The realization punches me in the gut. Maurice's words come back to my mind. Perhaps he was right. I'm not good enough for someone like Kathryn. Especially knowing the type of love she once had. Why would she want me? Sobering thoughts for me once again, and I can't help but feel as though I've been bombarded with them tonight.

Chapter 11

Holding Kathryn's wedding picture in my undeserving hands seems wrong to me. I am an uninvited guest on her memories. I slowly return the picture frame to its rightful place. However, my eyes don't want to let it go. They stubbornly stay focused on the picture of pure wedded bliss until I finally manage to turn my head.

Sitting close to the picture is a magazine-sized shadow box that catches my attention. I hadn't seen it before, but there is no overlooking it now. A shiny silver Olympic medal is displayed inside the wooden encasing. It lies proudly on a backdrop of black velvet.

Jean-Paul's medal. A piece from her past and housed prominently.

Feeling haunted by this ghost from Kathryn's late husband, I retreat from where I'm standing. Distance is needed. I can't help but wonder: Has she moved on? Or does she still grieve his loss?

In the short time we've been together, I've never noticed any sorrowfulness in the way she acts. In fact, exactly the opposite. The best way to describe her disposition would be serene, assured, and confident.

Sadness doesn't seem to be part of her make-up. Which gives me hope she's moved on from this man she obviously loved deeply. Besides, Kathryn had mentioned being in an off-and-on-again relationship with Frenchie, the man we met at the Nectar Café.

Knowing her relationship with Frenchie is currently in the off position gives me reason to hope I might have a chance with her.

I feel like an awkward schoolboy, an unusual place to find myself in. Especially since I've stopped counting how many women I've fucked over the years. But tonight, when I can't seem to remember another woman's face but Kathryn's beautiful one, my previous behavior is nothing to be proud of.

I've never needed or wanted a woman to like me in the conventional sense. I never encouraged those kinds of relationships. Ever since I was a teenager, women were drawn to me with no effort on my part. The only requirement from me was showing up. Nothing more, ever.

But Kathryn's appeal to me is much different. She's more than a sexual conquest or a pretty face on my arm for the night. The one thing unknown to me: Does she want me?

All I have to go on are her actions so far tonight. She didn't turn me away at the sidewalk when she came out of her apartment building. There's no denying she looked shocked to see me leaning against my Escalade. Maybe a touch annoyed I was stalking her, but she still let me into her private world. Which is more than I could've asked for considering she'd been warned against me. And those warnings were all sadly based on the truth, too. The rumor excuse doesn't work tonight. I've pretty much confessed to being a roguish bastard intent on my own pleasure.

Even knowing my carnal nature, she allowed me to hold her hand as we walked the streets. She chose to stay with me after Frenchie tried to persuade her to dump my player ass. We enjoyed a dinner together at a restaurant where the owners are like her family and hated the sight of me. A place she's never taken another man before tonight.

But the most meaningful concession was when she allowed me to kiss her passionately in Maurice's office, and then again in the elevator. Each time she returned my kiss with as much passion as I put into it, but pulled away too quickly for things to escalate.

Maybe it's my number-centered brain, but I can't help adding up all these positive points in my favor and believe they're a good sign for me. Here I am, a thirty-two-year-old man who's never really pursued a woman outside of sex once in my life. The attraction between us is like nothing I've felt before. She even admitted to it after our first kiss, but chose to call it lust. All I've ever known when it comes to women and sex is lust. But the chemistry Kathryn and I have is more than pure lust. Now I just need to convince her of this fact. How quickly the tables have turned.

Glancing at my watch, I realize Kathryn's session with pretty boy Eric will soon be over. Just a few more minutes left until he walks out of her harem-looking office and leaves the apartment. He better not have a smug, I just fucked your woman look on his face or things might get ugly.

Walking back over to the coffee table, I see the other two books she gave me to read lying there. One book is called, Tantric Sex, Spiritual Sex. The title almost makes me laugh, even if I'm a bit curious about the outlandish comparison. Grabbing the book and flipping through the pages, I discover this book contains more photos than the first one I read. Since reading didn't work to well the first time, the pictures might be a better option.

I know Kathryn told me not to just look at the pictures, but I want to know what might possibly be going on down the hall. Nothing I'm seeing on the pages appears out of the norm. A couple of charts display wheels of some kind running along a woman's body. The caption for the picture doesn't make a bit of sense to me, though. The different-colored wheels are Chakra points, or centers of energy.

Confused, I keep turning the pages until one photo catches my eye. It's of a couple, both are scantily clad but not nude, the man's legs are crossed in front of him while he is seated on a mat. The woman sits on his lap facing him, her legs tightly wrapped around his hips. In a way it looks like they're dry-humping, cock to pussy while moving against each other with their clothes on.

Was this what Kathryn and Eric were doing down the hall? The possibility of Eric's erect cock pressing into Kathryn's crotch is a disturbing visual for me.

Before my rational thinking kicks in, I'm walking toward the hallway leading to her office. I swore I'd be good, and standing outside of the room isn't too bad. Just being curious. But even I know that's a lie.

Approaching her office, faint music floats through the air. The music has an erotic feel to it, the sound of sex. Music to fuck by, I've called it before.

I want to hear more, and I do what I promised Kathryn I wouldn't—I totally misbehave and place my ear against the hardwood door in an attempt to make out any sounds coming from Kathryn and her pupil.

The only sound emitting from the room is music. So I push my ear harder against the wood in hopes of hearing more, but the door moves with me in its casing. The result is a loud and noticeable rattle that I'm sure Kathryn heard.

Completely busted.

I fly back to the living room and dive into her overstuffed chair. My heart's racing as adrenaline pumps through my veins. My palms are even sweating. Damn this woman and her ways of making me edgy.

I grab the books from the table again, needing to look like I've been engrossed in them when she walks out of her session. Maybe I should find a pencil and start taking notes.

But before I even get that far, I hear her coming down the hallway with Eric. Their conversation is indistinguishable, and I keep my head down, buried in the book. I check to make sure it's not upside down, and thankfully it's right side up.

When they enter the living room area, I wait a few seconds before glancing up, hoping to look surprised they're standing there finished. When I do raise my head, Kathryn appraises me. There's no denying she knows what I was up to outside her door; she's shaking her head subtly. Without saying a word, I shrug. There's no pulling the wool over her eyes at this point. No reason to even try.

The disapproving scowl isn't the only thing I notice about Kathryn. She has changed into sheer, tight workout clothes bordering on obscene. I want to take my sports coat and throw it over her shoulders. Her black sports bra and clingy yoga pants leave little to the imagination.

Which in turn makes mine run wild. Her perfect ass, gorgeously round tits, and slender waist are on full display for me, not to mention Eric. I knew she had a body, but this unrestricted look at her curves brings everything together in a mix that awakens my dormant cock. Especially when I think about her long legs wrapped around my waist like the dryhumpers in the Tantric book. I hope like hell she and this Eric guy weren't doing the bump and grind in her harem tent.

Eric stands by her side in typical guy jogging attire, the bag that he had earlier is slung over his shoulders. He changed from the business casual look he wore here tonight. Thankfully, his clothes aren't edgy. His blonde hair remains in place, just as it was earlier. His composure isn't amiss either. A warm and kind smile graces his face. Nothing about his appearance says, "I just got off with her." A slight conciliation I grab onto, which gives me a little relief.

"I see you've been reading?" Kathryn asks, arching a brow at me. At least she has acknowledged me.

"I was getting ready to start taking notes." I answer enthusiastically and she gives me a little huff in return. Yes, there's no fooling her.

Rising out from the chair, I make my way toward them.

"Eric, I am glad Melanie is coming next week, too," Kathryn says while gently placing her hand on Eric's shoulder. "With a couple more sessions, I think you two will be able to work through any other issues on your own." Eric's eyes seem to light up at the mention of his girlfriend's name.

"Thanks for everything, Kathryn. You know I'm going to ask Melanie to marry me. I have you to thank for helping me get my head on straight." Eric pulls Kathryn into a big hug similar to the one when he greeted her. "And you will definitely be invited to the wedding. Assuming she says yes."

"Of course she'll say yes." Kathryn replies with a smile. "I've seen the two of you together. You are meant to be."

Eric turns my way, all happy and boyish smiles, and holds out his hand to me. "Mr. Kingsley," our hands connect firmly, "you have quite the woman here."

He's smiling, and I'm left speechless. Well how the hell to do I respond to this? I agree with him totally; Kathryn's quite the woman.

Going with the flow, I say, "Thanks. I couldn't agree with you more." Why disrupt his happy mood with my uncertainties. I choose to generalize what he said. This approach might be more palatable for Kathryn. "Any man would be lucky to have her at his side."

There I said it.

"Such flattery from both of you." Kathryn laughs. "Two charmers under my roof at one time."

"Well, this charmer needs to get back to his girlfriend before it gets too late. Might need to show her a thing or two." Eric winks and I tense up. Again for the millionth time wondering what she taught him that he now has to share.

"Thanks again, Kathryn." Eric begins heading to the front door with Kathryn right behind him. "We'll see you next week. Same time."

"Looking forward to it. Please give my best to Melanie, too." Kathryn gives him a brief hug. Their bodies aren't as close this time, which suits me fine.

"Nice to meet you again, Mr. Kingsley," Eric adds while he's turning the door knob. "You two have a good evening."

He gives Kathryn and I a wink before closing the door. Being a man who's learned a few things about Kathryn this evening, I choose to keep my mouth shut and wait for her to speak.

She turns toward me with her hands already on her hips. A pose I know very well and usually means trouble for me. A laugh and smile grace her lovely face. She's amused at me, and I'm sure I know why.

"So what did you really do while I was working with Eric?" Her question isn't really a question but more like a trap with claws.

Rubbing the back of my neck, I say, "Answered a ton of emails. Called my housekeeper advising her to take a few days off. We need to assess the security of my penthouse and building before I'll allow her to be there." Not lying at all. I deflect as best as I can by giving her a list of innocuous activities.

Kathryn slowly approaches me, her head tilted to the side, analyzing me. "Anything else?"

"I read a bit from the books you gave me." Trying to sound like they were the most fucking awesome things I've read in ages, I continue. "There was a great chapter on the human touch. Really made me think."

"Oh, is that right?" She moves even closer now. It's that magnetic pull between us. With each step the strange energy I always feel when I'm close to her increases. "So what did you learn about human touch?"

"Mainly that touch is essential. The book claimed it's the most powerful force on earth, but I'm not quite buying that theory yet." I'm not sure why I added that last part. Whenever I speak to her, it's like a truth serum is running through my veins. The big bullshitter in me hides away, locked in a closet, whenever I look into her eyes.

"You did read. And here I thought you were just leaning against the door listening to what I was doing with Eric." She laughs once she's finished exposing my bad deeds. "Were you listening for moans or cries of passion? I'm sure you were disappointed as neither one happened here tonight." She smirks and then adds with a quick wink. "Unlike last week."

Fucking minx.

"All right, you caught me. I admit I listened for a second. Seriously, all I could hear was some music, but I wanted to hear more. And the door moved when I tried to get closer. I figured you heard me. So I didn't stand there waiting for you to come out and ream me out."

"It's okay." She giggles. "Seriously, tonight I used my years of psychologist training with Eric more that my Tantra expertise. I just wanted to see you squirm as I nailed your nosy ass to the wall."

"Who knew you were such a sadist?" Damn, I love teasing this woman. It really turns me on. Well everything about her does, but this challenging part of her really fires me up. Makes me want to kiss her into next week.

"No one has ever accused me of being a sadist before. But I do like getting the best of you. I enjoy putting you in your place. Feels like a tiny victory for all womankind when I do."

"Too funny. But I'm really not that bad of a guy. I swear." I hope I sound convincing.

"No, I suppose you're not. But you do have some growing up to do. Maybe I just see the potential in you, Kingsley."

Well, what can I say to that one? She sees possibilities in me. I can't help but be encouraged by her words. At least she's not writing me off completely.

"Potential, huh?"

"I believe so. Do you want to hear what I really think, though? It might make you more than a little uncomfortable." I take a strand of her soft hair and gently rub it between my fingers. I can't seem to keep my hands to myself.

"Please. Hit me with it." I'm dying to know her thoughts. I realize this is one of the first times I've been uneasy hearing a woman's perception of me. Another first for me tonight.

"Okay. Here goes." She takes a deep breath and looks me dead in the eye.

"From what I've seen and heard from you tonight, I'm convinced somewhere deep down inside there's a decent man in there." She brings a finger up to me, points and lays it straight on my chest, over my heart. "He's been hidden away for years while you pursued sex, money, and all the power you could grab. During all of these chases, a public persona was created, entrapping you. But I wonder if all of these gains in your life have brought you the happiness you hoped for."

I'm blown away at her assessment. Processing her words for a moment, I pause before responding. I have no idea what the hell to say, because I have to face the facts. If I wasn't standing here in her living room right now, I'd be at another location all by myself with no one to help me through the craziness of this day. No one to care about how I'm really doing as a human being. That reality is sobering and a fucking depressing thought.

"You really don't mince your words, do you?" Whoever said "the truth hurts" was the wisest damn person alive.

"Sorry. I tried to warn you first, remember?" Her hands touch my arms as she speaks. Rubbing me assuredly. Her touch is always so comforting to me. "Listen, I don't mean to beat up on you. It's been a shitty day. What do you say we change the subject?"

"Sounds good." Between dwelling on the demons surrounding my mother, discovering Kathryn's wedding picture, and realizing I might be the biggest shmuck on the planet, I welcome a topic that doesn't leave me so raw and exposed.

"I have some chocolate ice cream. How's that for a change?" She raises a brow in question.

"Do you have some whipped cream to go with it?" I wiggle my brows in return.

"Haha." She moves down the hallway, and I follow her dutifully. It's like there is a leash attached to me keeping me by her side. I don't like being far away from her. Normally this thought would scare the shit out of me, but not tonight. Maybe it's those tight yoga pants of hers. Damn, her sweet little ass fills them out so fine.

"Two scoops or one?" she asks as we enter her kitchen.

It's the first time I've been in here since arriving at her apartment. Sub-zero refrigerator. Viking stove. Granite counters. No expense spared in its design. For New York City, it appears to be a cook's kitchen. Rare because most professional people eat out or have dinner delivered. Truthfully, I only need one large kitchen drawer. A place to store my silverware and takeout menus.

"Two scoops for me, please." I point to the pots hanging over the six-burner stove. "It looks like you actually cook."

"I love to cook. After living in Paris for more than a decade, it's impossible not to pick up the Parisian's love for cooking." She bends over retrieving the chocolate ice cream from the Sub-zero's lower freezer. Her lush ass prominently on display, waking my cock up with a slight twitch.

"I love to eat, you love to cook. Who knows, this thing between us could work out after all?" She stands up after I finish speaking. Her eyes lit in amusement.

"This thing?" She chuckles as she places the ice cream on the counter and stretches to reach the bowls on the shelf. I intercept and help her with them. My body presses up along her backside. The Shalimar perfume hits my nose, and it takes everything I have to pull away from her once I have two bowls in my hand. After depositing the bowls on the counter, I stay close by leaning my back on the counter next to her. Kathryn gets a scoop from the drawer by the freezer and opens the ice cream carton.

"Yes, this thing. I'm not sure how to define it. Care to help a guy out?" She pauses with her hand on the ice cream scoop and looks up at me, searching my seriousness. I can tell she's thinking too much and is probably over-analyzing everything I just said.

"My guess is you don't do ice cream with women much. Right?" She hits the mark as usual.

"No, not in a casual way like now. More likely the ice cream I eat is served in a silver bowl on a crisp linen tablecloth."

"So talking and hanging out with me is something new for you. I doubt you've ever been friends with a woman, either. Correct me if I'm wrong."

"No, you're right." I suddenly find it sad to think I've never even thought about having a girl or woman as a friend. Sure, they act friendly to me, or more specifically my cock. But on a human level, person-to-person, I've never had more than a fleeting acquaintance or a professional working relationship with a woman.

"Maybe we should start with friendship." Kathryn finishes filling the bowls with ice cream and returns the carton to the freezer. I watch her bend over once again and suppress a moan. But I do my best to focus on our conversation even if I'm distracted to the point where I can barely think straight.

I clear my throat. "Okay, friends. I can do that. Maybe I should pass you a note like we're back in grade school."

"Dear Kathryn, will you be my friend? Please circle yes or no."

"I'll need you to add a maybe to that one. Verdict's still out." She smiles and pushes a full bowl of ice cream toward my chest.

I take the bowl. "Oh, come on. Remember those kisses from earlier? Surely we are at least friends now." I patiently wait for her response. She takes a bite of chocolate ice cream while closing her eyes and licking her lips after swallowing. The simple act is nothing short of erotic to me.

"God, how I love ice cream," she practically moans. Opening her eyes, she looks at me dead serious. Gone is the ice cream high, which melted away quickly. "Let's just call those kisses getting friendly."

"Works for me." Silently I hope for more chances at being friendly tonight. But I'm truly enjoying just talking with Kathryn.

"I thought it might." Her smile gleams at me, full of amusement. She knows me so well already.

She exits the kitchen area and extends her index finger, beckoning me to follow her, which I do willingly. Back in the living room, she jumps on the couch and tucks her legs under her body. Since she weighs so little, her body bounces with the impact, along with those magnificent breasts. The act is almost more than this guy can take, but I swallow hard and hope things below my belt behave.

"I have a TV in the cabinet. I hardly ever watch it, but the news comes on in a few minutes. Do you want me to turn it on?"

"I'd like to see what the media's saying. When I saw the ancient TV in Maurice's office, I didn't even want to try. But if you don't mind. My PR head emailed with details about what was being spouted, along with our official response. But I want to see it for myself."

"Of course. I'd like to see it, too."

Kathryn places the now-melting ice cream on the coffee table and walks to a cabinet adjacent to the bookshelf displaying her photos. She opens two large doors in the middle of the cabinet. A large-size flat screen television appears as she slides the doors to the side. A remote control sits on the wood base in front of it.

"I only watch movies on this contraption. I abhor television." She flips on the television; the channel menu appears and she struggles to find the correct news station, or any one for that matter.

Having inhaled my ice cream, I put down my empty, bowl. "Here, let me help with that."

She hands me the remote and immediately I find my favorite news channel. "Voilà!" I say in victory.

"Men know their way around remotes. I think it's in your DNA." She huffs as she returns to the couch and her soupy ice cream.

"I tend to be good about pushing a woman's buttons." Kathryn responds by rolling her eyes.

"You're freaking hilarious." Her eyes show her mirth even when her words don't. She flops down on the couch. "So can you turn up the volume, too? Or is multitasking too hard?"

Ignoring her jab, I carry the remote back with me and purposely sit down a little closer to her this time. "Ice cream was great. Thanks."

"You woofed yours down. I'm glad you liked it. Nothing like eating some chocolate at the end of a sucky day." Her eyes soften, appearing more affectionate as they lock with mine. She likely has no idea how much her concern means to me. She holds my gaze for a beat and then turns back to the television and I do the same.

Both of us stare at the screen as the eleven o'clock news gears up. The newscast begins with the female lead anchor starting with the first report of the night.

"Good evening. In an unusual and frightening turn of events, this evening the New York Public Library's annual gala was interrupted by a lone gunman."

Chapter 12

My throat constricts and tightness grips my stomach as the lead story unfolds. I rub my hands across my trousered legs as my palms begin to perspire.

Sweating again. How many times have I encountered this new trait in the last two days? I've begun to lose count.

"It's the lead story, Kingsley." Kathryn doesn't look my way as she speaks. Her eyes are glued to the story on the television. "This is unreal."

"You're telling me?" I scoff at her comment but focus on the screen. "I wonder how far the reporters will go with this story? The police haven't released the threat Simon made on my life yet."

"Hush, I can't hear." Kathryn swats at my leg and I promptly close my mouth. A reporter in front of the historic library is covering the story.

"This evening around seven p.m., Tom Duffy, Executive Director at Kings Capital, and his wife Lois, were confronted by Simon Edwards. Edwards, a former executive partner at Kings who was recently fired, confronted the couple as they were exiting their vehicle to walk the red carpet into the New York City Library Gala, held at Bryant Park. Sources say Edwards allegedly approached the couple with a gun drawn and pointed directly at them."

One shot was fired but the bullet embedded in a nearby car and no one was injured. Edwards reportedly fled the scene by the time authorities arrived. One eyewitness said they heard Edwards shout threats at his former partner, Tom Duffy. What those exact threats were isn't being disclosed by the NYPD at this time. However, there is speculation that Edwards' forced departure from Kings may have fueled tonight's attempted assault.

Police cordoned off the area and shut down the BDFM subway line for more than two hours. The search for Edwards remains active.

An NYPD spokesman had this to say about the investigation."

My mind races in disbelief as I try to comprehend what I'm hearing. Simon wanted me dead. He could've killed Tom and Lois. Or Tom and then left Lois to raise their unborn child by herself. The child would've been just like me, fatherless. The thought sickens me.

The camera cuts away to an interview with the police spokesman. I put aside the thoughts of what could have happened, for now.

"The investigation continues as we try to locate Simon Edwards. We have reason to believe he may have left the New York City area. Currently, the remarks he made during his assault have led us to conclude that his target tonight was specific, not general in nature."

The police spokesman's clip is brief and still leaves many questions unanswered. The reporter reappears on the screen and finishes her report by summarizing the events.

A photo of Simon flashes on the screen. It's Kings Capitals' official publicity photograph of him. The man I have known since I was nineteen is someone I never really knew at all. How did I not recognize his obviously murderous hatred of me? Surely there were signs before his betrayal, but nothing comes to mind. The reporter continues in her description of Simon.

"Simon Edwards is a thirty-two-year-old Caucasian male, six feet tall with dark brown hair. If you see Edwards, police ask that you call 9-1-1 immediately. Do not approach this individual on your own."

The evening's annual library gala was delayed more than an hour as police combed the building, but the show did go on as planned. The gala hosts for the evening, Ron and Nancy Smyth, reported a record-setting night of donations, indicating the incident outside didn't deter those gathering to support the New York Public Library. Susan Masters reporting live at Bryant Park for Channel 4 news. Back to you, Melissa."

"Thank you, Susan. In other news…"

The anchor's voice fades away as I reach for the remote and push the off button. I've heard and seen enough about this whole clusterfuck to last a lifetime, but the words of the reporter and the photo of Simon's face replay in my mind.

I rest my forehead in the palm of my hands, with my elbows digging into my thighs, supporting me as I collapse, mentally drained. Whatever mask I normally wear in these situations is nowhere to be found. My controlled life is falling away. These vulnerable feelings can't be disguised anymore.

Why did Simon snap? Why does he want to kill me? He wasn't one to show any emotion, ever. Love or hate were not passions in his vocabulary; he was a man of indifference. Nothing seemed to penetrate his cold disposition. What has occurred tonight is a display of shear hate directed toward me alone.

"I'm so sorry, Kingsley." Kathryn's words soothe me. She places her hands on my slumped back and begins to gently rub circles. Her fingers lightly skate over the fabric of my shirt, marking a needed trail of comfort against my skin.

"Do you want to talk about it?" she asks me, her voice barely above a whisper.

Raising my head off my hands, I bend my neck slightly and look into her familiar blue eyes. A man could lose his mind staring into them. I've never needed or wanted a friend more than I do right now. And I couldn't ask for a better or more beautiful one than Kathryn.

I take a deep breath before I answer her. "What would've caused Simon to react so violently toward me? He was already planning on leaving the company to join the one he was giving secrets to. So when the reporter says his recent firing was the cause of tonight's assault, well, it doesn't make any sense to me."

"Something definitely triggered his behavior. I've seen people respond violently in my practice before, although not this dramatically. Occasionally, individuals who snap from reality can become desperate and lash out at people. You may be the person he blames for his misery, even if you had nothing to do with his situation."

"I hope you're right." I run my fingers through my hair and shake my head in an attempt to free the weight of our discussion from my mind. Turning my attention back toward Kathryn, I smile warmly at her, hoping she'll let me change the subject.

"I'd rather not discuss Simon and his craziness anymore. It seems pointless to keep rehashing it until we know more about his motives. However, there is something I would like to talk about. Something I've been wondering all night." I lie back against the couch's cushions. They welcome me, and my upper body relaxes into them, looking for a modicum of rest from the tension. Kathryn appraises me curiously.

"There's something different about you, Kathryn, in a good way. You're confident, serene, and seem to have a strong, unflappable inner peace. I'm curious to know if it's a result of you practicing Tantra?" I prepare myself for her response, as I have no idea how she'll answer my query. She gazes at me with a sweet smile. She appears to be happy with the question. Hopefully she'll accommodate me with an answer, because I'm dying to know.

"Are you curious because it involves sex? Or are you wondering why I chose to practice it?" Her question makes me contemplate my motive. What is the reason behind my curiosity?

"I'll be honest with you. I am interested in the sex angle, and why you practice it and the effects it has on you."

"Fair enough." She looks at me with a keen understanding and shifts closer to me. "I think most people wonder the same thing when I tell them about my association with Tantra."

She glances down at the couch, as if she's collecting her thoughts before continuing with her explanation.

"A few years ago I was in a dark place personally. I mentioned my late husband last night at the bar when you asked if I was French. Remember?"

She pauses and looks at me to answer her.

"Of course, I remember. You surprised me with that answer. It was definitely unexpected." Part of me wants to tell her I'm sorry for her loss, sympathetically acknowledge his death. But I remain silent because she appears ready to resume talking.

"Before I continue, how much do you know about Jean-Paul? You seem to know almost everything about me, and I don't want to bore you with details you're already aware of."

Without thinking, I glance over to the bookcase where Kathryn and Jean-Paul's wedding picture sits along with the encased silver medal. I turn back to her, and I can see that her eyes have followed mine. She realizes I looked at her memorial to him when she left me alone earlier.

"Okay." I start my confession on the extent of my knowledge concerning her late husband. "I know he was an Olympic skier who died a few years ago in a skiing accident. I have to admit I looked through your pictures and saw your wedding photo. You two seemed very happy." Her eyes gaze beyond me like she's leaving the here and now in a dreamy way. I know she's reminiscing about him and what they had together. I watch a slow smile form on her lips at she remembers him.

"We were very happy." She turns back to me now. The smile still lingering on her lips. "I was gutted when he died. I sank into a deep depression. Even getting up to go to work was too much most days. His death was traumatic for me on so many levels. It left me shaken and all alone. From the day he and I met, we were inseparable. He was my life. We were each other's worlds."

I want to envy him, hate him even, but I can't. The feeling doesn't come to me. Instead I feel sad that she lost someone so dear to her. After my mother's death, I know losing someone you love deeply is nothing I'd wish upon anyone. I reach for her hand as her eyes fill with tears. When our fingers connect, I realize how much I missed feeling her soft skin against mine.

"He died skiing in the French Alps. An Olympic skier gliding down a semi-steep hill should've been nothing out of the ordinary, but he must have hit an unseen mogul. He lost control and veered off course and headed straight into a thick patch of trees. I was watching his movements from above as I skied down toward him."

She closes her eyes; a few tears fall down her pale cheeks. I move on instinct and wipe them from her face. Their presence is too much for me to stomach. She opens her eyes again and forces a smile through her tears. I want to pull her into my arms and soothe away the pain, but I hold off and wait, choosing to comfort her with words.

"I'm so sorry, Kathryn. I can't think of anything more horrible than being witness to the accident." I think back to my nightmares, the ones that still haunt me, and wonder if she has anything similar to them. Imagining the pain Kathryn went through watching her husband die right in front of her eyes; it's horrific.

"Thanks, Kingsley. I'm sorry to drag you back to that dark place with me. But that's when I discovered Tantra, or when it saved me. It brought light back into my life." Her tears are dry now, but I'm still holding her hand, not wanting to let go.

We've moved even closer to one another. Our bodies turned toward each other on the couch with our legs now touching at the knees. We've once again succumbed to the magnetic pull between us, an unseen energy we can't seem to control.

She takes a few deep breaths, trying to regain her composure. Her eyelashes still wet from her tears, but her face doesn't show a trace of the sadness she expressed a short moment ago.

"So Tantra helped you get beyond his death?" I ask, encouraging her to continue.

"It did. The man you met today at the café, Jacques LeBaron, was a fellow psychologist with me in Paris. We've known each other since our doctorate studies and remained friends after graduation. Jacques worried that I was withdrawing from life after Jean-Paul's death, and he feared I wasn't coping with my loss. I knew he was right, but I had no idea how to feel again. I was very numb at that point. Going through the essential motions of existing. Jacques had practiced Tantra for several years and persuaded me to come to a meeting with him. I agreed to go, but just as friends."

My jaw tenses at the mention of Frenchie's name. Jean-Paul is a ghost from her past, but this other man is here in her present. And I don't care for him being in her life now, sticking his nose in her business like he did earlier when I was with her. I don't like it, or him, one fucking bit. Over the course of twenty-four hours, I've turned into a green-eyed monster. It's a foreign feeling to me.

"So is this when you began seeing him? After your husband's death?" My brows pull together; I can't conceal my feelings for Jacque.

"Jacques and I have never been together in the true sense of the word. This may be hard for you to hear, but he and I have practiced Tantra together for the past two years. Jacques is very special to me, but I will never love him beyond being my dear friend. Our relationship lacks chemistry, that spark needed for love and a basic attraction. It's missing, and we both acknowledge it. We respect and care for each other, but without that deep chemistry we'll never be more than occasional lovers."

Part of me wants to punch the couch pillows beside me. The other part wants to shout for joy that she doesn't feel anything more for him than she does.

"I can tell you're having a hard time with me mentioning Jacques' name. But enough with the double standard, Kingsley. I'm looking past your countless one-night stands right now." She crosses her arms over her chest, standing her ground.

"Touché," I agree with her assessment and throw my hands up in surrender. "Please, go on."

She brings her arms back down to her lap and leans toward me. The same stance she had before I went all caveman.

"Let me tell you what happened to me emotionally and spiritually when I started practicing Tantra. I'll leave out the physical part with him. It seems to make you uncomfortable."

"You picked up on that, did you? Perceptive woman." My sarcastic laugh follows, lightening the mood between us. "I'd appreciate it. Besides, we have some wild chemistry, don't you think?"

"You're winning me over in that department, Mr. Kingsley." Her eyes dip to my lips, and for a moment I think she's inviting me to kiss her. But her eyes rise again to mine and her plump, tempting lips move instead. "There is definitely something going on between us. My conclusion on what it is exactly is still pending."

"All right. The lady finally confesses." I pump my fist a few inches in the air like I just scored a touchdown.

Her eyes fill with laughter as she giggles. "Back to Tantra, you distracting man." God, I love to hear her giggling. It's music to my ears.

"Please continue. Seriously, I want to know how you became the emotionally strong woman you are today."

"Charmer has to be your middle name." She teases while reaching for my hand and squeezing it lightly. "Back to my story. During my first meeting, I was so much like you. Curious but unsure what Tantra was about. Also my mood was foul that day. I had grueling counseling sessions with clients and just wanted to go home and sleep. The thought of hanging out with a bunch of people talking about feelings, sex, and love was the last thing I wanted to do, but I went anyway. More like I dragged myself there."

She continued. "I endured the meeting and stuck it out. I'm so thankful that I did, too. At the end of the session they had us participate in a simple exercise. Nothing too sexual, more about opening yourself up to someone. Connecting on a basic human level."

"So no sex lessons the first time?" I ask her, surprised. I was expecting something more down and dirty like the picture I viewed in the book with the couple dry-humping each other.

"Nothing like that at all. I sat across from, well, you know who." She speaks the words out of the side of her mouth cutely, trying to skip over Frenchie's name, and I'm glad.

"Yes, he who shall not be named."

"Yes, him. Anyway, the simple exercises the instructor had us do made me reconnect with my feelings. I'd totally shut them off. I thought it would be better to feel nothing than the pain of my loss. So I locked the door to them and became numb. Tantra was the key that opened the door up for me. All the emotions I'd stuffed away came tumbling out." Her eyes have a sincere look, and she takes both my hands in hers. "It all started with opening myself up and feeling again."

"I'm not sure I understand what you're talking about." Confusion has to be plastered all over my face. "Care to show me?"

"What? Now?" Her eyes are wide in surprise. My request obviously isn't what she expected.

"This will not come as a shock, but I'm more of a hands-on learner." I wiggle my brows suggestively. "Possibly the engineer in me, who knows? Whatta ya say?" Kathryn bites her lip as she decides on an answer. But I can't wait and I push her to respond. "Come on, say yes. Please?"

"On one condition. No laughing. Tantra means a lot to me. The thought of you not taking it seriously bothers me. You laugh and my teaching stops. Capisce?" There is no arguing with her menacing threat. She loves to end with a punch that puts me in my place.

"You love the word, capisce, don't you?" I pause for a second and watch her beautiful face. "But I'll be your willing student. I'll only laugh if you tickle me."

"You're ticklish?" She smiles devilishly at me. Her hands wander up my sides, and her fingers start tapping eagerly against my ribs. She huffs when I don't respond with even a slight chuckle.

"Nah, I'm not ticklish. Well at least not there." She punches my arm lightly. But if she glanced down at my crotch, she would have seen how much her touch did affect me.

"You're just hilarious." She stares at me pointedly. "This type of humor is what I'm talking about, though. If I introduce you to Tantra, you have to be serious. I mean it."

"Settle down," I say. "I sincerely promise. If it's that important to you, I'll be good. Maybe just an occasional smile or two. Surely that would be all right?"

"Of course you can smile. But that's where I draw the line." She lifts herself off the couch. Her sweet ass right at my eye level. No lines appear on the curve of her yoga pants, so my mind immediately wonders if she's wearing anything under them.

She bends over and takes our ice cream bowls. "Let me rinse these bowls out and I can give you a simple intro session explaining Tantra. Unless you're too tired?"

"Not at all. I'm wide awake. See?" I blink my eyes rapidly, trying to show I'm alert and ready. I'm rewarded with a sexy toss of her lovely hair over her shoulder.

Damn, how I want this woman.

"Why don't you go ahead of me?" Kathryn begins to walk toward the kitchen. "Change into the pajamas I mentioned earlier in the guest room. My brother's pair. You need to get out of your stiff monkey suit."

"When a woman tells me to take off my clothes, I always obey." My remarks get a half-hearted laugh.

Before disappearing into the kitchen, she looks at me over her shoulder. "When has a woman ever had to ask you to take off your clothes?"

"Touché," I say mostly to myself as I once again concede her point, silently wondering how much I've missed in life by acting the way I have with women. Having this kind of teasing banter with a woman makes me want more of it, and with this woman in particular. I never knew what I was missing until now. It is becoming clear to me how much I want to impress Kathryn, and show her that I am worthy of exploring what we might have beyond the palpable lust, something I never bothered with before tonight.

Gathering up my suit coat, I quickly make my way back to the guest room in search of some borrowed pajamas. After shutting the door I disrobe, removing my suit pants and wrinkled dress shirt. I lay them over the edge of the bed.

The bed I would prefer to only have my clothes lying on tonight. I can't help but hope Kathryn will give into me in some way and quit trying to fight this pull between us.

Our being together seems as inevitable as the sun rising and setting. She wants me, although she still hasn't completely admitted to it yet. I more than want her. I've made this fact abundantly clear.

The inability to gratify the desires I have for her drives me crazy, too. When has my cock not gotten its way? I have to reach back pretty far to recall a time.

High school was the last memory I have of denying myself, but even then I usually had some girl at my beck and call. Until Kathryn, I've never used the words "waiting" and "sex" in the same sentence, nor have they been put together as a thought in my head.

All it's taken is a beautiful, alluring, and feisty woman with a mind and body fit to be worshipped to completely unhinge me.

Walking over to the dresser, I open a drawer and find a pair of black pajama pants and a T-shirt. I glance at the tag and see Kathryn was correct in guessing my size matched her brother's. Maybe I should say they didn't fit and wander into that harem tent of hers in just my boxer briefs. Fuck, I might do it anyway.

Only issue with wearing just my briefs is that my dick has been at half mast almost the entire time I've been in her presence tonight. I wouldn't be leaving much to the imagination.

The barely-there clothing she's wearing is to blame. Her sports bra dipped seductively low on her chest and exposed the full mounds of her breasts. So round, real, and perfect. She has more than a handful, and I hope to find out how much more soon.

My cock comes alive at the thought of her breasts in my hands and her nipples against my tongue. If I'd walk into her office right now, even covered in these pants, she'll see how tightly wound up I am for her. But she wants me to be serious, so I remind myself to be good.

After dressing in the pajamas, I glance at my reflection in the mirror over the dresser. I'm in all black from head to toe, but when I look closer at my face, I see something strange in my eyes. There's anxiousness in them, something unfamiliar to me.

Sighing, I chalk it up to the entire day I've endured.

One thing is for damn sure: I need to get back to the real me. The man who makes grown men tremble at the boardroom table. Who cowers to no one, not even a vixen he's desperate to fuck.

Standing tall with my head held high, I walk out of the guest room with a renewed purpose and decide to quit acquiescing to Kathryn and all her wishes. It's time for her to give me what I want, which adds up to more than a couple of kisses for the night.

But I scoff at my own thoughts. If I'm being honest with myself, my ability to live up to this declaration is highly unlikely. Not where Kathryn's concerned.

Once I'm out in the hallway, I notice the door to her office is slightly ajar. My bare feet are quiet as I walk over on the dark wood floor. Stopping in front of the door, I lean forward and listen for any sounds coming from inside. Erotic music plays softly and the room appears dark from what little I'm able to see through the cracked door.

Not wanting to enter without Kathryn's acknowledgement, I tap my fingers on the wood.

"Come in, Kingsley." Her voice is breathy and low, almost unrecognizable.

I place my hand on the door but restrain myself and slowly push it open just a couple of inches. There are candles burning faintly on small accent tables, but I can't see where Kathryn is yet. Golden lanterns hang in various lengths from the silk-draped ceiling. A subdued glow filters through patterns punched into the lanterns' metal.

I push the door open the remaining way and gasp. Kathryn comes into my view. She's kneeling on the large cushion in the middle of the room. Breathtakingly beautiful.

Her pose is one of pure submission. Kneeling as she faces me with her sweet ass resting on the heels of her feet. Her delicate hands, the ones I want touching me, are placed flat above her knees as her body leans forward.

I'm still absorbing the scene in front of me. Kathryn is waiting for me while the flickering light casts shadows across her skin and hair.

"Come join me, Kingsley." Kathryn curls her lips into a sexy smile, and with a gesturing motion of her hand she invites me to join her. At this moment, I'm powerless and will do whatever this beautiful woman kneeling before me wants.

The magnetic pull I've felt since I met her last night draws me to her. I'm powerless against its force. Walking across the rug-covered floor, I arrive at the pillow she's gracefully kneeling on. Without another thought, I bend my knees and reflect her pose. Willingly, I submit.

Chapter 13

"Are you ready?" Kathryn asks me with a quizzical lift of her brow. The fact I'm here kneeling quietly and waiting for her to start should be a good enough sign for her.

"Ready as I'll ever be." I look deeply into her eyes as shadows play across her face. With silk tapestries and flickering light surrounding her, she takes on an ethereal presence as if she belongs in another world. My hands itch to reach and touch her soft skin. Yes, Kathryn, I want to say, I'm ready and willing, totally spellbound by you and your beauty. But I hold my tongue.

"I'm going to start at the basic level with you tonight. I like to call it a curious beginner's session." Her voice is low, and I have to concentrate to make out the words as they float together in a whisper. "Any time you have a question, please let me know. It's how you'll learn."

I only nod, not saying a word.

"Tantric sex is an art that is taught and learned. But there isn't one set teaching method universally practiced by everyone. The variations of Tantra remind me of the world's major religions. One main belief for each one, but countless ways of observing it."

Some Tantra practitioners prefer a completely fundamental approach, balking at those who try to introduce modern concepts. Others are more liberal, like me, and bring the contemporary world into their teaching and mix the two together. Are you following me?"

I nod my head again. My life experience is limited as far as religion is concerned, but the concept she's speaking about makes sense.

"I believe most people need a balance between the ancient and contemporary to practice Tantra in their everyday lives. I bring my training as a psychologist into the mix, too. Tantra focuses on touch and connection with your partner, something missing in our world and its daily hustle. It requires people to slow down by stepping out of the rat race and reconnecting with their lover."

"Giving your time and openness to your partner is the only requirement needed to experience Tantra. There are no sexual aids or equipment. The human body contains everything needed for tantric sex. Hands for touching." Her eyes travel to my hands placed on my legs, mirroring hers. "Arms for embracing, lips for kissing, tongues for tasting, and eyes for seeing into each other's souls."

She stops and gauges my reaction to her words. Just sitting in front of this beauty with her talk of tongues tasting and lips kissing has me hard and wanting to fuck her like never before. Kathryn's gaze lowers toward the junction of my thighs and sees my definite interest in what she's saying about Tantra. She remains silent, waiting for me to make the next move, so I break the silence.

"I like the tools of your trade. Tongues, especially."

"Your juvenile response is what I feared. Try to act like a grown-up, please?" She shakes her head in disapproval. Her words are meant as a chastisement to my smart mouth.

"You're right. My apologies, Kathryn." Dammit, why did I spout off like that? I'm so used to using trite words with no effort to win over any woman I want, and I guess my brain hasn't digested the fact that Kathryn isn't just any woman. I bow my head once to her as I try to make amends. "I am extremely interested and want you to continue. Please?"

"Thanks, Kingsley." Any annoyance in her eyes thankfully disappears. "What I want to focus on with you tonight is the human touch." She reaches out her hands and encloses them around mine. She lifts them up only a couple of inches above our knees.

"Tongues are good, but hands are even better. They're the essential instrument for what I'm going to teach you tonight." My cock twitches with those words.

She slowly caresses her thumb over the top of my hands and lowers them back down to my legs. Then her fingers begin to lightly move up my arms. Slowly and carefully she makes her way up my forearms. The feeling of her touch leaves the hair on my arms standing up straight like I've been electrocuted. My eyes close in reaction as I try to absorb the sensations I'm experiencing.

"Look into my eyes." Her voice is commanding and not her usual tone, but I obey nonetheless and open my eyes. I find her staring back at me intensely. Without any of the gentleness from a moment ago.

"Sacred Indian texts teach us that human energy is controlled by nine areas called chakras that run a vertical line straight down our bodies." One of her hands travels down my body from my neck to my lower abdomen, but she stops her downward progression before making contact with my dick, which is feeling very neglected at the moment. There's only so much I can take with her fingers all over me like this. Her hand returns back to my arm, and she continues caressing me like before. I hope my cock survives all the sensory overload.

"The goal in Tantra is to unite different areas into one as we, I mean, couples make love. The aim is to open our minds and spiritual side while having sex, combining the two. The key word is open. Freeing oneself."

As much as I'd like to understand what she's saying to me, I'm not sure what she really means by opening myself up. It's a completely foreign concept to me. My life is orderly and controlled. I only share necessary interactions and exchanges with those around me. The sharing of feelings isn't what I do. The thought we're about to go down that road right now makes me want to stop the session. But I make myself stay here with her, totally unable to leave this woman. I'm rooted to this spot by the sheer weight of her seductive presence, her willing pupil in anything she wishes to teach me. I'm hers for the taking.

"Tonight we are focusing on this part of your body." Her hands quit massaging along my arms and she places them over my chest. Lightly pressing into me. Her featherlike touch is so faint I can barely feel its weight against my skin. "This area over your heart is an important energy spot according to Tantric teachings. If it is blocked and closed, then your entire body's energy can't flow. Your heart is the core of your being. So we will start there."

"Our session is not about achieving but about receiving. For someone who constantly strives for results in their life, this concept may seem foreign to you, Kingsley. So try not to think about holding on to your feelings. As I touch you, focus on how it feels and relaxes you. Receive those feelings. Don't try to fight them."

I do as she bids me, but I'm so tempted to close my eyes and get lost in her touch. Or possibly hide myself from it. I'm not sure which. However, I force myself to keep my eyes open.

"I'm going to guide you through a mental exercise while I continue running my hands over your skin. My touch will be light, but purposeful. You need to stare into my eyes the entire time. Do not break our connection by turning away from me or closing them."

Where is she leading me with this so-called mental exercise? It should concern me. But if it means she continues to touch me like she's doing, I will try to comply and go along for the ride with her.

"I'll focus." She has to know I completely trust her at this moment, which for me isn't a normal occurrence. I'm giving her free rein without any control or stipulations.

"Think of the last time in your life you felt loved by someone. By the word felt I want you to think of their touch, too. Perhaps when you were younger. A comforting touch from long ago. Remember how you received that love and their touch. What it felt like, how you responded to their love."

Her command is not one I want to process inside my brain or my heart; I'd rather concentrate on her touch alone. Going back in my past to when I felt a loving touch is dangerous. It will expose a dark place I've locked away. My body stiffens even as her touch tries to coax me into obeying her instructions, but what she's wishing me to do, right now, may simply be too much. I don't know if I can do it.

"You're resisting what I've asked. I can feel it. There has to be a moment in your life where you felt this kind of connection, but now you're not willing to reach back and bring the memory to life. Why?"

"You're asking me to do something, think of things, I've refused to dwell on for years." Our eyes are locked on each other with an intensity I never knew possible. But I believe she understands my confession and knows how difficult this is for me.

"You do remember a certain time you felt that comforting touch, don't you? You're fighting it, I can see. Your entire body tensed up as I was touching you. Even the muscles on your face are strained and tight." She stops and stares deep into my eyes. Her gaze penetrates me, reaching deep inside as if she's trying to draw my secrets out. Those I'm not willing to share.

"Do you want to know what I see in your eyes right now?" I don't respond to her question. I'm sure she's going to let me know her assessment regardless of my reply. "A scared man. Scarred, too. You may have conquered Wall Street, but you've not conquered your own demons. They lie repressed inside of you. Releasing them will heal you. It's like a cancer eating away inside of you. Keeping you from experiencing life to its fullest. Believe me, you can do this, Kingsley. Let them go."

"How?" I know she's right. I can't even form an argument to deny what she's said. And honestly, the fight within me to hide myself from her requires more energy than I have tonight. The day has left me raw with my defenses down. I'm afraid I'm about to crumble at her feet and reveal more to her than I have even to myself. Would she want me if she knew I was broken, unable to open up?

"Can you think of one time where a touch was so powerful you can almost feel it again just by reliving the memory?" She's back to rubbing my hands. She has no idea she's encouraging me to go back to the one person who has loved me the most, my mother. I never mention her name aloud to anyone. Even after her death, my friends stayed clear of the subject. It's a gamble for me, and I have no idea what the consequences will be if I talk about her, think about her, and remember her.

"There is one person who loved me like you're talking about. But the memories I have with her are something I prefer not to think about." I try to draw a line but it's vague at best. Kathryn will try to erase it and have me cross over it. I can feel her pulling at me now. Leading me toward some cliff where I'll likely free fall.

"You have a simple choice right now. Go back to those memories, open the door to them or we can stop right where we are. There's no reason to continue, and I can't make you think about this person or the memories. The choice is yours."

The choice to bury my mother's memory is how I've gotten through the last ten years knowing I was the reason she took her own life. No matter how warped her reasoning was, she believed her suicide was the best thing for me, that it would free me. How fucking wrong she was.

"I don't want to end what we have going on here, but I don't know if I can go back to those memories. I've embargoed them for years."

"Because they're too painful?"

"What other reason would there be?" As cruel as I sound, I don't care if she's offended by my tone.

"Fair enough." Her words are conciliatory. "We can quit if you'd like? It's getting late anyway."

"I shouldn't have bitten off your head. Please, I'll try." I speak quickly before I really think about the ramifications of what I've said. Can I really do this?

"If you are sure?" I nod and express the same response with my eyes. There's no turning back now. The cliff I've imagined is in front of me, and I may be taking her down with me. "If it's all right with you, I think it's best if you remove your shirt so I can have direct contact with your skin."

I gladly comply with her request and pull the T-shirt over my head in a flash. I'm sitting half-naked in front of her now, but I've never felt so bare or exposed in my whole life. Never have I given my nakedness a thought around a woman, but with her, right now in this moment, I am totally vulnerable. My skin a flimsy covering to the mess inside, as my warring emotions are trying to break free.

"I'm going to move closer to you." Kathryn scoots my way on the cushiony mat. Her nearness feels good to me. If I'm going to do this, I want her as close as she's willing to be.

"Normally, in my private teaching session, everyone keeps their clothes on. What you're doing is out of the ordinary for me. And I'd like to take it one step further if possible. Although knowing you, I'm sure you'll have no issue with it." A cute smirk marks her face. "What I'd like to have you do is cross your legs in front of yourself."

My mind drifts back to the Tantra book I browsed through and the image of the couple with the woman straddling the man. My cock gets hard just thinking she may intend for us to be in a similar position. But I may be too distracted, having her so close and wrapped around me, to continue with this mental exercise she's trying to teach me. Will I be able to control myself and keep my hands away from her? Looking at the tent in my pants, I know my cock is going to be a problem, too.

I swing my legs out in front of me, trying not to knock into her as I do. I lean back on the mat with my hands behind me for support as I cross my legs in front of me. Now I'm in position, just liked she requested, sitting with my back straight.

"Now, I'm going to sit on your lap and with my legs going around your sides. I never do this when I'm teaching Tantra, only when I'm practicing it with someone. But I think we need this intimacy for you to open up to me, and for you to finally go back to that place in your past. Normally, I would press myself against your, um, your penis." She looks down where my penis is located and her brows rise. My arousal can't be missed. I'm big by most standards in this department from what I've been told, so my erection is definitely on her radar now.

"As you can see, I'd be fine with that." She's likely not going to appreciate my sex-laced comment. But hell, I'm a man with one damn painful hard-on for this woman, and the thought of her pussy coming into contact with me sounds damn fine.

"I can see that," she says looking down at my crotch with a knowing smile. "But please try to rein yourself in as much as possible. Our time is about receiving not about achieving, and you're used to achieving when you're in this kind of state, that's for sure."

Kathryn climbs onto my lap, her pussy comes dangerously close to my aching cock, but to my disappointment doesn't directly touch me. It appears there will be no bump and grind for now. But I swear I can feel the heat of her sex now that she's opened to me. I can't help but wonder if she's wet, and turned on like I am. Never have I been this close to a woman with her legs spread without removing her clothes and thrusting balls deep into her. Control might be more than I can handle, as my body wants to react on memory due to the countless times I've been in this position before.

"I'll try to calm myself down, but I don't think there is much hope with you sitting this close and practically dry-humping me. Truthfully, I want to rip your damn clothes off. So yes, I'm having a hard time right now, pun intended."

"I don't mean to make this difficult for you, and I appreciate you being honest with me as well. We need honesty for this session to work, so please tell me how you're feeling even if you don't think I want to hear it. I'll try not to torture you, and remember it's best not to focus on sex, instead focus on trying to open up a memory locked inside you. I'm going to teach you a Tantric breathing technique that will help you concentrate on something else besides sex. Hopefully it will help."

"I sure as hell hope it does, too." My remarks are a sarcastic plea.

She places her hands on my bare shoulders and spreads her fingers out over my skin, making small circles. I react with a little shiver, although I'm sure it didn't escape her trained eye.

Kathryn has to know what she's doing to me. It's crazy. A few simple touches on my skin and I feel like it's the most intimate contact I've ever experienced with a woman in my life. I wonder if it's not so much the contact that makes it different, but whose hands are driving me wild. Either way, I pray she continues.

"Follow my lead here. I want you to breathe the opposite of my breaths. When I inhale you exhale. Let's try it, and remember complete eye contact, at all times."

Kathryn breathes in deeply, then exhales slowly with a full blow. She bobs her head for me to follow. I breathe in and out to mirror hers, while our eyes remain focused on each other. The only movement is a slight rise from our chests as we breathe, and her hands as they continue to touch me.

Our transposed breathing is sensuous; it feels like a sexual rhythm of in and out. A push and pull. The technique's erotic feeling further stimulates me, which is the exact opposite of what Kathryn hoped for. But it's arousing in a different way. Sure, I want to pound into her right now, but there is also an unusual feeling over my whole body. A relaxing sensation, one I've never experience before having sex or in any other situation for that matter.

"You're doing well. Keep it up." Her hands continue to rub over my chest. Splayed out and lightly massaging me.

"I'm feeling strange, good, but strange." She smiles knowingly back at me, and to my surprise kisses my cheek.

"That's good. It means you're finally starting to relax and let go. When you become more relaxed you will be sensitive to the erotic side of our intimacy." Her lips tickle my ears as she speaks, and her full breasts press against my bare skin. It's almost too much for me to take at this point. "Now try to focus on the breathing. It will be just enough to distract you. At least I hope."

"I'll try, but having your beautiful breasts in my face is killing me." She pushes back, and her perfect tits are no longer touching me. Why did I have to open my big mouth? I want to tell her they were fine pressing against me and please bring them back, but I keep my thoughts to myself.

"Back to our breathing, okay? And quiet. Listen to the music playing. Do you feel the beat?"

"Yes," I say. I almost don't recognize my voice; it's weak but so relaxed as her hands continue their sweet torment against my skin.

"Breathe and exhale on the beats. Get in sync with the music. Let your senses become involved, come alive."

A little too much of me has come alive right now, and there doesn't seem to be a thing I can do about it. I'm powerless with her this close to me, rubbing her hands all over me. And, holy fuck, I can feel her hips starting to move on my legs. They're circling to the beat of the music. I want to press up into her, relieve my ache. It would just take one swift move of my hips for my cock to get some relief and touch her.

I hold back but it becomes worse. Focusing on the breathing and following her lead will hopefully help, but it's likely impossible at this point.

Minutes seem to float by as we continue breathing. Kathryn keeps massaging me. Our gazes stay intensely fixed, neither one of us looking away. All of these sensations combine together and make me feel something I can't quite name. I've never meditated before, but my centered concentration makes me wonder if this is what it feels like. All my energy seems gathered and focused as if the world around us has faded away.

Maybe that's the point, bringing all my conscious thoughts to a place where I'm in a trance-like state. A lover's high only reached by Kathryn's hands sliding over me, her hips undulating with the music as she straddles my legs, and her eyes leaving me weakened and defenseless to stop what I'm feeling.

"Kingsley," she whispers. "The touch from earlier. Think about it now."

Her voice draws me out of my altered state of mind. I know she's asking me to think back to the touch from a woman whose memory haunts me, but I feel completely powerless to resist Kathryn's demand. She's mesmerized me with some kind of Tantric magic. I'm bewitched without an ounce of fight left within me. She knows my dilemma, my hesitancy to surrender and loosen the grip I have on my past, and she's won.

My resistance vanishes as a memory starts to surface. A time when I was sick as a child. It's bubbling up inside of me. Deep within my gut, I feel my muscles constrict. The tightening makes me hold my breath as I struggle with the discomfort. I fight to keep my eyes focused on Kathryn, but my eyelids are starting to flutter.

Just when I'm unsure if I can continue with whatever the fuck I'm experiencing, Kathryn rescues me. She grips my jaw, holding my head in place.

"Let go, Kingsley," she whispers to me, calling the memory out. I obey and release the first knot in my stomach. The ache spirals to my chest, tightening and intensifying. I feel as if a weight has been dropped on me. The feelings I'm experiencing are so intense, no matter how hard I try, my eyes won't stay open. When I give in and close them, the memories come flooding back.

My mother sat next to me on my small twin bed. I was about ten and very sick, a rare occurrence for me. My beloved Batman sheets were tucked snuggly around me. She took my hand and told me I was going to be all right. I felt her fingers run through my hair, gently caressing my scalp. Calming me, loving me. I was weak from fever but her touch gave me strength. The smell of her perfume drifted all around me. She smiled warmly down at me, her beautiful face reflecting a mother's love.

Then she began singing to me, a song from my childhood. Her voice was angelic as she sang the familiar words I remembered so well.

My mother's melodic voice turns into a sound of pain, a beseeching cry from deep down inside her soul. The gut-wrenching sound, more like a howl, jolts me from wherever my mind has traveled to, and it's then I realize the sound I heard was my own.

Chapter 14

My eyes fly open in disbelief, my screaming fading away as my senses return. It was the desperate cry I wanted to voice at my mother's grave, but it remained buried until now.

Kathryn is still in front of me, her eyes swimming with tears. They're streaming down her beautiful face, but her expression doesn't contain any sadness; a genuine happiness radiates from her instead. Her encouraging smile intersects with tears as they trail down her face. It's then I realize the tears she's shedding are for me.

"Oh, Kingsley. You sweet, sweet man." Her words are so tender and loving.

Her arms encircle me as her soft body folds and melts into mine. The legs, once loosely lying by my side, now hug me tightly around my hips; her heels dig almost painfully into my backside. But I welcome the feeling because it affirms her feelings for me.

Desperate to hold her, I greedily wrap my arms around her waist. Nothing stops me now, including her. My hands meet as they encompass her tiny frame, one drifting lower as I grasp the sweet ass I've dreamed of holding. I move the other hand higher and cup it behind her neck. I entwine and weave my fingers through her soft hair. Drawing her tightly to me, her body feels so fragile and delicate next to my hard chest.

We cling to each other while she continues to soothingly caress my skin, nothing is holding her back now. Murmurs escape from her sweet lips as they move gently across my throat, kissing a path to my ear. She speaks so quietly, I can't fully hear what she's saying, but I know the meaning regardless. She wants me, finally.

I bring my head down to hers and bury myself in her hair. Her smell. Her scent. Like an aphrodisiac, overloading my senses, making me feel high, almost drugged when I inhale. I can't seem to get enough of her so I push myself deeper into her raven-colored silk, needing more, feeling as though I'll never get enough.

"You were wonderful." Her voice floats around me in a haze of sensations. "And I don't what this to stop."

I want to tell her the same thing, but I'm unable to speak. My voice is lost because I'm still too overcome from what I just experienced with her. Kathryn runs her hands all over me. Pulling them through my hair. Fingernails grazing my back. She moves her lips across my jaw, down my neck, and stops at my chest. The very place I felt something inside me break loose as I cried out. The cry lifted the weight of suppressing ten years of guilt. How this could even be possible is beyond me, but it's truly gone.

I have no time to process the difference I feel as her lips find mine. Passionately we connect, our tongues tangling. Our kiss is so different than the others we shared tonight. It's free and uninhibited. No guessing if I'm doing the right thing, or if she'll allow me to ravish her, because she's in the lead. Where she's taking me, I don't know, but I'll gladly follow.

Now, I have her body in my hands, the one that has tortured and teased me since I met her last night. Finally, she relinquishes to me and every intimate part of us connects. The ache I felt for her vanished the second her hot sex made contact with mine. Normally contact like this would make me want to push my cock roughly into her pussy, but I don't care about myself right now. Instead I want to soak this moment in, capture it in time.

She pulls away, and I moan at the loss of her touch. "Look at me, Kingsley." I obey instantly; I would do anything for this woman.

"Breathe with me again."

The cycle from earlier begins again. Breathe in, and exhale out. But this time when her hips circle, her sex strokes against mine in an up and down motion. I give into the feeling, following her. Our moans mix; the heat between us building.

Our movements are beyond dry-humping. I feel as though I'm buried deep inside of her with each thrust of my cock against her covered sex. The connection between our bodies mimics the act I thought I knew so well. I realize now how right she was. I knew nothing.

"God, Kathryn." I groan, the build-up for my release closing in.

"We're going to slow it down." I want to beg her to continue, as I felt my balls starting to tighten. My release was seconds away. Now I fear they're turning blue. "I know you're close, that's why we're pulling back, slowing down, to only build back up. Trust me."

"You're killing me," I groan, resting my head on her shoulder.

I'm beginning to think Tantra is another word for torture at this point. Emotionally and physically, I've never experienced anything like the grueling intensity I'm submitting to with her. But the physical part has changed since I went back to those memories of my mother. I don't understand it, the change in intimacy, but our contact together is deeper, more intense.

"You'll thank me." She winks and slows her gyrating hips. They sweep past me slowly, painfully slow. My orgasm was on the verge, but somehow my desire has picked up, the delay driving me crazy with need.

She kisses me. Our tongues moving in sync with her hips and my thrusts. Pulling away from me, Kathryn takes the barely-there sports bra in her hands and lifts it over her head. Her chest now completely exposed. Beautiful round breasts, full with rose-colored nipples standing before me. Ready and waiting. I nearly come on the spot. It's as if she's cast a witch's spell and given her body unbelievable power over me.

"You're so beautiful. Perfect." Her seductive smile lets me know my words are appreciated, and her breasts are mine for the taking. So I take them.

I'm almost shaking as the passion flows through me. Ready to burst when I come into contact with the sides of her breast. One in each hand, I hold them delicately, worshiping them.

Thumbing her aroused nipples, I'm in heaven. Hard and taut without even my touch. They stiffen further as I pull and twist, elongating them. Her hips pick up speed as I continue to tease her. I reach down and pull one nipple into my mouth, sucking and flicking it with my tongue.

I hear her crying out for more as I do. She forces her hips harder against my erection. Her need for more as desperate as mine. Fuck, how I wish I was inside her, feeling her wetness all around me. The thought alone is enough to make me come.

My moans now join her as I shove myself up into her, grinding against her hot pussy.

She cups my jaw and pulls my head away. "Look at me when you come."

Her eyes are dark and hooded, so full of arousal. Likely no different than my own. Our grinding hasn't ceased and I'm getting close again. Not far from the end for me, but I'm enjoying this ride with her. I don't ever want it to stop.

My breath hitches as I feel her fingers undoing the ties of my pants. Loosening them until they're free and hanging open. She places her hands on the area above my boxers and gives me a devilish look. One, which promises to undo me. I keep eye contact with her, though; I've learned to follow rules tonight.

She sneaks around the elastic of my briefs, and I hold my breath praying she doesn't stop. And she doesn't. I feel her hands exploring further, deeper until she's taken me fully into them and enclosed her fingers around me. I moan when she begins to move her hands up and down. It's the sweet friction I've been craving.

I've wanted this moment with her since I met her last night. Dreamed of it even. But now that's she's finally here, in my arms, with my cock in her hands, it's different than I imagined. Damn, it's incredibly so much more.

I want to get her there with me, so I place my fingers palm up onto her pussy. She's practically pulsing with need, and fuck, she's hot and feeling slick even through her yoga pants.

"I want to touch you, too." I need to get underneath these damn yoga pants like it's the last thing I'll ever do.

"Hell, I've already crossed so many lines..." Kathryn says, husky and breathy. It was all she needed to say.

In a frenzy, I flatten my hand and delve inside her yoga pants. They're tight but no match for me. I push my hand down her toned stomach, my fingers glide over her bare pussy. Bare. Damn, my favorite kind. I then slip my fingers down into her heat, cupping and possessing her entirely. I watch her eyes roll backward as I find her clit and feel the wetness.

Right now, possibly for the first time in my entire life, I want a woman. I don't just want a fuck or quick head. Then it suddenly dawns on me and I understand what she's been trying to tell me about sex versus fucking. I see the difference now. It's as clear as a sunny day.

She moves against my hand, and I can't help but smile as we stare into each other eyes. I've desired and lusted after this beautiful woman, and for now she's all mine. I've never known a craving like this before.

I need to be inside her somehow and feel that connection. So I enter her with two fingers as I rub my thumb over her clit in circles. Pressing harder, she rocks and finds a rhythm. The whole time I've been stimulating her, she's had her fingers wrapped around me, stroking my cock. My orgasm now only seconds away.

"Come," I plead as my face shows my desire to bring her with me over the edge.

My one word is followed by more pressure onto her clit, and a slight curl of my fingers inside her. She holds me tighter and moves her hand faster and we both fly off into the beginnings of our release.

Everything connects inside me with the force of my orgasm. My whole body spasms with each beat of my heart. I cry out in an unfathomable ecstasy. The sound echoing around the tapestry-covered walls.

Chapter 15

My body begins to calm and come down from its high, my cries of pleasure now faded away and replaced by another sound—an uncontrollable laughter. It's coming from somewhere deep within me as an indescribable exhilaration courses through me from head to toe. I can't contain this wild feeling of needing to belt out a laugh, and I don't have the power to suppress it. Though one thing is certain—I've never laughed like this in my entire life. It's completely foreign to me.

Kathryn gazes at me as I laugh like an idiot, a brilliant smile shining on her face. I look into her tear-filled eyes as we both laugh together.

I wrap my arms around her and bring her against me again, skin to skin, her full breasts pressing into me. I hold her tight and rock our bodies from side to side, trying to show her how much she means to me right now. Then I fall backward onto the mat behind me, taking both of us down in a swift move, the mat's cushion softening our fall.

Our laughter continues for a few more seconds but then slowly subsides into occasional giggles as we lie there holding one another. I gently caress her back with the tips of my fingers, enjoying the feel of her soft skin.

But sadly, Kathryn moves away from our embrace, breaking the moment between us. She places her hands by my sides and raises herself off my stomach to straddle me. She reaches for my discarded T-shirt at the edge of the mat and uses it to clean off my stomach, the result of having the most explosive orgasm in my life. I watch her lovely breasts, ones I'm quite familiar with now, sway with every movement she makes, her hair wild around her face. When she touches my stomach and sides, my laughter starts up again.

"I thought you weren't ticklish." Kathryn teases me.

"Shit, I don't know what I am right now," I manage to say, my gut getting sore from laughing so much. I can't seem to stop it, and frankly I don't want to. She lies on top of me again, returning to where I want her to be. I encircle her with my arms, and an odd feeling of completeness hits me as I do. The only movement we make is the gentle shaking corresponding with my quiet laughter, although it's more of a child-like giggle at this point.

I feel her lips kissing my neck, their touch as light as a feather. She runs her fingers through my hair and pulls on the strands. The sensations I'm feeling from her helps to still the laughter in me. It's finally dying down, but the excitement from my whole experience with her remains.

"What the hell just happened to me?" I ask as she raises her head off my chest. She peers at me with smiling eyes. At least whatever the fuck I experienced makes her happy, too, but I hope she clues me in because I have no name for what transpired.

"What you went through was amazing, and I'm not fully certain I even know what was going on with you. No one I've worked with in Tantra has reacted to quite the same degree as you just did. It was nothing short of spectacular." She brushes her hands over my cheeks and chastely kisses my lips. "But whatever was blocking you from opening up to others, well, I think you chased those demons away."

"It does feel as though a weight has been lifted off me. A weight I didn't know existed. And here I thought my life was going along just fine." I push the hair away from her face.

"How is what I felt even possible? Seriously, I feel great, but that was some freaky shit. I sensed my gut twisting right before a heaviness hit my chest. Next thing I know I'm crying out as if, well, as if I'm dying. Then what we did after that… Touching you finally, it felt as though I'd never touched a woman before, or had one touch me. It meant something different."

"It's amazing what sex can be like when there is meaning behind it. How things have changed since I met the cocky Mr. Kingsley of last night." She's right, I'm not sure how, but I feel different right now. Those words I spoke last night, about fucking for a release, I can't imagine saying them to her now. Not after what just happened between us.

"Don't remind me of what I said to you. I might even confess to being embarrassed about ever speaking them." I'm not ready for a full-out confession yet. I still have my pride, even if I know she's got me wrapped around every single one of her fingers.

"It's amazing what one intense Tantra session can do with our emotions, how tied they are to touch and intimacy. I believe there's a life force behind the practice. I had a similar experience to yours, although nowhere near as dramatic." She takes a deep breath before continuing, as if she's preparing herself to go back to the night she's describing. "At my first Tantra session, I cried a river of tears. I think the grief I'd bottled up after Jean-Paul's death came spilling out of me. The numbness went away and left me from that moment on. I started to heal and return back to a normal life. I don't know where I'd be if I hadn't gone to that first session."

"All I can say for now is wow." I see such understanding in her eyes. "It feels as if I've had a bath on my insides, if that makes any sense? Likely a horrible description, but I can't think of any better way to explain it."

"I'll put on my psychologist hat for a minute." She gives me a subtle wink with a little gleam in her eyes. "You were so closed to receiving from others and giving yourself fully to them. When you finally let go and felt things you hadn't in years, the results were mighty powerful, thus your scream. I cried tears, and you cried out instead. I admit it was painful for me to hear you in such torment, but it needed to happen. You're better for it now."

"And speaking of a bath," Kathryn continues. "It's getting late and you've had quite the night. From death threats to our little mind-blowing event here tonight. What do you say we head for the shower?"

"We, as in us together?" I ask with the hope of a thousand praying saints.

"Yes. Unless you have an objection," she says in a sarcastic way while she rises to her feet and steps off the mat. Once standing, she reaches for her sports bra. I'm waiting for her to put it on and cover up those luscious tits, but instead she turns to face me still bare-chested, hair cascading around her shoulders. A raven-haired temptress. God, how did I get so fucking lucky?

"Damn, woman, you'll get no objections about sharing a shower from me." I love how she stands before me exposed, so free and open with her beautiful body. I can't help but wonder if the touching beneath clothes we did together was out of the norm for her. She said she'd crossed so many lines with me.

"What we did tonight? Was that what you had planned? I mean the sex part?"

"Can't say I planned it, but it felt right. Don't you agree?" She gives me a seductive smirk while placing her hands on her hips with her breasts extending out at me. Does she know how she's driving me wild right now?

"Of course, I agree." No doubt, the easiest answer of my life. "There's something between us, I've been feeling it since we met last night. It's like a strange pull or energy whenever you're near me." I want to tell her being near her like this makes my pulse race, but I don't want to push it too far. "I thought it might take a little longer to convince you of the same."

I've risen off the mat, so I'm standing directly in front of her. I bring my hands to the sides of her breasts, holding the weight of them in my palms. I look up at her, trying to gauge her feelings about what I'm doing to her, but her eyes urge me on. Her breasts are too alluring to stay away from them, and thankfully she doesn't stop me. My thumbs and fingers flick over the tip of her nipples as she lets out a small moan of pleasure.

"You can't stand there uncovered and expect me to keep my hands to myself." My words are spoken softly, and Kathryn responds by throwing her head back as I continue to work my fingers over her. I bend to bring my lips to her ear and whisper to her. "You feel this thing we have, don't you?"

I don't wait for a reply; instead I bring her into my arms. I cup one hand around the back of her neck while my other arm finds the small of her back. I kiss her passionately, pulling her closer. She returns my hunger by pushing her lips against mine. I close my eyes tightly, enjoying the pleasure of feeling her in my arms. The taste of her against my lips works through me, spurring me on. Who knew a kiss could have this much power behind it?

"Thank you, Kathryn." This time I break our kiss and speak. She needs to know how much tonight means to me. Her head rests on my chest as I weave my fingers through her hair. "Now about that shower…"

"Follow me," she says as she moves out of my arms and turns toward the door. She peeks over her shoulder, waiting for me to follow.

"Where you lead, I'll follow." I chuckle to myself, knowing what I just said is the utter truth. She totally owns me. After tonight, I'll never tease Tom about being pussy-whipped again. I think instead we should start comparing notes.

"Oh, the candles." She begins scurrying around the room, blowing them out. I help her by extinguishing a couple near the sound system. Since it's still playing music, I switch it off, too.

"Thanks." She opens the door and waits for me.

"My pleasure, beautiful," I say with a devilish look in my eyes, and she responds with that musical giggle of hers.

I smile down at her when I arrive near her by the door. "After you, my dear."

We walk into the hallway, and I look at the room where my clothes from today lie over the bed and wonder if I'll be sleeping there tonight. She stops at the door to the room, too, dashing my hopes. I want to say, what about that shower, but decide to wait.

"Why don't you find some clean pajamas and join me in the master bath. I'll get the shower going." Grinning like a loon, she shakes her head at me and rolls her eyes. I watch her walk toward her room with her sweet ass sashaying, and her hair swaying across her bare back. What a sight to behold.

"I'll be right there," I call after her as she disappears into her room, and truer words have never spoken. Hell or high water can't keep me away from being alone with her in a shower. Just the thought of watching water cascade down her body revives my erection.

I remember that I left my T-shirt in the harem tent and quickly return to the room to retrieve it. Once back in the guest room, I quickly remove my pants and find a replacement pair in the dresser drawer. I don't even bother with a shirt this time. And who gives a fuck about briefs? I could care less, so commando it is.

I decide not to get dressed before jumping into the shower. It seems pointless, so I amble my naked ass to her bedroom. I toss my pants on her bed in hopes I'll be sleeping there tonight. I hear the water running from behind the cracked door leading to the bath. Pushing the door open, I see a breathtaking sight in front of me. Grabbing onto the door's frame with my hands, I need the extra support at the sight of her before me.

The bathroom is dimly lit, but Kathryn stands in the middle of a glass-enclosed shower with a light above her head acting as a spotlight. Her body is turned to the side, so I'm at a great angle to peruse all of her curves while the water streams down them.

I'm dumbstruck by her body. Her legs are long and slender. That sweet ass I've been lusting after since she walked away from me at the bar last night is even more perfect than I imagined. Every flawless inch of her blows my mind and draws me across the tile floor to the shower's edge. I press my palm up to the glass wall and watch as she turns around to me. A lazy, sexy smile makes its way across her face as she sees me standing there before her, no clothes on, and fully erect.

She moves her eyes to where my palm lies flat against the glass and brings hers to mirror mine on her side. Streams of water fall down around her hand. Slowly she turns her head back toward me and our eyes reconnect.

I'm not sure how this simple act between us could feel so intimate, but it does. Neither one of us stirs. I'm not even sure if I'm breathing at this point. The sound of the running water is the only thing filling the room, until she breaks the silence and calls to me.

"Kingsley, join me."

I remove my hand from the wall of glass as she opens the door for me. I step into the shower, and the warm water hits my overheated flesh.

She takes me by the hand and brings me closer to her. Next she reaches for a bottle on a ledge built into the shower's back tiled wall. Popping the container open, she tilts it upside down while I watch the contents slowly trickle into the palm of her hands. Unceremoniously, she drops the bottle beside us, out of the way. Her hands gather over my chest, running a similar path from earlier tonight, caressing me tenderly. She migrates up to my shoulders and arms. The body wash is like oil, making her fingers glide over me.

I close my eyes, unable to keep them open as the day is finally catching up with me. My body is exhausted from all the events I've endured, both the good and bad, and this relaxing touch of hers makes it all hit home. I think even my erection is gone which is saying a lot with this beautiful woman massaging her hands all over me.

"You're completely exhausted." I hear Kathryn announce as if she's reading my mind. We seem to be so in tune with each other, she may be reading my body instead.

She kneads my shoulders, and I slump into her hands as she works the tension away.

"You're a psychic," I say, but my eyes remain closed because I feel as if I could curl up in her arms and sleep the night away. "Maybe it's obvious since I'm behaving and keeping my hands to myself."

Kathryn stands to the side so the water can more directly hit my skin. My eyes remain closed, but I feel her hands skating over my body and washing away the suds.

"No one has ever treated me like this. Thank you." My words are honest but almost pathetic to my own ears. Here I am a thirty-two-year-old man who's fucked countless women over the years. But soberly, I realize the attention she's been giving so freely to me tonight means more than all those fucks added together.

"You're welcome, Kingsley. I think it's time to get you to bed, though. You look like you're about ready to collapse." She turns off the water, and I open my eyes as she gives my arm an encouraging squeeze. "Wait here. I'll grab you a towel."

She wrings the water out of her hair and gracefully exits the shower. I wait for her return in the exact place she left me, watching in awe as her naked body moves toward a shelf filled with plush white towels. She removes a couple of them and turns my direction once again.

The sight of her unclothed and unashamed, like Eve in the Garden of Eden, nearly makes me drop to my knees. I don't think there's another word but beautiful for Kathryn.

She lays one towel on the ground outside the shower and secures the other one around her body. She picks up the discarded towel off the floor, re-enters the shower, and begins to dry the water from my skin. I fight to keep my eyes open, but I lose the battle as she gently rubs the soft towel over me. Front to back until she finishes by wrapping the towel around my waist.

I open my eyes to find her smiling kindly up at me. "Why don't you get dressed and meet me back in my bed? Skip the guest room. At this point you've officially graduated to the master suite."

"I like the sound of that." I dip down and kiss her forehead in a sign of gratitude.

She pats my towel-covered ass as I walk past her. "I hope there's more where that came from," I say responding to her playfulness as I leave the bathroom and find the pants where I left them on her bed. The one I'm sharing with her tonight.

"Hey," I yell to her. "Which side of the bed is yours?"

She appears at the bathroom door wearing a deceptively innocent pink negligee, which ends at the top of her thighs. Everything of importance covered, but the outlines of her nipples stand out clearly, teasing me.

"The side with the alarm and all the stacked books. I like to read before I fall asleep." She nods in the direction of the nightstand, and I see her books there. Some of them are worn and likely re-read favorites.

I climb into the other side of the bed and fully appreciate her love of finer things. Because her sheets feel divine as I stretch out my legs and pull the top cover over me. She turns off all the bedroom lights. Unashamedly, I watch her walking around the room in the skimpy pink nightie. Since I'm lying in her bed as an invited guest, I fully believe I've earned the right to stare.

The covers move as she joins me in the bed, although I can't make her out in the darkness. She scoots over toward me and nuzzles her back up against my front. I instinctively place my arm around her waist, and we fit together like pieces of a puzzle. I break the dark silence and speak.

"You know this is my first time actually spooning. And I'm rather enjoying myself, although it's likely related to the beautiful company I'm keeping."

"Go to sleep, charmer." I feel her ass wiggle wickedly against me, and I retaliate with a little pinch on her backside through the covers.

"Hey. What was that for?"

"You know very well what it was for, you little minx." She responds with that darling little giggle I'm beginning to love.

I feel my eyes getting heavy and sleep approaching me, but there's something I want to know from her before we drift off.

"Why are you being so good to me? I'm not sure I deserve it."

"Remember earlier when I said you were a scared and scarred man. Well I left an important description off the list. Good. You are a good man, Kingsley. Beneath the cocky exterior and finesse, you're a good man."

"No longer a boy then?" I ask with the biggest smile on my face.

"Yes, I believe you've graduated to manhood, too." She giggles again and snuggles closer into me. I fall asleep breathing in the lovely scent of her hair.

Chapter 16

My eyes open as I wake to absolutely nothing. Not a single damn nightmare or even a welcomed dream visited me in my sleep. For two nights in a row, the tormenting dreams I've endured for the past ten years have vanished.

Looking over at the beauty sleeping next to me, I'm convinced she's the reason for my restful sleep. She makes me feel safe and secure. The Tantra experience we shared last night still blows my mind. Going back to those memories, fully reliving them and the peace I felt when I finally did.

Kathryn is some type of sexy sorceress, and I have no desire to let her go anytime soon. Hopefully, she's okay with my plans, but the thought of what she feels or doesn't feel for me is unsettling.

Me, the consummate player of Manhattan, worried about a woman's affections? How the fuck did this woman bring me to my knees in such a short time? With one quick perusal of Kathryn's sleeping body, the answer is obvious.

Even though she's facing away from me, I have one breathtaking view. The downy soft sheets have become tangled between her legs, while her silk pink negligée gathers above her hips, giving me a perfect view of her sweet ass in her sheer panties. My needy fingers are itching to reach out and touch her, but I don't want to wake her just yet.

Impure thoughts of last night are producing some issues for my dick. I discreetly adjust myself beneath the sheets, hoping not to move the bed too much. I glance over her shoulder to the see the clock on her nightstand. It's not quite seven thirty, but for me it might as well be high noon since I'm usually up well before six.

I need to call Mrs. Carter and let her know I'll be arriving especially late this morning. She should already be sitting at her desk by now, likely staring at my empty office, wondering where the hell I am and worrying about the news of Simon from last night.

Plus, I'll likely have scores of emails and texts to catch up on. Rubbing my temple, I think hard about where I left my phone. With everything that happened last night, I can't seem to think straight. Then it quickly comes back to me: the guest room.

I'll need to leave the bed quietly and retrieve it. With one last look at Kathryn, I inch to the edge of the mattress and swing my legs around to meet the floor and gingerly stand. Looking over my shoulder as I tiptoe toward the door, Kathryn is sleeping away, undisturbed by my movements.

My phone is located on the dresser where I placed it, but the battery wasn't charged overnight, which is something I would never let happen. Ever. Instead of it bothering me, I shrug it off with a smile.

Using the remaining battery I have left, I read my many missed texts, calls, and emails. I scroll through the list and start reading an email from Peters, marked urgent.

Your car is impounded until tomorrow at eight a.m. I've advised Eddie to use the spare company car for today.

Your bodyguard, Jordan Hayes, met Eddie this morning and will escort you EVERYWHERE starting today. He's licensed to carry and conceal a firearm and will be packing a gun until Simon is detained. No complaints or protests on this issue, it's non-negotiable.

Detective Harold Baker, the NYPD lead investigator on Simon's case, will come to your office at two for an informal interview. MacDonald hired a personal attorney familiar with high profile cases like yours. He will be there to counsel you before, during, and after the detective's questioning. MacDonald will arrive with him at a quarter to two for an introduction.

The latest Intel on Simon has his credit card being used in Canada. I saw the video of him from last night when he was allegedly getting gas outside of the city. It appeared to be a man fitting his description. Height, weight, and hair color match, but I didn't directly see his face. However, the police suspect Simon's fled the area. Per Mrs. Carter, you have an event this evening, and I believe you can still attend; however, I need to discuss this further with you in person.

Since several texts, calls, and emails have gone unanswered, I'm assuming you're still at Kathryn Delcour's apartment. Please advise on your whereabouts ASAP. I'd like to confirm you're still alive.

I fire off a quick email to Peters, hopefully satisfying his knowledge I'm among the living while asking him to meet me in my office at ten thirty. Next up is Eddie.

"Hello, Mr. Kingsley." As usual he picks up after the first ring. Always dependable Eddie.

"Hey, Eddie. Man, I'm glad you're answering my calls this morning." I say teasingly, trying to lighten the tone of our call. "I can't tell you how sorry I am about last night. You all right?"

"Yes, sir. I'm okay now, but I was rather upset last night. Mr. Edwards shooting off a gun, screaming and yelling crazy nonsense… Thank God Mrs. Duffy and everyone else was okay. Simon seemed possessed. By what, I don't know?"

There was no disguising the fear in Eddie's voice. Witnessing the entire scene has left him shaken up. I'll need to compensate him and his wife for all his troubles. Perhaps a nice vacation abroad when this all blows over. Maybe Paris, since Eddie has mentioned wanting to take his wife there.

"I'm not sure either, Eddie, but I'm glad no one was hurt. Police believe he fled the area. Let's hope they're right." Something in the back of my mind nags at me. Simon's too smart to be so blatantly obvious, but I'll have to trust Peters and the NYPD on this situation for now.

"I understand you have the company car and my bodyguard is with you, too. I need you to pick me up at nine thirty where you dropped me off yesterday. You know, the apartment building we camped out in front of for a few hours."

"I remember it very well. Beautiful lady, sir." Eddie breaks the stanch professionalism he usually upholds with me. He knows very well Kathryn isn't the typical woman I've pursued in the past. He's never witnessed me pursue anyone, really. Sure he's heard me fucking plenty of women in the backseat, likely seen an eyeful or two over the last couple of years, but my actions with Kathryn are so out of character for me, even normally silent Eddie can't seem to keep his comments to himself.

"Her name is Kathryn, and beautiful doesn't even come close to describing her." I grin thinking about her last night in the shower. As long as I live, I don't think I'll ever be able to forget the sight of her at that moment. It's seared into my brain.

"Well, sir. I hope you don't mind me saying this, but I'm happy for you. When I met my wife, no other woman existed for me after that day."

"So you knew when you met her that something was different?" I need to hear more details from Eddie, because I want to compare notes with him. I have no real frame of reference for what's happening between Kathryn and me.

"Pretty much. There was just something about her. I couldn't really put my finger on it at the time. But I'm convinced now, looking back, it was love at first sight." I hear a definite smile in Eddie's voice.

"Thanks, Eddie. Will see how things go." I don't want to get my hopes up as I'm charting new waters with Kathryn, but I haven't been the same since I first met her. "See you at nine thirty sharp. Have the bodyguard meet me in the lobby."

"Yes, sir." Eddie replies quickly before I end the call.

I decide to email Mrs. Carter and let her know I will be late to the office and instruct her to clear my calendar for the day. I need some time to wrap my head around the events of the last forty-eight hours. Maneuvering and conquering my day-to-day meetings will have to wait until Monday. I'll just stick to catching up and answering emails.

After reading through a few emails from my public relations department and head attorney, I see they have everything under control. I have a good group of people around me: smart, talented, and fully capable of handling a crisis like this. My employees are treated with the utmost respect and enjoy the above-average pay scale I provide them.

I turn off my phone in hopes the battery will last until I make it to the office, then return it to rest on the dresser. A hunger to be with Kathryn again hits me, and I believe it may be time for a little breakfast in bed. I smile to myself, appreciating my little double entendre. A sweet little bite of Kathryn sounds quite delicious to me. The thought of tasting her against my tongue makes my cock twitch.

Walking the short distance back to her bedroom, I reenter her suite to see the bed empty. My hopes of rejoining her under the covers are dashed. As I stand there pouting, she exits the bathroom suite and comes to a stop when I catch her eye. The mere sight of her increases my heart rate.

Her hair is a disarray of raven curls. Her pink nighty becomes almost translucent as faint rays of sunlight escape from cracks in the drawn curtains, illuminating her curves.

She's looking at me shyly with her head tilted to the side. I detect a slight uneasiness in her mood as she eyes me. I grin reassuringly at her and watch her face light up in a smile, too. The confident Kathryn has returned.

I move toward her without even a thought and take her into my arms. I grab her face in my hands and kiss her deeply, wanting to possess her completely.

I kiss the corner of her mouth, and my lips make a trail to her neck. She tilts to the side, allowing me better access as I lightly nibble on her skin. Kathryn relaxes in my arms when her back sways, and I know she's mine for the taking. And dammit, I want to take her back to bed; there's still time before I have to leave her apartment and face reality.

"Did you think I'd left you?" I whisper into her ear, kissing and sucking on the small lobe. "And didn't even leave behind a note of thanks. Would that have upset you?"

"Not particularly," she answers me with her lips against my ear now. However, the answer isn't what I was expecting.

"What do you mean? 'Not particularly'?" Her words send a blow to my pride, even if I did egg her on for an answer.

"Something told me I wasn't just a one-night stand with you." She emphasizes her point by poking a finger in my rib. I'm certain there was a mischievous glint in her eyes, too.

"Touché, once again." She knows exactly what effect she has on me. "You're the first woman I've awaken to see the sun with."

"For some reason, I find this fact rather sad versus flattering." Her gaze is now one of tenderness as she rubs my jaw soothingly with her fingers.

Truthfully," she continues, "I heard you in the guest room talking to someone on the phone. I figured you were tending to your empire and couldn't be bothered." She raises her head looking up at me, since I'm now standing tall, towering over her.

"The empire is still afloat. No sinking ships at the moment." I twirl a strand of her hair around my finger. "If you hadn't heard my voice, you still wouldn't have been a little bit concerned?"

"Nah." Kathryn scrunches her nose. "I figured you'd show up at my doorstep again. I believe I have something you want," she replies in a sassy, singsong way, but goddammit, she's right. I want her like I've never wanted anything else in my life, and it may be turning into more of a need for me. Ironic, since I've never wanted or needed a woman before meeting her.

"What if I said I want that little something right now?" I try a vague and sneaky approach, but I want in her panties desperately. I soften my question with a smile and nearly shout for joy when she returns it.

She gazes up at me through her long dark lashes, fully challenging me to take what I want. I reach for her hand and guide her across the floor. After a couple steps, we arrive at the edge of the bed.

"Sit down, Kathryn." She willingly complies and sits, her large blue eyes gazing up at me expectantly. I gently make a path down the front of her body with my fingers, making sure they run directly over her erect nipples as they push against the silk fabric. I place my fingers on the bottom of her pink negligee, gathering up the hem and lifting the silky garment over her head.

Kathryn's biting her lip innocently as I look down at her perfect breasts. Her rosy peaks are pebbled, appearing eager for my touch. I graze my fingers slowly across her breasts, touching her hardened nipples as I lazily explore. My fingers trail underneath the fullness of her breasts, then I bring them back up again, grasping her nipples between my fingers in a slight pinch. Kathryn flinches and moans, letting me know she likes how I'm playing with her.

Working my hands upward, I cup them over her shoulders, lightly rubbing my thumbs over the delicate skin on her throat. I hold her in my grip and ease her backward so her upper body is lying flat on the bed. She wiggles and moves up the bed, resting her head on a pillow. Her black hair flows angelically around her, a dark contrast to the white sheets. A sexy smile forms on Kathryn's red full lips, one worthy of a devilish angel who plays a tease but delivers in the end.

She grabs hold of my pants and tries to pull them down as I stand next to her. Not one to keep a lady waiting, I loosen the tie to my pants, push them down my legs, and step out of them. While Kathryn's eyeing my full-fledged and eager erection, I focus on the tip of her tongue as it appears, licking her decadent lips. The sight makes me want to pounce. I restrain myself and edge onto the bed, kneeling beside her bent legs. Needing her fully bare before me, I bring my hands to the band of her panties.

"Why did you even put these on?" I ask with a wink of my eye.

"Now, lift up your hips." It's more of a demand than a request. Kathryn willingly complies. My heart races as I ease them down her legs with anxious hands.

Her panties gone and tossed to the side, I kneel between her legs as I rub my hands down her slender thighs. She catches on quickly and parts her legs wider in invitation. I lower my hips down to hers, my cock finding her wet heat. Perching over her, I look deep into her longing eyes. I'm unable to restrain myself, and I begin rubbing my cock against her sex. She grasps my arms, diverting my attention from the moment. I fear she's going to put an end to what we're doing, but I still my movements anyway.

"I've not made love since his death," she says, her voice only a whisper as she turns her head to the side, away from me. The shyness I see reflecting from her is the same thing I saw when I walked back into her room. She's unsure about giving herself to me, and I can't really blame her. "The times I've practiced Tantric sex, well, it was nothing more than what we did last night. Mutual touching. Nothing more."

To say I'm ecstatic is an understatement. She hasn't technically fucked Frenchie. I feel a true sense of relief knowing she's not had sex with that fucker, and I'm sure my face-splitting grin clues her into my feelings.

Then a thought hits me and makes me worry about where things can go between us since her practices of sex differ so greatly from mine. Granted, I'm a fuck and run guy, but I'm willing to learn. Right now I'm a newbie on the whole Tantra business, though I loved the little taste so far.

"Are you okay with having sex outside of your harem tent?" I hope she says yes.

"My harem tent?" She giggles sweetly. "Funny description, but the truth is I haven't wanted to have regular sex with anyone until now. That is, if you're willing?"

Hell yes, I'm fucking willing! is what I want to yell, but I play it cool instead. However, I'm still a horny guy, so I start rubbing my cock against her sex again.

"I might not be up to speed on Tantra, but I'll aim for bliss." I grin at her after saying the word bliss. The very word she used when describing her goal of sex the night we met. An amused expression crosses her face. "Will that be good enough for you?"

I don't give her time to reply as my lips crash down upon hers. I know there's no turning back for either of us as her legs wrap around mine and her hips start thrusting up into my erection. Her wet heat slides up and down me. I close my eyes and raise my head high as the connection between us rushes through me, making me moan at the sensation. But I want more than just touching, and this morning I have other plans. So I force myself to break away as I start to venture downward toward my first goal: tasting Kathryn and having her come against my tongue.

"I want to properly thank you for last night," I say seductively as my fingers start exploring her pussy. Her legs widen for me, and I find the sweet little spot I remember from last night, aroused and ready.

I capture a nipple in my mouth and suck on it, adding a slight scrape of my teeth. She arches her back, pushing her breast hard against my mouth. In response, I give her nipple a quick bite. Kathryn cries out, her body jerking off the bed.

Leaving her breast, I trail kisses over her stomach. Kathryn's body moves restlessly as I stop to suck on the skin along her ribs and sides. She brings her hands to my head and weaves her fingers through my hair, pulling and playing with it. I've been watching her face as I work my way downward, hoping she'll open her eyes. She finally does, and they're a haze of desire, needy for more.

My lips find their way to her bare sex as she lies open and unashamed before me. It's a remarkable sight. I look up into her eyes again, and she's conveying two words to me: trust and want.

I use my fingers to part her fully, and lick her clit with my tongue. She arches farther off the bed and tugs my hair hard as I work her over. Her taste is incredible and I can't get enough. I press my aching cock into the mattress, seeking relief at the sight of her starting to come undone. The only relief I'll have will be when I'm buried deep inside of her.

"Has it been a long time?" I ask, half a question, half a knowing deduction.

"God, you have no idea," she gasps. The intensity she's feeling leaves her nearly breathless.

Determined to make this good for her, I wrap one arm around her hip and use my position to push her toward me. Her legs start to shake and tremble, so I know she's edging closer to her release.

I pull back from her clit and gently blow over the sensitive flesh. Kathryn moans and grabs the sheets, clutching them tightly. I return to touching her clit with my tongue. Circling it. Flicking it. Then sucking it between my lips. I feel her body starting to let go as her hips start to press up in tiny thrusts.

She moves her hands back to my head and pushes me down roughly against her sex. The woman wants more and I'm happy to oblige, so I add one more sensation to the mix.

My fingers.

I plunge two of them inside her and twist them forward, hoping to connect with her G-spot. I begin fucking her with my fingers, and it's then that she screams out and succumbs to her orgasm.

Her face is etched with satisfaction, or dare I say bliss, as she comes down from the high. It feels great being the man who put that look on her lovely face.

I kiss my way back up her beautiful body and wait for her breathing to return to normal.

"God, Kingsley." She's laughing now, so very similar to my uncontrollable laughter last night.

"I love hearing you say God and my name together. But I'd prefer you screamed Adam instead." I tease her, only making her laugh more. Though I wonder what it will take to get her to call me by my first name.

"Hmm, I'll take that under consideration. Come here, you." She reaches out to me, and I partially collapse on her and roll us over onto our sides. We're facing each other now, and she's smiling in contentment at me. "That was, well, spectacular might come close, but I would say a definite top ten for me."

"Not a top three, though. So I have room for improvement?" We laugh for a second at my silly joke. Staring into each other's eyes, I stroke her hair. Kathryn brings her lips up to mine and begins to kiss me, slowly and sweetly. I feel her hand wander toward my cock, and I am growing harder in anticipation of her touch.

When she wraps her hand around me, I close my eyes and lose myself in the sensation, relishing the feeling of her hand.

Then something begins to tickle my stomach. I open my eyes and realize where she's heading. I guessed right, as her mouth draws me in. She places a hand on my stomach and pushes me onto my back.

Now that I'm lying flat, she has a better angle and can take my cock into her mouth deeper. She curls her hand around the base and works it in an opposite rhythm of her mouth. The feeling is unbelievable.

I'm itching to run my fingers through her hair, grab onto her head, and help her move faster up and down. I refrain and grab ahold of the sheets instead. She's not like the other women who've given me head, so I'll let her be in charge, even if it fucking kills me.

Kathryn's mouth and hands move faster, and she adds her tongue, giving the tip of my dick a little swirl as she pulls up. Damn, she's good. A fucking expert, and I know I'm not far away from coming, but I'd prefer being inside of her when I do.

As if she was reading my mind, she pulls her mouth away from my cock and looks up at me.

"Stay there," she says to me, her lips red and swollen.

"No, please, come back." I plead with her, practically begging with my eyes. Kathryn gives me a sexy smirk and pats my leg, but doesn't return to my now-throbbing dick. I throw my arms over my head in frustration, wondering if this woman will be the death of me.

"Condom," she says flippantly over her shoulder.

Fuck the damn condoms, is what I want to say as she moves completely off the bed to open her nightstand drawer. She digs around in search of them, moving unseen objects out of the way.

"Here you go. Take your pick." Finally, she presents an unopened box to me with a proud grin on her face.

The sight of her makes me smile. She's standing there completely naked, looking like some beautiful sex goddess as she hands the box to me. I suppose she thinks I'm the expert, and she's likely correct. I have to laugh at the ridiculousness of our situation. I usually go through a box of these in a month, but I'm wondering if the box she gave me is expired.

Once I peel back the box's lid, I see untouched foil packs perfectly lined up in a row. I take one out and throw the box onto the floor. I start to sit up but Kathryn climbs back on the bed and roughly pushes me back down. I look up at her in surprise.

"Put that thing on, I'm ready for a little cowgirl." Holy shit. She's going to ride me, and I'll be damned if I can't get the fucking condom on fast enough.

"So this kind of sex is okay with you?" I don't know if cowgirl's acceptable in Tantra, but I'm praying it's allowed.

"I've heard it's good to mix it up. I haven't had a chance to try something different until now. And this was always my favorite." She positions herself on top of me. She's straddling me, her legs spread wide, and I feel the need building as I'm sheathed, fully erect, and waiting.

I begin to speak, but she intercepts me. "Hush, I've got a cock to ride."

Fuck me! Dirty talk? Now she's even the woman of my wet dreams.

She peers wickedly at me while she places my cock at her opening. I slip inside of her as she lowers herself down the length of me. Damn, she feels so good and as tight as hell. After all, it's been a couple of years for her. I feel her clenching muscles, and I moan as she circles her hips and grinds around me.

I need more contact with her so I bring my hands up to her breasts, rubbing my thumbs across her nipples. I cup the weight of them in the palm of my hand. I want to reach up and take a nipple in my mouth, but her hands are placed on my chest for leverage and I'm not about to fuck with that.

Instead I watch as the she rides me with abandon, and I'll be damned if it isn't the hottest fucking thing I've ever seen. Her hooded eyes are filled with desire as she looks down at me. I have no idea how long I'm going to last, and I fear my stamina will be embarrassingly short.

Kathryn starts really rocking against me. A sweet pace is set as she does. I try to meet her movements, a rhythm between us beginning.

As we continue staring into each other eyes, something deep passes between us. I have no idea what this feeling might be called; I've never felt anything like it before. But it's profound and makes me want to hold on to her tightly and never let go.

Kathryn draws me back into the moment with a deep drop of her hips. My need to let go starts to build. I don't know how close she is yet, but I sure as hell want her coming with me. The thought of her clenching around me when she climaxes makes me almost lose control.

I feel down where we are connected together with my fingers. I lift my head higher and see my dick sliding in and out of her. It's almost too much; I feel my balls starting to tighten up. I hold off the feeling as best I can while rubbing her clit with the tips of my fingers. She jumps as I begin to press against her harder, rubbing faster.

Kathryn leans back a little, giving me better access to her. What she does next makes me come undone. She begins to play with her own nipples, elongating them, pinching, and pulling them. Fuck, I've never seen anything sexier. Nothing compares to watching her toy with herself.

"Damn, Kathryn. Do you have any idea how much you're turning me on?" I practically moan my words as real moans start to follow. I simply can't control them any longer.

I feel her muscles close in tighter around me. Kathryn's pushing harder against me in her movements, too. I hope she's close because I'm seconds away. When she throws her head back and begins to scream, I push up into her with all my might. Finally finding my release with her. My muscles start tensing as I spill into the condom. The strength of my orgasm is nothing like I've experienced before, and my mind goes blank.

Kathryn collapses on top of me, both of us totally spent. Our breathing, ragged and deep. I push her hair out of the way and gently glide my fingers along the skin of her back. She's so soft and delicate and shivers under my touch. Even after our shattering orgasms, a simple touch from me can affect her. A fact I like a lot.

"Kathryn, I…" I'm uncertain how to continue as words fail me. A large part of me wants to know how she feels. Was it the same for her, too?

"I don't have words either yet. Maybe it's because I haven't had sex like this in years, but…" Her voice sounds funny, maybe even a little choked up. I feel wetness on my chest next to where her face is. I lift her head up with my hands and see that she's crying. Her tears kill me, the deep emotions I feel from seeing them cloud her eyes are unparalleled for me. I've never experienced this level of concern or feeling for another human being in my adult life.

"Kathryn, beautiful, what is wrong? Did I do something?" I say, my voice filled with concern.

Chapter 17

"I'm fine, really," she says sniffling. I'm not convinced she's telling me the truth. Actually, she's telling me nothing at all.

"Something made you cry?" I hate to pry it out of her, but I can't stand not knowing. I'm concerned I might have something to do with her tears. "Please talk to me."

"I feel that after two years, I've completely moved on from his death. Us, being together, and making love, gives me that feeling. My tears are more from relief. I'm definitely not sad. Just the opposite, in fact." She rises up off my chest and looks down at me with a contented look in her eyes. Our faces are only inches apart, and I can see that her tears are gone.

But I'm at a loss with no idea what to say back to her. Glad you're over your dead husband doesn't seem like the right response. The truth is she was married to a man she deeply loved; who I'm certain loved her, too. What fool wouldn't? She watched him die tragically, and people don't get over heartbreak like that easily. She's waited two long years to make love to someone, or in this case let me make love to her. I just don't know how I ended up being the lucky bastard she chose.

"I understand losing someone you love." I finally respond. Kathryn eyes me, likely wanting to know more about my loss.

But I'll save that for another time, if ever. "There's no pain like it."

"Thanks, Kingsley. I'm sorry to dampen the mood. What we just shared was wonderful. I wouldn't change a thing." She leans down toward me and kisses me quickly on the lips. "Especially those last two orgasms. You're really rather talented."

"Oh contraire, beautiful. That mouth of yours. Then your tongue." I feel myself getting hard at the memory, and shit, I realize I still have the fucking condom on. She's had me so damned mesmerized, I hadn't given it a thought or noticed. Normally, that damn thing is off the second after I come.

"Hey, I need to take care of a little something." I point toward my dick. Though she's lying on top of me and can probably feel me getting hard anyway. She lifts up and looks down at my half-mast erection.

"Oh, that." I can tell from the surprise in her voice she knows what I'm talking about now.

"Yes, that," I laugh. "Maybe a shower, too?"

It's getting late, and I barely have enough time to get ready before Eddie arrives. Although I don't want her to think I'm dashing out too quickly. God knows I'd rather stay in bed with her all day. The thought is very tempting, but I have to head into the office.

"I think that's a great idea," she says while handing me some tissues off the nightstand.

I discreetly remove the condom. God I hate those fucking things, but I've never been a one-woman man, and the women I fuck are pretty much tramps. So it's been my official coat of armor for years. That said, I'd love to be with Kathryn without one. Feeling her with nothing in the way, damn, I can't even imagine it.

"So what would it take to not use condoms?" I know I'm sticking my neck out asking her. I lift myself off the bed and follow behind her as we head to the shower.

"Well, the burden of proof is on you. I've been a good girl for two years. I doubt you've been a good boy for two days." She's talking over her shoulder as I trail behind her sweet ass.

"I'll work on that. The burden of proof, that is." I start to make a list in my mind of what I need to do to prove I'm clean. "Would an official letter from my doctor be enough?"

"You're serious, aren't you?" Standing in front of the glass shower, Kathryn turns toward me with her hands on her hips and a skeptical look on her face. I'm a bit distracted by the fact there isn't a stitch of clothing covering her delectable body.

"You sure make it hard for a man to concentrate." I gaze up and down her body. "But yes, I'm totally serious. What would it take?"

"For starters, I'm not going to even consider it for now." My hopes crash to the ground, but I can't blame her. She has no reason to trust me. "Second, I don't think a man like you can change your ways so quickly. You know, the old leopard can't change his spots thing. You were so cocky the other night and even left with Lizzie."

I wince. Fuck, hearing her say that name stings. I did make a gigantic mistake with Lizzie, and probably scores of others, too. What's going on with Kathryn is night and day from what I've had with all the others, every last one of them. But she's right, there's no reason for her to trust me yet. It's a sobering fact.

"What if I've changed? It can happen, right?"

"Let's just say we're in a holding pattern. I'll need more than a few days of monogamy to believe you're able to stop screwing around." There's something in her eyes. I see a woman who wants to believe but is too leery to hope for what seems out of my character.

She enters the shower and turns on the water. I step in right behind her. Kathryn stands under the water and the spray cascades down her body. I have to practically put my hands behind my back to keep from touching her. My cock disobeys as usual and stands at attention. Fucking traitor.

Kathryn pours some shampoo onto her palm and hands the bottle to me so I can use it. I join in and we both get the lather going, but it's too damn quiet for my liking, so I speak up.

"Can I finish washing your hair?" I can no longer keep my hands to myself. It's a losing battle, and massaging the shampoo into her hair is safe. At least my hands are busy.

She nods and I begin to gently rub circles against her scalp. She remains still, not moving a muscle as I continue. Kathryn turns to face me while tipping her head under the streaming water to rinse out the suds. She raises her hands to her head and weaves her fingers through the strands, attempting to rinse out the last of shampoo.

With her hands placed on top of her head, her breasts lift higher, making them stick out closer to me, and my control slips. I finally reach out to touch and cup them. My thumb and fingers begin pulling on her wet, hard nipples.

She slides her hands up my arms. Her fingers find mine as she takes my hands in hers. I'm not sure what to make of her actions. Is she trying to stop me from touching her? If she is, I may have to protest.

"Hold me, Kingsley," she whispers so softly I barely hear her above the sound of the water splashing against the tiles.

I comply willingly and encircle my arms around her. We stand there under the spray for a long time until she finally looks up at me, her eyes searching my face. For what I don't know.

"Do you think you can really stop sleeping around?" Her words are more like her wish for me, one that I want to fulfill.

"Yes," I say without a second of hesitation, because I know it's true. I don't want to be with anyone else but her. The feeling is remarkable, and nothing I would have ever expected. But I have to ask myself a question: Can a player's ways really die that quickly?

It's surprising to me, but I think that part of me died and was buried over the last few days. The thought of having sex with anyone but Kathryn seems wrong and abhorrent to me.

"I may need to alert the New York Times with an official death notice. You've killed the manwhore in me." We both laugh, but what I said couldn't be more true.

She looks up at me. "Yes, I'm deadly." She throws back her head and giggles, and damn I love the sound.

"Yes, you are. At least tc me; however, it's been the sweetest death." Cupping her jaw, I bend down and kiss her with all I have in me. Making sure she knows I mean what I said.

She detaches her lips from mine and smiles sweetly at me, and I swear my heart melts more for this beautiful woman. She turns off the shower's faucet and goes through the same routine of gathering us towels as last night. I could really get used to us showering together.

"Are you a coffee drinker?" I watch as she rubs the water off her body and yes, my damn cock is hard again.

"Yes, I've been one since my days at MIT." I stand close to her with my towel wrapped around my waist.

Kathryn walks to a closed door on the bathroom's far wall, opens it and enters. It's a nicely sized walk-in closet, and I stand at the opening, watching her pull out silk black panties and a matching bra.

"I'll brew some then." She's pulls a pair of dark-colored jeans up her legs as she's facing away from me. I love watching her wiggle that sweet ass into them. I also love how they fit her so snuggly, highlighting all her curves. She slips on a gray T-shirt and turns around toward me.

"Thanks, I could really use some before I head out into the jungle. I should get dressed, too. My driver, Eddie, is picking me up at nine thirty." Kathryn looks up at me surprised. I know I'm cutting it close, but I'll make it. I always do.

"You better hurry," she says and flies past me like she's running a race. "Good thing I have one of those quick brew makers."

I return to the guest room and slip on my clothes from yesterday. I have a few spare suits, shirts, and boxers at the office. But I have to laugh that I'm doing the walk of shame today.

Once dressed with my cell phone in hand, I head to the kitchen, the smell of freshly brewed coffee leading the way. Kathryn's at the counter slicing up a bagel, then pops it into the toaster. She sees me out of the corner of her eye and turns to me with a welcoming smile.

"Let me pour you a cup. I have a to-go mug here, too." She scurries around preparing a cup for me. "How do you like it?"

"A splash of milk with a scoop of sugar. And thanks."

There are a couple barstools on the other side of the granite countertop. I sit on the one closest to me and turn on my phone. The battery is nearly drained, but I'm able to scroll through a few emails. From what I read, Mrs. Carter has cleared my calendar for the day and Peters will be at my office at ten thirty as requested.

But damn, how I wish I could stay here with Kathryn. I'm tempted to text Eddie and tell him to turn the car around and forget picking me up, but I can't slack on my duties today. One good thing, though, it's Friday, which means we have the weekend ahead of us. The thought lifts my mood considerably.

"So, Kathryn, do you have any plans for the weekend?" My question comes out more timid than I meant it to be. I'm right back in high school again, before I realized I didn't need to ask a woman for anything. They found their way to me.

Kathryn hands me a coffee cup before she answers. "Thanks, it smells great." I begin sipping from the cup, and it tastes as good as it smells.

"You're welcome. Did you have something in mind for the weekend?" Kathryn plays coy, but it's clear she's trying to pump information out of me.

"Yes, I have something in mind." I wink, and she smiles knowingly. "I'm not sure if I can do anything in public, though, so I may have to resort to private activities."

I grab my coffee, rise off the stool as I stuff my phone in my pants pocket, and walk toward her. I wrap my free arm around her, drawing her tight against my body. I bend down so my lips are next to her ear.

"Here's what I want to do this weekend." She stills in my arms. I have her full attention now. "Have you teach me all about Tantra. A hands-on demonstration in your harem tent. What do you say?"

She leans her head away from me, and I see a sexy smirk on her face. Everything about her tells me she's okay with my idea.

"Do you think you can handle it? It could mean hours and hours of lessons and practice to get it right." Kathryn is toying with the lapel of my suit coat. Running her fingers under it like she did the night we met at the bar.

"Hours of practice?" I ask, teasingly, giving her a knowing smirk.

"Yes, hours of me touching you and you touching me. Clothes are left outside the door, too." She presses herself against my erection. Just the thought of hours alone with a naked Kathryn has me hard and ready to go. It's become a constant side effect when I'm near this woman.

"I think you can feel my answer," I say with a little chuckle. She boldly reaches between our bodies and palms my cock, her fingers wrapping around me through my pants, right here in her damn kitchen with a coffee in my hand, and Eddie likely waiting for my horny ass downstairs.

"You do seem like a willing student, and I'll promise to be a very thorough teacher." There's no missing the devilish twinkle in her eye.

"God, you're driving me mad," I say with a sigh, but it's practically a groan. It's true, my need for her is maddening. "I wish I could stay here and get started on your lessons, but Eddie is waiting outside for me by now.

"Okay, I'll get started on my lesson plans. There's so much I want to teach you." Her eyes get a faraway look in them, and I can only imagine what she's dreaming about. She leads me to the front door, and I'm saddened knowing our time together, for now, is about to end.

"Maybe I can see you tonight. I'll give you a call later." I stop myself when I realize I don't even have her phone number. What an idiot. "But I'll need your number first."

I open up my phone and thankfully it hasn't turned off yet. I pull up my phone's contact screen and add Kathryn as a new contact. I punch in her name as "Beautiful." I hand the phone over to her after the keypad appears.

"Here, put your number in my phone." She takes it in her hands and slowly smiles up at me.

"Beautiful, huh?" She taps in her number with the tip of a finger.

"Yes, very beautiful, actually." I take the phone back from her and save the information, and just as I do a text comes through for me. It's from Eddie, likely concerned because I'm never late. I return his text with a two simple words: "three minutes."

"Text from my driver. He's outside, so I really have to go." I think she's a bit down I'm leaving, too. The smile fades from her face. "But I'll call you later, I promise."

"I'm sure you promise all your hook-ups that." Her voice is laced with too much sarcasm for my liking. How could I convince her what I'm doing with her isn't some random hook-up for me?

"Actually, I never promise them anything." I look her hard in the eyes. She needs to understand how serious I am about this subject. "Nor do I stay over at their house and share morning coffee. You're the exception to everything, Kathryn."

Her smile has returned, and I breathe a sigh of relief. I hate her second-guessing what I'm feeling for her.

"Slick as ever, Kingsley," she says, in jest I hope, while opening the door for me.

I walk toward the door and turn around as I cross over the threshold. Kathryn's leaning against the wall with one leg bent. Her hair falls down around her, almost touching the tips of her full breasts. She's grinning at me, seductively.

I sit my coffee cup down on the floor quickly and dig in my pocket for my phone. I need a picture of her to look at during the day.

"Hold that pose," I say to her, excitedly. "And the smile. I love it."

By some miracle, my phone hasn't died on me yet, and I'm able to snap a couple of shots. She laughs at me when I finished, but now I can take a piece of her with me today.

Finally, I am in the elevator, making my way to the lobby after I gave her one more kiss for good measure. I wanted to leave her with one last good memory, and hopefully I did.

Once in the lobby, I scan the area for the damn bodyguard. Peters didn't give me a description, and I don't want to wander around, either. I'm beginning to get super frustrated until I see a tall man, who looks like he could bench press a horse, walking toward me. This dude has to be my bodyguard.

When he's about two feet away and still approaching me, he sticks out his hand. Looks like I guessed right.

"Good morning, Mr. Kingsley. I'm Jordan Hayes." His grip on my hand is firm and a hair away from being painful.

"Yes, Mr. Hayes. I would say it's nice to meet you, but under the circumstances..." I shrug at him instead of completing my train of thought. "However, I appreciate you being available on short notice."

We head for the exit, Hayes plastered to my side, walking with me stride for stride. I hate his presence near me already, but I'll have to endure it until Simon is apprehended. I don't think Peters will relent on the subject of added protection. Hopefully, they'll find Simon soon, because this fucking monkey, or Goliath, on my back is going to get old quick.

When we hit the open air, Hayes extends his arm and stops me before I walk to the car. He's looking all around, his face as serious as shit. Hell, he's one scary motherfucker. I suppose that's a good trait in a bodyguard, but he looks like he eats small children for breakfast.

"Hold up." He commands and I comply. I'm tall at six foot three, but I'm not about to cross him. "When we are outside, I need you to follow my lead. Actually, it might be good to do so at all times."

He has no idea how hard it is for me to follow anyone or their orders. Well anyone expect Kathryn. I'd follow that woman and her sweet ass anywhere.

"Okay," I say through gritted teeth.

Finally, we're in the company car and heading to my office building in mid-town. I pull out my phone and it's officially dead now, with nothing registering on the black screen.

"Eddie, do you have a spare charger?" He passes one to the backseat and I swiftly plug in my phone. I'm desperate to see my beauty's photo while we weave through Manhattan traffic. It takes an excruciating amount of time, but finally my phone comes back to life and her image displays before me, perfectly casual with an alluring smile. The sight of her makes me want to tell Eddie to turn the car around and head back to her place. But once again, I have a billion-dollar business waiting for me, not to mention families across the globe tied to the company's success. At least I have a portable version of Kathryn with me.

We arrive at my building, and Eddie pulls up to the secured underground entrance. It's guarded and only accessible after obtaining clearance from the on-site attendant. I'm sure my bodyguard loves the tight security. It's totally impenetrable as far as Simon's concerned.

Hayes instructs Eddie where he wants us to be dropped off. I frown thinking Hayes has become my new sidekick. At least I can make him stand outside the doors of my office for some privacy. I don't do well with anyone breathing down my neck.

I lean my head back as the car descends the ramp into the building's underground area. I fear it's going to be a long-ass day since I can't seem to get Kathryn off my mind. All my thoughts keep meandering back to her.

Hayes and I arrive at my office suite right before ten thirty, and I see Peters perched on Mrs. Carter's desk. They're interacting casually, and Peters seems to be very familiar with her as he leans over the desk. I cough as we approach and watch them jump apart at the sound.

Good God, Peters is flirting with her. Could he have the hots for Mrs. Carter? They're both divorced and alone. I wonder how long this attraction between them has been going on. Maybe I just didn't notice it before.

"Good morning, Mrs. Carter," I say congenially while scowling at Peters. He, after all, has hired this ginormous shadow stalking me everywhere and is now making moves on my assistant.

"Peters, come with me." I raise my arm and motion for him to follow me into my office. "And Goliath, you can wait outside here."

I swear Hayes smiles at my nickname. "I hope that tag doesn't offend you."

"Believe me, sir, I've heard worse." He laughs. Who knew this scary fucker had a sense of humor? Maybe I'll survive his hovering over me after all.

"Good, as no offense was meant." I walk with purpose into my office, throwing off my suit coat on a couch. I need to change out of yesterday's suit immediately.

"Have a seat, Peters, while I change," I say to him as I walk into the private bedroom I have off my suite. I've only used the space to catch up on a few hours sleep when I've had to stay and work overnight. My office is off limits to extracurricular activities with women. Well, except for Kathryn, of course.

Yes, I'd break the "no sex at work rule" with her in a heartbeat. As I change, I imagine her arriving at my office in a stylish coat, locking the door behind her, and discarding the coat on the floor as she makes her way to my desk. And of course she has nothing on underneath. I zip up my slacks and laugh at my already growing erection. I hope I'll see her tonight; otherwise, I'm going to have a struggle on my hands, literally.

Back at my desk, with my work face firmly in place, Peters goes through a litany of security requirements he's placing on my life. No social activities: too public and accessible. No dining out: too many people for Goliath to watch over.

Until there is confirmation on Simon's suspected whereabouts, I'm a prisoner with two places as my jail cell. My office and my penthouse.

I agree to Peters terms and happily wish him farewell as he leaves. No doubt stopping at Mrs. Carter's desk on the way out.

Scores of issues were sent to me via email. I work through lunch trying to put out fire after fire. Mrs. Carter has to walk to the deli across the street for my favorite pastrami sandwich. Goliath said no deliveries were allowed. She was nice and included him in the order. I suppose it's better to feed the beast.

Lost in a problem overseas at one of our software manufacturing plants in China, I'm startled when Mrs. Carter buzzes me over the intercom.

"Sorry to interrupt, Mr. Kingsley, but Mr. Peters is on the phone for you. He says it's important." I sigh deeply and reach for the button on the phone so I can answer her.

"Thanks." My answer is short, as I was knee deep in the problem and hate being disturbed.

"What's up, Peters?"

"The police detective needs to move his appointment with you back until the end of the day. Around five thirty or so. Will that be a problem?" he says like I have a choice. Personally, I've always deferred to those wearing a badge, and I'm not about to cross them now.

"Yes. Let my attorneys know."

"Will do. I'm at your apartment and working on the security here. I think I'm on the management's shit list." He laughs, and I find no humor in his reaction. I'm of a mind to slam the damn phone down in his ear.

"Do what you must." I end the call and get back to work after emailing Mrs. Carter about the change. I ask her to pass the information on to Hayes, too.

The afternoon hours breeze by as I work. At five, I come up for a little air and give Kathryn a quick call before the detective arrives. I want, no strike that—I need to hear her voice. It's amazing how much this woman has gotten under my skin in just three days. However, the last few days have felt more like a month in time with so many fucked-up things being thrown at me.

"Hello?" She answers my call, but I hear hesitancy in her voice.

"Hey, beautiful. It's Adam."

"Oh, I didn't know who it was. How's your day been? Slain any giants today?"

"Haven't slain any giants, but I do have one as a bodyguard. Dude's probably six eight and three hundred pounds. Scary mother."

She's laughing and giggling at me. I smile at the sweet sound. It's one of my favorite things about her.

"Well, I'm glad you've got protection. I don't want anything happening to you." I do love hearing that she may care for me and want me around for a while.

"Is that so?"

"Yes, I have plans for you," she responds seductively, making me wonder what she has in mind.

"I like the sound of that." My mind wanders back to this morning. I close my eyes and see her riding atop me again, ecstasy on her beautiful face. "Hopefully, I can see you tonight. I have to get my bodyguard settled into my place after I leave work."

"I'm meeting a friend for happy hour and should be finished by seven."

"Is this friend someone I know?" I ask for details in a roundabout way, hoping she will tell me this friend isn't male. I hate feeling jealous, but shit I'm jealous as hell thinking I might have to share her with another man.

"Wouldn't you like to know?" I can see her smirk over the phone. "It's an old friend from my childhood. He's flown in from San Francisco."

My blood begins to boil as I rise out of my chair to stand. I begin pacing the floor behind my desk. I don't want her meeting any man, old friend or not. But what can I say, I don't have a claim on her yet, but I sure fucking want one.

"So this friend, an old flame?" I can't help myself and ask for more details on this man and what he is or was to her.

She's giggling into the phone. "More like my gay best friend."

Oh, that's a big relief, and I have to laugh at myself. The whole boyfriend thing is a new experience for me. And so far, I'm failing miserably at it.

"Is it bad that I'm happy he's not interested in you that way?"

"No, it's rather sweet. And I don't think I'd like you having drinks with a woman tonight, either." She seems a bit terse, but as silly as it sounds, I'm thrilled she would be jealous, too.

The intercom buzzes on my desk. I know what it means. I have to go and prepare for the detective's questioning.

"Hold on, beautiful," I say while covering the receiver and pushing the intercom button.

"Yes, Mrs. Carter?"

"Sir, Mr. MacDonald's here."

"Okay, send him in."

I return to Kathryn. "I have to go, but keep tonight open for me. Please?"

"Same goes for you."

I end the call with a shit-eating grin on my face. MacDonald enters my office and looks at me in surprise; maybe shock is a better term, as I'm not my normal impassive self today.

"Who blew sunshine up your ass, Adam? You have a smile as big as Texas on your face. What gives?" MacDonald appears stunned to see me in such a jovial mood. I should deflect my Kathryn-induced high, but I have no desire to even attempt it. This is one high I don't want to come down from.

Chapter 18

NYPD Detectives Harold Baker and Jason Simpson sit across from my attorneys and me at the wooden conference table in my office. The room is completely silent except for Baker rustling through the folders in his hand. He's scattering paper left and right in front of him. He sets downs an 8x10 printed photo, and even though the image is upside down, I instantly make out who it is: Simon. The dark hair and tight smile are a dead giveaway. The same photo was used on the news last night.

Was it only last night? So much has happened in my life, the days feel more like weeks.

Baker shifts in his seat, preparing to speak. It appears he's the lead detective as Simpson assists him while they prep for the interview. I turn to MacDonald and Marcus Rhodes, my newly hired personal attorney, with a cocked brow and see that they, too, are amused with the display of disorganization from the detectives.

"My apologies, gentlemen." Baker looks up from his paper shuffling to address us. I can tell he's a bit flustered, though I have no idea what would cause such confusion.

"We've had some loose ends to tie up in this case. All of them surrounding motive."

Motive? The word sparks my interest, and I lean forward, hoping Baker will disclose more to us.

"Mr. Kingsley, I know you're a busy man." I watch as he scans around my large office suite. I know it seems opulent, and likely double the size of the average apartment in Manhattan, but I make no excuses for its grandeur. I've worked impossibly hard over the last ten years, and my office's size and scope reflect my success. "So I won't keep you long. After all, it's late in the day on a Friday, and a young man like yourself has to have plans for the night. Perhaps a lady friend waiting for you?"

A man like yourself? A lady friend? What the fuck does he mean by that? I don't care for the tone of this interview already, and the smirk on the detective's face is getting under my skin. I find no humor in the circumstances surrounding Simon's threat on my life and nearly ending Tom's. The detective should conduct himself more professionally. What have I done to deserve this type of treatment? Shouldn't he be on my side?

"Detective, I am a busy man, and any remarks about my social life are not helping us find my former partner any faster. The way I live my life is not the issue here." Baker smirks at me even more, if that's possible. I can't figure out why this man is showing such contempt for me. "But please continue, you have my undivided attention."

With a smug expression on his face, Baker folds his hands on the table while giving me a shrewd look. I wish he'd just get on with the interview and skip the dramatics.

"As I said, we, Detective Henley and myself, have been working on a possible motive today. We conducted a thorough search of Mr. Edwards' apartment. Quite a grand place, by the way, but he didn't leave much of a trail for us. He took all of his computer equipment, but we found this in his office. Actually, it's a photo of the evidence we found there."

Evidence? Baker produces a sheet of paper out of the pile in front of him. He looks it over carefully and passes it to me across the table. I reach my hand out as the paper glides toward me.

Righting it, I see a photo of myself. It's my official photo given to media outlets. I'm posing formally with my arms crossed over my chest. The picture was taken in my office with me standing behind my desk. It was meant to make me look commanding, but what's drawn on my face takes any of that thought away. An unmistakable bull's-eye is printed over my face, marking me like a target from a firing range. To say this photo is unsettling would be an understatement; it clearly shows Simon's hatred for me.

"We know he was fired from your company two days ago, or left to pursue other interests. I believe that's the more corporate way of putting it." He stops and laughs at himself. The other detective joins in with a slight chuckle. It's a dueling pair of comedians.

"Get on with it, gentlemen." I say as these two are really starting to piss me off. I can feel my temper starting to flare.

"Or course, initially we believed he acted out of revenge for your company firing him. However, we interviewed his ex-fiancée today, and a new development took us down another road, so to speak."

"What kind of development?" Why do I feel like Baker wants a pound of flesh from me? I'm the injured—or least the endangered—party in this matter. The road he's leading me down makes me wonder what he found out from the ex-fiancée. My side of the table remains silent for now.

"Here's a photo of Marta Llewellyn, Mr. Edwards' ex-fiancée." Again we do the shuffle and pass with the photo. I take the photo in my hand and see a stunning woman. Straight blond hair hanging down to her breasts. The dress she's wearing is cut dangerously low, exposing what appear to be a pair of large surgically enhanced breasts. Glancing back up to her face, her brown eyes have a scheming nature to them. After dealing with so many women, I've learned to be leery of that look, as it usually spells trouble.

"I've never met Ms. Llewellyn," I remark after viewing the photo and setting it aside. "What does she have to do with Simon going crazy?"

"Are you sure you've never met her?" Baker asks with a definite gotcha attitude, like he's trying to outsmart me. This man totally has it out for me. There is no disguising it now. I glance at my attorneys, who both have puzzled looks on their faces.

"No, I've never met her before," I say emphatically.

"You have a home in the Hamptons, correct?" Baker already knows the answer to his question; it's public information. Any detective worth his salt would know this fact.

"You know I do," I say with a snap back at Baker. I feel the hand of Rhodes, my attorney, on my arm, giving me a subtle but unmistakable hint to keep my shit together. I turn to Rhodes and convey a look meant to tell him I'll control my temper.

"Well, Ms. Llewellyn remembers meeting you. About a year ago, last June, to be more precise. There was a Parrish Art Museum benefit at a large estate in the Hamptons that you both attended. I've confirmed with the museum's benefit committee that both of you were in attendance at the event."

"I said I have no recollection of ever meeting her. I may have been there; I'm a major contributor to the Parrish. I also have a house in the Hamptons. During the season, I'm out at there often. I usually attend two similar events per weekend."

"She had this photo of the two of you." Baker quickly hands me another photo. I gaze at the image, still not familiar with the woman. Rhodes seizes the photo from me.

"Detective Baker, I think you've made your point clear on the facts of my client and this woman being at the same event. Could you please get to the point of this discussion?" Rhodes speaks with an air of superiority and confidence.

"The long and the short of it?" Baker looks at us from his side of the table, his shoulders pushed back, his back ramrod straight. "Your client, Mr. Kingsley, allegedly took this woman home for the night, or I should say for an hour or so, after the event. Then he proceeded to, as Ms. Llewellyn explained it, 'fuck her brains out in his study'."

What the hell? I recall fucking many women in my study in the Hamptons last summer, but not a single face or body stands out to me. So what the detective is proclaiming could be true.

"Ms. Llewellyn said she believes Mr. Kingsley and she had some kind connection that night. One that was never fully explored since she left shortly after the act, due to Mr. Kingsley needing to take a conference call." Baker is definitely mocking me and poking fun at my excuse to get the woman out of my house. "Supposedly, she snapped these photos of your bathroom before your driver took her home."

Rhodes takes the photo from Baker and places it on the table in front of me. I see my guest bathroom, the one closest to my study. The details are still hazy, but there's no denying it now. I nod to Rhodes in confirmation that it is indeed as the detective says.

Baker rubs his fingers across his chin. His attitude toward me remains condescending, but under the circumstances, what is my defense? "Ms. Llewellyn appears to have been hell-bent on meeting Mr. Kingsley again. So much so that she lured Mr. Edwards into a relationship in hopes of getting close to Mr. Kingsley."

"She appears to be obsessed with Mr. Kingsley. When a dinner date with Mr. Kingsley, her then-fiancée, Edwards, and herself didn't happen, she'd had enough and broke off the engagement. Vowing to meet Mr. Kingsley some other way."

Shit, shit, shit. The missing pieces of the puzzle have become crystal clear to me, and the reality I'm confronted with reveals the selfishness of my actions. Everything I've been facing over the last few days is the result of my own behavior. Granted the girl is nuts, but if I'd never fucked and dumped her, these officers wouldn't be here grilling me now. I'm to blame for setting the wheels in motion.

"We asked Ms. Llewellyn if she told Edwards the true reason why she broke up with him. She told him everything down to the last detail. It seems as though Mr. Edwards blames you." Baker nods his head in my direction with his brows knitted together in a scowl. "Apparently, he cracked when he realized she was using him to get to you. She gave us some emails he sent to her. It's clear he's hated you for years, even referencing you in their correspondence."

Another paper makes its way across the table, and I don't want to acknowledge it. I'd prefer this interview to be over, and the detective, along with his cohort, gone from my sight.

"This printout is the last email Edwards sent to Ms. Llewellyn. There is no doubt in our mind he had some type of mental breakdown and is determined to get at Mr. Kingsley."

The rest of the interview is a blur to me. I feel overwhelmed with guilt and remorse for my choices. Unaccustomed feelings for someone so used to instant gratification and impenitence. But it was true, I was careless and cared for no one but myself. Now someone I've known for almost half my life wants me dead because he thought I took from him the most precious thing he ever had: his lover and future wife.

Finally the room is empty. The detectives and attorneys have left, and I'm alone with the detective's papers sitting in front of me, reminding me of my self-indulgence. I lean my elbows on the table and bury my head in my hands. Not remembering the woman's face and the intimate acts I did with her sickens me, but I know she's just one of many I've used and forgotten. Other than my beautiful Kathryn, there isn't a fuck I'm proud of. What a fool I've been.

Chapter 19

The glow from the evening sun shines through my office windows. The view from the top floor of my building showcases the brilliant sunset as it flickers over the Hudson River. Normally, I stare in awe at the colors blazing across the horizon, but tonight I've moved far away from the display and the conference table with its incriminating evidence. Instead I've found a soft couch and a bottle of scotch to keep me company as I hide from the world. The couch is comfortable; the scotch is a familiar and numbing friend.

I rest my feet on the coffee table in front of me and lay my head back over the top of the couch as I await a call from Kathryn. I sent her a text around six thirty, hoping she might be able to meet me earlier than we discussed. She returned my text promptly, saying she would call me in about thirty minutes. The time is now ten after seven, and my palms sweat as I itch to call her. I pour myself another glass of scotch, very conscious that waiting is a game I'm not accustomed to playing.

Holding my phone in my hand, I feel it begin to buzz. I sit up straight, removing my feet from the table, and look down at the phone and see the photo of Kathryn I took earlier in the day filling the screen.

"Kathryn," I say her name quietly as my voice strains from all the tension I'm under.

"Kingsley, is everything okay? You sound funny." I hear the concern in her voice and close my eyes as I realize she does truly care about me. At this moment, she may be the only person in the world who does.

"The police were here earlier and…" I can't seem to tell her what I learned today about myself and Simon's motive for wanting me dead. "I need to see you."

"You're scaring me." Now her voice reflects a touch of fear, but I don't want her worrying about me.

"I know what's behind Simon's actions now." Without giving her the ugly specifics, I say, "But I'd rather talk to you about it in person."

"Of course. You're not in more danger now, are you?"

"No, the police are convinced Simon has fled to Canada, and until they know he's back on American soil, the case has been put on hold."

After enduring the detectives' attitude toward me, I'm convinced they feel I've brought Simon's revenge upon myself and don't care to waste their time going through the hassle of working with the Canadian authorities.

"Well, that's good news he's not in the area at least. But something else is bothering you. What aren't you telling me?"

"It's the motive behind Simon's actions. It's not what I expected at all. Where are you now?"

"I'm close to The Pierre at the Rose Club bar in The Plaza." She's only a few blocks from my penthouse, and I sigh in relief as my mind forms a plan.

"Let's meet at The Pierre. On 61st Street there's rose-colored marble accenting one of the hotel's entrances. Enter there through the revolving doors, and once you're inside the lobby head straight toward the back wall. You'll see a seating area with red velvet chairs ahead of you. Sit down in one of them and face the lobby entrance. You won't be able to miss me when I arrive; I'm sure you'll notice Goliath, my bodyguard, first. Join me when you see us walking closer to you. We'll ride up the elevator together."

"Are you sure it's okay?"

"Yes, my security guy has been working at The Pierre all day. The inside is likely safer than the White House."

"It will only take me a few minutes to walk there. Are you still at your office?"

"Yes, but I'm leaving now." I rise up from the couch, grab my discarded suit coat off a nearby chair, and head to my office's outside door. I can't decide whether to bring the papers on the conference table or not. For now I think it's best to leave them. What I have to say to Kathryn won't need a picture.

"Then I'll see you in a few minutes. And Kingsley, everything's going to be all right."

"Thanks, beautiful. I hope you're right."

Her words soothe me and give me hope. She has no idea how I long for them to be true. But for now, I have to face the reality of the situation. Simon's loose, and until he's caught I'll always be looking over my shoulder. My carefree lifestyle, with its laissez-faire freedom, is gone.

I'd love to take Kathryn out for an elegant dinner tonight. Nothing would make me happier than to parade her on my arm. But for now my apartment will have to be our meeting place.

Heading out of my office, I see Eddie and Goliath playing cards on top of Mrs. Carter's abandoned desk. Eddie is seated in Mrs. Carter's chair, and his brow furrows as he concentrates on the cards in his hand. Goliath is perched on the edge of the desk. He too appears consumed by the game, and neither of them moves a muscle as I stand there observing them.

I pull the door closed behind me; the handle makes a clicking sound against the metal, startling them. Their eyes shoot up from their amusement, and on reflex they immediately stand when they see it's me. Goliath walks toward me as Eddie nervously stuffs the cards back into the box.

"Mr. Kingsley." Stopping in front of me, Goliath towers over me; his expression is unreadable. "Finished for the day, sir?"

"Yes, I'm ready to leave." I have spoken no truer words today, as I can't wait to get the hell out of here, especially knowing that Kathryn is waiting for me.

Goliath takes longs strides as he leads the way to the elevators. Eddie and I dutifully follow behind him since Goliath is in charge of getting me safely to my next destination. And as annoying as it is having someone shadowing my every move, I'll just have to get used to it for now, because my gut feeling is that Simon will be on the loose for a while with no one actively pursuing him.

The police insinuated the case is in limbo until Simon returns to American soil, so I need to discuss an alternative plan with Peters. Perhaps he can hire someone to search for Simon in Canada. It's amazing what money can do, and I'd be willing to pay a king's ransom to have my freedom back.

On the way to my penthouse, I give Tom a call. He was off work today to stay home with Lois and make sure she was fully recovered from the trauma of Simon's attack on them last night.

"Adam. " Tom seems to be in a good spirits. I breathe a sigh of relief hoping this means Lois is doing all right. To think a stupid choice on my part could've killed them makes me ill.

"Just checking in with you to see how Lois is doing." I pause and wait for him to answer. I hear what sounds like the heels of Tom's shoes clicking against tiles.

"Sorry, I needed to step away from Lois. I've tried to avoid talking about last night unless she brings up the subject. But she's doing fine. After we left the library last night, she calmed down. I think it was the initial shock of Simon firing the gun at us, followed by his threats. It was too much for her."

"Hell, it's too much for anyone. I'm relieved she's doing okay. Especially in her condition, and what she's already been through…" I don't finish my statement, but Tom knows what I'm implying.

"I took her to her favorite restaurant for lunch, followed by a mini-shopping spree at Barney's. She's just starting to show and needs new clothes. Overall, I think she's doing fine. So don't worry." He clears his throat. "Did you find out anything more about Simon? The news didn't cover it tonight, so I wasn't sure."

Hell, how do I answer Tom's question and tell him what I found out today? Normally, we meet at nine each Saturday morning for a game or two of squash, but obviously that's not happening tomorrow. I feel like what I need to say to him should be done in person. The details I have to disclose aren't going to be welcomed, and I sure as hell don't want to spoil his current good mood.

"He's still on the loose for now." I leave out the facts about Simon's motive. "I can't meet for squash tomorrow morning. Too public. How about meeting me at the office tomorrow at nine instead?"

"Sure thing," Tom replies quickly. "I better get back to Lois. She's trying to decide between Chinese or Italian for take-out.

And in pursuit of domestic harmony, I agreed to watch one of her chick flicks."

"Have fun," I say with a chuckle, but mostly I'm laughing at myself. A couple of days ago, I would have made a jab at Tom. Telling him how Lois has him wrapped around her finger, but now I get it. Kathryn has me under the same spell.

As Eddie makes a left off Madison Avenue onto 61st Street, Goliath tries to swivel in the front seat and turn around to see me. It's almost comical watching his giant frame twist.

"Sir, let's go over our plan for exiting the car and entering the building."

Who knew that opening the door and getting out on my own would be a luxury?

"I'll exit the vehicle first. Do a quick scan of the sidewalk and those standing around the entrance. Once I'm convinced the coast is clear, I will open your door. You need to exit quickly when I do, so be prepared to step out. Skip the revolving doors; we will use the set of doors to the right of them."

"Sounds simple enough. I have a friend, Kathryn Delcour, meeting us in the lobby. I stayed with her last night when Peters said I couldn't go home. She's no danger to me."

Eddie catches my eye as he looks into the rearview mirror. He gives me a big smile at the mention of Kathryn's name. He knows what I'm doing with Kathryn is out of the norm for me. Same woman two days in a row is a record breaker.

"Will she be going up to your penthouse with us?" Goliath asks, now facing forward and appearing more comfortable in the front seat.

"Yes," I say quickly with one simple word. I don't care to discuss any other matters concerning Kathryn with him.

I can see the entrance for The Pierre through the front windshield. We are almost there. I feel the anticipation building knowing Kathryn is only moments away from my sight, and as soon as the elevator doors close, my arms will be wrapped around her.

Eddie begins to stop the car in front of the entrance, and Goliath is out the door before the wheels quit turning. He's in full-on bodyguard mode now as he walks around the car to the door closest the sidewalk. He motions one of the doormen away from the car with his arm, indicating he has things covered and needs no assistance from them.

Goliath opens the passenger door after scanning up and down the street. I do as he instructed and exit quickly. With hurried steps, we make our way toward the building's entrance. Once inside the lobby, I glance in front of me looking for my reward, and I make out Kathryn in the distance. But people are traipsing through the lobby, walking through my line of sight and partially blocking her from my view.

Finally I've passed the hustle and bustle of the front desk and our eyes connect. The buzz I feel whenever I'm in her presence begins again. I'm pulled across the carpeted floor to her. Poor Goliath is having a hard time keeping up with me, but I give him no mind at all, because the only thing on my mind now is Kathryn.

Gracefully, she stands and begins walking toward me. She looks stunning in a black wrap dress that hugs her every curve. The gap narrows between us until I'm beside her.

"Hey, beautiful." My heart races as I extend my arm and take her delicate hand in mine. I feel her fingers enclose around mine and give my hand a gentle squeeze. Who knew a simple touch could help calm me? But it does.

"Hi, Kingsley." She smiles up at me, and its brilliance dazzles me, leaving me breathless. I run my fingers through the hair lying over her shoulder, righting a strand that's going astray.

"Excuse me, Mr. Kingsley, but we need to proceed to the elevators." Oh, yes, I almost forgot Goliath.

"Of course," I say through clenched teeth, upset that our perfect reunion was interrupted. "We'll follow you."

"At your side is best," Goliath mutters to me.

"Kathryn, I'd like for you to meet Jordan Hayes, my bodyguard and shadow." I introduce him with a stab at some humor; it seemed to work when I called him Goliath to his face earlier.

"Nice to meet you, Mr. Hayes." Kathryn reaches out her hand to Goliath. Being no fool, he takes it in his own for a quick shake. It's not every day a beautiful woman like her is in your presence.

After the quick exchange, Goliath returns to guard mode, looking around the area for good measure. Kathryn and I walk hand in hand toward the elevator with Goliath escorting us. He's standing awkwardly close to me with his hand behind my back in a protective move. So much for being discreet; his purpose of protecting me is likely clear to everyone's eye.

We stand before the elevator and wait for the car to descend to the main floor. I rub my thumb gently over Kathryn's hand as we gaze into each other's eyes. Even though I've had a shitty day, there's still something primal between us, and I can't help wanting to get lost in her embrace.

We step into the elevator, and Goliath bugs off a couple that want to ride up with us. He appears obsessed with controlling the situation. I produce the key that overrides the keypad and insert it into its lock. Now I can successfully push the button for my floor. The residents and a few workers are the only ones with access to the floor I live on. It keeps curious hotel guests from wandering around where they're not invited.

We are standing behind Goliath as he faces the door. He insists on being the first off. Once the car begins to ascend, I turn my attention back to Kathryn and rejoin our hands. But handholding simply isn't enough for me, and I sweep her small form into my arms, crushing her to me. I bury my nose into her hair and breathe deeply. Her scent, the perfume I love, fills my lungs, and I feel the day's stresses fading away for a second.

"Why does it seem like days since I've seen you?" I murmur quietly in her ear. The weariness I feel can't be hidden.

She doesn't answer my question with words; instead she pushes herself closer against my body, telling me all I need to know with her actions.

We stand in this position quietly embracing each other, rocking from side to side, until the elevator doors open up onto my floor. Momentarily, I almost forget about my troubles.

I give her a quick kiss on the forehead as we reluctantly pull apart and prepare to exit. My penthouse is one of only two residences on the top floor, so we turn to the right and make our way down the long hallway to my door. Goliath, my constant shadow, for once follows behind us.

"Are you sure you're okay, Kingsley? You seem so different to me. Sad, actually." Kathryn gazes at me; her brows knitted together in concern.

"It's been a hell of an afternoon. I'll tell you all about it once we're inside my apartment and settled." I squeeze her hand in reassurance.

As I unlock my door, I see a surveillance camera perched above my door. Peters must have installed it today; another sign he's doing his job.

We walk into the foyer and are greeted by Peters himself. He's all grins when he sees Kathryn with me.

"Hello, Peters." I wrap my arm around Kathryn's shoulder and draw her to my side in a definite 'she's mine' move. Peters isn't fooled and chuckles to himself. Likely shocked to see me being openly affectionate to a woman. He's known me for years, and this type of behavior isn't anything he's seen before.

"This is Kathryn Delcour. Kathryn, this is John Peters, my security expert." I want to say, 'and pain in the ass,' but I refrain and keep it civil. After all, he's doing a good job trying to keep me safe, even if he insists on having a giant follow me around.

"Nice to meet you, Mrs. Delcour."

"Nice to meet you, too," Kathryn replies as she stands poised and perfect in my living room. Outshining all the expensive artwork surrounding us.

Peters turns to me and puts on his serious business face, as the introductions are over. "I'm going to get Hayes settled in the guest room off the kitchen. He'll be staying here for the time being. I've set up cameras and a closed circuit television network for your residence, the hotel's lobby, and the sidewalk in front of the entrance. Also I've made sure the hotel's employees, especially the doormen, as they're our first line of defense, have copies of Simon's photo.

"I trust you'll do what you feel is necessary, but I'd appreciate it if you'd remember I want to have a life of some kind." I try not to come across bitter, but I can't mask it. Being a virtual prisoner in my own house upsets me. Fuck, the whole ordeal has me on edge.

"I'll try to make all the changes as painless as possible. But for now you need to stay out of public places. I'll handle getting Hayes familiar with things from here. You two enjoy the rest of your evening. Hayes and I will make ourselves scarce." Peters effectively dismisses us and motions to have Goliath follow him toward the kitchen. I'm thankful to be free and finally have some time alone with Kathryn.

With our hands still joined, I steer Kathryn toward my bar. It's off the main room on the way to my study. Fuck, I'm avoiding that room at all costs as the memory of today's interview comes back to my mind.

"How about a drink or glass of wine?" My voice still sounds tight as we stand before my vast supply of alcohol. I grab a bottle of Glenlivet and pour a glass.

"I'd love a gin and tonic. Bombay Sapphire if you have it."

"You bet. One gin and tonic for the lovely lady."

I give her a quick kiss on the cheek when I hand her the drink. But she's observing me with a keen eye, likely wondering what's up with me. I know it's time to talk to her about Simon, but I'm apprehensive, a new feeling for me. The confident, I-can-take-on–the-world Adam has seemed to escape me.

"Let's go to my bedroom so we can talk." She raises her brow at my suggestion. But for once the word bedroom doesn't bring sex to my mind. "I'm serious—about talking."

"And I'm here to listen, Kingsley." She gives me a quick kiss. "I can tell you have a lot on your mind. I've been worried about you since our phone call." Her eyes are full of compassion, and I realize it's exactly what I need right now.

Chapter 20

Holding my glass of scotch, I place my free hand on the small of Kathryn's back and guide her down the hallway to my bedroom. My Italian dress shoes hit the teak wood floors making a heavy sound as I walk, reflecting my mood. I don't stop along the way to show her the various rooms. One blends into another until we enter my bedroom suite at the end of the hall. I don't turn on the lights, preferring to speak my secrets in the dark like a coward. The room is full of shadows as the city lights filter through the windows, giving enough light to illuminate our way in the room.

The bedroom is modern and sparsely decorated but large at nearly twelve hundred square feet. My favorite part of the room, and my penthouse for that matter, is the room's wall of windows, giving me a million-dollar view out onto Central Park.

I take her hand and walk to the glass wall more out of habit than for any other reason. It always fascinates me to see the lack of materialism found in Central Park, especially in a city that's built on it. The view I have here calms me. It's so far removed from the hustle and bustle of my life.

"I'll never tire of this view. It's incredible," she says while gazing out the windows with me and placing her palm against the solid glass.

"It's nothing compared to you." I draw her closer, careful not to spill my drink, as she wraps her arms around my waist.

"Thanks, Kingsley. That was sweet, and maybe a little cheesy." She looks up at me with laughter in her eyes. "I haven't seen much of that cocky, rich player since we met two nights ago."

Kathryn starts unbuttoning my shirt in the area over my chest. After releasing a couple buttons, she separates the material and lays soft kisses on my exposed skin. I groan at the tingling sensation of her touch.

"Oh, Kathryn, the things I want to do to you. But I swear this isn't why I brought you in here."

"I know. There will be time to talk. I want to touch you, and I think you need it, too."

I can't disagree. Her touch lifted a weight off me last night, and I need to go back to the same place of peace again. I'm convinced only Kathryn has the power to take away the hollow feeling I have inside. She's my miracle worker.

I should pull myself away, take her hands off me and tell her what I learned about Simon and myself, but my will to stop her isn't there. Selfishly, I crave her healing touch more than I need to confess my misdeeds to her.

In complete surrender, I close my eyes and tilt my head back as she removes my tie.

"Let me have your drink." Kathryn takes my untouched scotch and sets it down on the side table where she put her own drink.

Kathryn turns back to me, her eyes blazing. Even in the semi-darkness of the evening, her blue eyes seem to burn seductively. The same hunger I feel for her is mirrored back at me in her eyes. There's no denying the chemistry we have; it practically glows like a flame between us.

She places her hands on my shoulders and slips my jacket down my arms. She glances down toward my belt and starts to unbuckle it. Kathryn grabs onto my buckle and roughly pulls the leather through the loops of my pants. My belt is tossed aside, joining my jacket on the floor. Her actions are possessive and hot. My cock stands fully erect as she pulls my shirttail out of my pants.

Needing to feel her, too, I run my fingers through her hair and lean down to press my lips to the top of her head, kissing her silky hair. Her spicy scent swirls all around me. Closing my eyes, I feel the usual rush hit me when I breathe in her perfume.

Kathryn glides her fingers over my chest through my open shirt with featherlight touches. She parts the shirt further and takes one of my nipples into her mouth. The sensation drives me wild, and I wrap my arms around her and pull her to me as uncontrollable desire fires through my veins.

I place my fingers under her chin and tilt her head up so she's looking at me. She glances at my lips, and I answer by lowering my lips to hers. We share a scorching kiss, our tongues weaving and dancing together.

"Kathryn," I mumble against her lips. "I want to make love to you."

Make love. Two simple words, but ones I've never uttered to a woman before. Until Kathryn, I've never wanted to worship a women's body and please her in every possible way.

"Please, Kingsley." Her voice sounds weak with need, and I know in this intimate moment she owns me, and I'll do anything she asks of me. Every part of me, but mostly my once-closed-off heart. The heart I forgot I even had.

Taking her hand, I lead her to my bed and gently turn her so she's facing me. I reach for the ties of her wrap dress and slowly unfasten them. Kathryn's breathing becomes labored and her breasts rise and fall in anticipation. But I want to take my time tonight. I plan to savor every detail of our lovemaking.

Much like how she removed my jacket, I ease the dress off her shoulders and let it pool onto the ground. Kathryn stands before me in white lace panties and a matching bra that have a silver threading weaved into them. The cool silver threads catch enough light to glimmer in the darkness, giving her an ethereal appearance. A sexy angel sent from heaven above to rescue me, my very own Eve.

I circle my arms around her ribcage as my fingers find the hooks to her bra and gingerly slide the straps down her arms. Her breasts are so full and round, her nipples so ready. I close my mouth over one of her nipples. Kathryn places her hands on my head, pulling me closer, and then moans softly as I continue sucking and toying with her. God I love how responsive she is to me. I switch to her other breast, giving it the same attention, and hear the same sounds of pleasure coming from her lips.

I kiss my way down her stomach, and I go to me knees before her. She feels like velvet, so soft and delicate against my lips. Kathryn's muscles contract in expectancy as I get closer to her sex. With two fingers hooking around the elastic, I ease her panties down her legs, inch by inch. My actions are deliberate and torturously slow.

Kathryn starts muttering. "Please, please." A pleading chant as I kiss her hipbone. I lick her skin, teasing my tongue across her stomach as I make my way down to her pussy. The scent of her arousal fills my nose and my dick becomes even harder. Everything about this captivating woman, her scent, her touch, and her beautiful body, turns me on.

With her hands still on my head, she guides me lower until I'm able to push my tongue through the lips of her sex and find her swollen clit.

"God, Kingsley. Yes. Like that." She tugs almost painfully at my hair.

Kathryn's legs begin to tremble as her climax nears. Protectively, I wrap my hands around her legs, trying to hold her up, but she is still in her heels and teetering on the verge of collapse. To help anchor her to me, I carefully raise one of her legs and bring it over my shoulder. I never lose contact with her clit, causing her whole body to shake even more.

For a woman who likes the gentleness of Tantra, she sure as hell has no problem with rough oral sex. And I aim to please her desires by sucking, licking, and touching her sex with my teeth.

I remember what tipped her over the edge this morning, so I place my fingers inside her, then add a little twist and rub over her G-spot. After a couple of passes with my fingers, Kathryn comes undone, her muscles tightening and clenching against my fingers.

I gaze up at her as she continues to ride the wave of her orgasm. Her beautiful face displays the pleasure I've given her. Her eyes close tightly and she moans through her high.

Kathryn collapses back onto my bed, panting, with her arms thrown above her head. Her hair is a mess of tangles over her face, but there is a definite smile of satisfaction on her lips.

Nothing could make me happier knowing I've put that look on her face. I'm learning the power of giving in sex, and it's a fucking mighty feeling when you know it's someone you…

Was I really about to slip and say that word? Even in my own head, I'm surprised at the level of deep feelings I have for Kathryn. But I can't really put what I feel for her into words yet.

To be in like doesn't seem strong enough. But to be in love? How could that even be possible? I've only known her a few days.

I'll settle on her being the person who means the most to me in this whole damn world. I'll debate the L words later. For now I just want her to be mine.

The bedroom is silent except for Kathryn's heavy breathing as she catches her breath and stretches out across my bed. Having risen off my knees, I'm standing at the bed's edge and begin removing my clothes, but my eyes never leave the beautiful woman in front of me with a content smile gracing her face. I return it because I feel the same. Content that my woman is satisfied and feeling blissed in her afterglow.

"I think you enjoyed that… a lot."

"Pretty sure of yourself." She smirks at me and raises up on her elbows, making her breasts jut out at me. And all I want to do is get my damn pants off and join her on the bed. "But then again, I don't remember it being like that. Maybe it's just been so long... "

Her reply makes the memory of her late husband come to mind. It's a fleeting thought, but I still wonder why she chose me? It seems impossible this sensuous woman hasn't been with a man fully since his death.

"I hope it was worth the wait." I take off my pants and socks and quickly add them to the pile by the bed.

"You have no idea. I think I'm sleeping with an oral expert." Her teasing is laced with dead seriousness, which surprises me. In my selfish sexual exploits, giving oral was something I did sparingly. I took more than I gave.

"Well, I can say the same about you, beautiful. No one compares or even comes close." I remove my boxers, the last bit of clothing I'm wearing, and I stand fully erect in front her. "Can I join you?"

Kathryn eyes my erection and hungrily licks her lips. I stroke myself a couple of times, pumping my cock. "See something you want?"

"Yes, but we need a condom."

I grab one from the unopened box in the nightstand, and when I turn around to face Kathryn, I'm expecting her to be eagerly awaiting me. Instead she has a questioning glint in her eye, and I wonder what I've done. She asked for the condom and I gave no resistance even though she knows I'd rather not use one. I'm sure as hell not going to press that point again tonight.

I respond to her with my own questioning look.

"So, you've never had another woman in your bedroom, but you have condoms by your bed?" She tosses back her head defiantly and stares at me speculatively. Her tone is pointed, and I'm completely blindsided by her remark.

"I bought them a year ago when I moved in. They're probably older than the ones in your drawer." I dig the box from my nightstand and hand it to her. "Here, you can count them if you'd like. There should be thirty-six, counting the one in my hand."

She peers into the box and sees it is indeed full. I hope the full box will convince her of the truth.

"You're the only woman I've brought to my place and definitely the only one who's been in my bed. There's been no one else, only you." My voice is low and serious as I try to make my case that she's it.

"You sound sincere." She's appraising me. "I guess I'll believe you. Maybe I'm easily convinced after that orgasm."

I exhale the breath I was holding, and she laughs that melodic giggle I love while handing the box back to me.

One trust disaster avoided. I breathe a giant sigh of relief as I stuff the box away in the drawer, minus one condom, of course.

She throws the black comforter back, pulling it completely off the bed. Gracefully easing herself up the bed, Kathryn lays her head on one of my pillows and turns toward me. Invitingly, she pats my side of the bed, and I climb in next to her, turning on my side to mirror her position. Kathryn stares deeply into my eyes as if she's searching my soul.

The room is quiet. And in this still moment, something shifts between us. Even though we are naked and ready, sex becomes the furthest thing on my mind. It's then I know the time has come for me to tell her about Simon. The delay has been long enough; there are no excuses or reasons left other than my cowardice, and she deserves to know the truth.

Her hair spills over the white pillowcase in a black stream. Unable to keep my hands to myself, I twist a raven strand around my index finger. It grounds me to her and gives me the strength to begin a story I'm not one fucking bit proud of.

"The detectives came to my office today to interview me about Simon." She's gazing with concern, hearing the wavering in my voice.

I start at the beginning: The night I met Marta Llewellyn in the Hamptons and how it was just a normal, common hook-up for me. One so ordinary I couldn't even remember her face, let alone her name. Not a single detail or fact is spared in my confession to her. She silently listens to me, as I pour out every damn detail. But to my relief she moves closer to me as I speak. I feared she'd do just the opposite and recoil in disappointment or even disgust. Because what she heard plays into what people have warned her about me, and I've hung myself with each word.

I finish and take a cleansing breath. She cups my chin in her hand, wanting my undivided attention. When I look into her eyes, what I find is complete understanding, not condemnation.

"What you did that evening was disgraceful and cheap, and obviously a horrible decision. I'll never understand that part of your life. But the woman agreed to be with you, she understood." Kathryn caresses my arm with her fingertips. "She was wrong to believe there was more to you then casual sex."

"I suppose, but my actions got the whole ball rolling. Simon could've shot Tom or Lois, and I can't seem to shake that fact." I close my eyes, trying to clear the ugly thoughts from my mind.

"Look at me, Kingsley."

I open my eyes to see her peering at me intensely.

"Nothing happened to them, though. Yes, you made a choice to have sex with this woman, but she was malicious. She deceived a trusting man. Simon fell in love with her, but she knew the entire time he was just a means to an end as she hoped to get near you. To me that is pure evil. She took a person's heart and twisted it. But the final blame lies with Simon. Not you. He didn't just change on a dime; maybe the break-up triggered something. Judging by his actions, I think he's been out of touch with reality for longer than you realized, and her betrayal pushed him off the deep end."

"I've wondered what I missed with Simon. He's always been extremely private, keeping everything to himself. We met our freshman year at MIT; all four us, Tom, Simon, myself, and Patrick. We lived on the same floor. Studied together and dreamed big dreams. We were young, idealistic, and ambitious." I rest my hand on her hip and rub my thumb over her skin.

"Your dreams seem to have come true." Kathryn pats my arm reassuringly and looks pensive. "Did Simon date much in college or after? I'm wondering if he had a lot of experience with women and heartbreak."

"Not that I know of. Simon liked to be behind the scenes; he was quiet and not your typical college guy. Even back then, he stayed in on the weekends. We would study like mad all week and go apeshit wild on Saturday night. I honestly don't recall him dating anyone before his ex-fiancée." I run my fingers through my hair and close my eyes, briefly remembering how the guys and I ran the streets of Boston while running into many willing coeds along the way. "Occasionally, Simon would come out with us. But he'd always ended up going home alone after we, um, hooked-up with some girls."

"Typical college behavior, but it carried on way past college for you." Her tone and words scold me; even her eyes carry a rebuke in them. "But not typical for Simon. His behavior seems anti-social. I really do think he's had issues for a long time."

"Well, Dr. Kathryn, I think you're right about Simon. He was more than just shy. At times I felt like he loathed people." I place my arm around her waist and pull our bodies together. The silky sheets help her glide easily into my arms. I bury my face in her hair, breathing deeply while kissing her exposed shoulder. "Thanks for being here for me. I don't know where I'd be right now without you, likely alone and working my way through a bottle of scotch."

"I'm here for you, Kingsley," she softly mutters while I nuzzle her neck and feel her fingers lightly scratching my back. Her encouragement and acceptance of me soothes me like a healing balm. I raise my head and brush a few strands of hair away from her face, then trace over her cheekbones with my fingertips.

"Thanks for not judging me and giving me a chance. I still wonder why you've let me into your life? Was it something your mother said?" I smile remembering how Mrs. Swanson attempted to play matchmaker with us the other night at the event.

"You know I'm a Vanderbilt, right?" I answer her with a shake of my head. Thanks to Peters' research, I knew this fact the first night we met. "I figured as much, you stalker. There appears to be something in my DNA that attracts bad boys. My mother, aunts, and cousins have all succumbed to one, however they managed to tame the tiger in them, too. The list of former bad boys in our family tree stretches for miles. I believe it's some mutated gene we Vanderbilt women carry."

"Beautiful, you don't have a mutated gene in this delectable body of yours." I run my hand down the front of her body, grazing the tips of a nipple, ending at the curve of her hip. Everything about her is simply perfection without a flaw or blemish. "Now me, on the other hand…"

"What about you?" She has no idea how loaded that question is. It's nothing short of a bomb waiting to be detonated. "I know nothing about your past or childhood. But you know everything about me."

She's gently trying to coax my life's story out of me, and I'll be damned, but I'm feeling like sharing it with her. If she could handle the craziness with Simon and didn't run away, that speaks volumes to me.

Maybe it's her training as a psychologist that has me opening up and talking to her. Although it's more likely she makes me feel safe and secure, because for the first time in ten years I'm willing to trust someone and crack open the door of my past.

And Kathryn's not just anyone; she's the woman who's given herself to me in every possible way. She led me through that intense Tantra session, and I felt a load literally slough off me.

Now it's time for her to know where those demons originated, and how my life was started on this earth.

"Kingsley, are you all right?" My back is to the glass windows letting in the city light. My position keeps my face in the shadows as we lie on the bed facing each other. She can't make out that I'm lost in thought as I contemplate how to start my story. I guess starting from the beginning and how I was conceived is the best.

Chapter 21

"If I tell you who my father is, then you'll understand why I'm the one with the mutated genes." I laugh half-heartedly, because there isn't a drop of humor in the facts surrounding my birth father. He's a cruel, selfish bastard. Before I start sharing the details, I place my hand on the small of her back and pull her tighter to me. I want to feel her skin against mine.

"My mother, Flora, was a beautiful woman, much like you." I bring my hand to her face and brush my knuckles against her cheek. Kathryn leans into my touch. "She studied at Parson's School of Design. The summer after she graduated, Vogue magazine offered her a job as an assistant to an assistant. Very low on the totem pole, but she had her foot in the door."

"Vogue held an event for the fashion industry soon after she started. That's where she met my, for lack of a better term, father. I don't know all the details surrounding their meeting, because I found out this information after my mother's death."

"Kingsley, I'm so sorry. How old were you when she died?" Now Kathryn is tracing her fingertips up and down my arm almost hypnotically, but even with her tender touch, I don't know if I can talk about this subject. Every time I even think about her death my heart races, and for years it's been the subject of all my nightmares. I turn over onto my back, sighing before I speak again. I need a few seconds to prepare myself.

"She died when I was twenty-two, right before I graduated from MIT." I take a deep breath and stare at the shadows dancing on the ceiling. "She called me on a Wednesday night saying she wanted to talk with me. It was unlike her to call mid-week due to my studies. Our usual calls were on Sunday night. Everything about our call seemed odd. Her voice was strained and weak. I kept asking if she was sick. She said she wasn't feeling well and likely wouldn't make it to my graduation the next week, saying she had a bad virus. But I wasn't buying it."

Kathryn moves closer to me and I tuck her into my side. She lays her hand above my heart and skates her fingers over my chest. I close my eyes to focus and absorb the power of her touch; the next part is the toughest.

"I hadn't been home once the entire semester, and I had this feeling in my gut something was up. She'd never miss my graduation. Not in a million years. She was the type of mother who came to every game, awards assembly, or band concert. So I hopped a shuttle flight on Friday from Boston to Philly. My finals were over and basically I was done at MIT."

Turning my head to Kathryn, I see her eyes filled with compassion, encouraging me to continue. I have to look away from her, because I can't face her goodness, knowing I was anything but good ten years ago.

"On the flight to Philly, a flight attendant shamelessly hit on me. She was pretty, so I returned her attention and flirted back. As she was preparing the cabin for landing, she slipped me a piece of paper with her name and hotel on it. She was staying at a downtown hotel near the airport and invited me to join her at the bar in an hour. I ended up going to her hotel. I stayed for a couple of hours. After I was finished, I left in a cab to my mother's house."

My chest starts to ache and my breathing becomes harsh as I get closer to the rough shit.

Dammit. Dammit. Dammit. I can't go back to this.

I shoot up straight on the bed as my heart starts to pound against my chest. Swinging my legs to the edge, I place my feet on the floor and vigorously run both my hands through my hair.

Bringing up these old memories during my waking hours is no different than when they visit me in nightmares. The same panicked reaction courses through me.

Kathryn scoots over the sheets toward me, her brows drawn together. The pain etched on her face is for me. No one, besides my mother, has ever shared in my pain, but having Kathryn here calms me down a bit.

"Kingsley." My name is a whisper on her lips; the pain I see on her face reflects in her voice.

"You don't have to tell me any more tonight." Kathryn moves to sit on the edge of the bed next to me. She places her small hand on my leg, and I cover it protectively with my own. I feel the connection between us in this simple touch.

"I need to tell you." I swallow hard. My throat feels parched and dry, and I wish I had my glass of scotch.

"When I arrived at my mother's house, the lights were off. The entire place was eerie. It wasn't even ten at night, so she should've been up. I called out to her and there wasn't a response. Just a still silence. I thought she might be in bed, so I hurried up the stairs. I switched on her bedroom light, and…" I pause trying to catch my breath and slow my heart down. My body is so geared up it feels like I just came off a five-mile run.

"She was lying on top of the bed's covers in one of her favorite dresses, but something was terribly wrong. Her hands were folded over her chest, and I glanced at her nightstand and saw some pills scattered over the top. It didn't seem possible, but I knew she swallowed some of them."

Kathryn wraps both of her hands around my single one. Her small gesture means so much to me.

"I'm at my mother's side in a second, and begin to shake her. But there's no response. In a panic, I pick up the bedside phone and dial 9-1-1. I can't tell you what I did until the paramedics arrived. They tried to revive her, but they were too late. They put her body on their gurney and covered her with a white sheet to take her away. 'The coroner said she'd only been dead about an hour. I might have been there to save her if I hadn't..." I'm unable to finish as I feel a couple small tears fall down my face. The first ones I've cried since her graveside.

"Kingsley, how horrible. I can't even imagine." She leans her head against my arm, and I glance over at her, wondering if my tears are hidden in the darkness.

"She had cancer; a Stage 4 Glioblastoma, an inoperable brain tumor like the one that killed Senator Kennedy. She didn't want to burden me with her terminal illness as she slowly died. So she took her own life. I'd planned to head to New York after graduation, and she feared I'd come back to Philly and take care of her instead. But I still can't shake the fact that I was fucking some strange woman while she was alone, dying." I lower my head in disgust at myself, wondering if Kathryn is disgusted with me, too.

"You can't blame yourself, Kingsley. You had no idea." I feel her giving me light kisses along my arm.

"How did I just find you now? Why couldn't you have come into my life ten years ago?" I release her hand and clutch her tight to me, never wanting to let her go.

"Hush, you sweet man. I'm here now." She runs her fingers through my hair and stops in the back where she twirls the ends around her fingers. I hum quietly, relishing in her soft touch.

"You don't know how much I need to hear that. I've never spoken about her death to anyone, just her attorney. He gave me a letter she'd written. He was instructed to give it to me after her death."

"So is this when you learned about your father?" I take a deep breath and plod on, knowing I've said all I can about her death tonight.

"Yes, for years I was told my father died shortly before I was born, but I found out that wasn't the case at all. Her attorney had a letter she'd written a couple days before she died." I close my eyes as I feel Kathryn trace her fingers tenderly across my back, helping me calm down.

"And in many ways, it wasn't a lie, because his only acknowledgement of my presence on this Earth was when he presented her with a check for ten million dollars. The only stipulation to cashing it was my mother had to sign away any legal recourse to sue him for more money. It was a paternity settlement, of sorts."

"I feel so sorry for your mother. And for you, too. How horrible to learn something like that after she was gone. The questions you must've had."

"You wouldn't believe the questions I had. They were endless. I'll never know the answers to them, either, because they're buried away with her forever."

"And because of this, it's difficult for you to put closure on her passing?" I nod. She's right, not having answers about my father and her death has kept me in limbo, unable to let go of those hard memories. I sigh deeply as she moves even closer to me, comforting me with her kindheartedness.

"Closure? That's something I will never have." I know the bitter truth of these words. Some things broken can't be fixed, and I'm convinced this applies to my situation.

"It's possible to have closure without having all the answers. The path isn't easy for this kind of healing, though. You would have to be willing to see a therapist. Talk through the past."

"Doubt that'll be happening anytime soon. There's no way I could talk to a complete stranger about this." The very thought makes my heart start racing.

"Sometimes talking to a stranger is easier than someone you know. Just something to think about, because I hate seeing you in such pain."

"I'll think about it." It's a vague promise I know I won't keep. Probably shitty of me, but I'm not ready for the psychiatrist couch yet.

"Good." She takes both of my hands in hers and gives them an encouraging little squeeze. "You do know who your father is. He must be a wealthy man to a give her such a large sum."

"Yes… the hush money." I laugh at the term, because it's anything but quiet to me. "He's wealthy and well-known. I've seen him at various functions, but I've made damn sure we've never officially met. I'm convinced he knows who I am, because he stops and stares at me with contempt when he sees me. I'm sure my look back at him is no different."

"So he still lives in the city and you see him? God, that has to be hard as hell, Kingsley."

"Well, it's difficult to hide from Xavier Thorpe, the mascot of New York City." Kathryn's entire body tenses up when I mention my father's name. I even feel her gripping my hand tighter. "What's the matter? Do you know him?"

"Yes, I know him." Her voice is shaky and she sighs while lowering her head. I sense she's not comfortable talking about him. Something odd we have in common it appears, but I don't know what it is. "Although I've not seen him since I was nineteen. I'm a close friend of his son."

"Oliver? Thorpe disowned him and exiled him to San Francisco when he came out, right?" She nods her head and a sad look crosses her face. Then a thought comes to my mind. She was meeting her gay best friend in town from San Francisco tonight. "Hey, the man you met for happy hour…"

"Yes, it was Oliver Thorpe." She bends over and wraps her arms around herself. She's clearly troubled by this conversation. "Ollie and I have been friends since we were… well I don't remember a time when I didn't know him. He's been in my life for that long."

"You two grew up together? It's unreal. What are the chances that you would even know my half-brother? What's Ollie like? Is he a good guy?" I lean down toward her, anxious to hear more. I've known about my half-brother since shortly after I learned who my own father really was. I've always been curious about him.

She's sitting back up straight now, but her arms are still around her waist. "Ollie's great and was there for me during the darkest period of my life." I wonder if she's referring to the death of her husband. "Maybe you could meet him someday? I don't want to push. But he'd love to know he has a brother. He's an only child, and I know you two have a lot in common where your X is concerned."

"Really? How so?"

"You both were exiled by your father. One for being conceived, the other for being gay." I can't understand how a man could be so cruel by rejecting his own offspring.

"I've watched Oliver's career out in Silicon Valley for years. He's done well for himself without the help of X. But I never wanted to intrude in his life. Maybe someday I could meet him. I have a few distant relatives, but I've not seen any of them since, well, since her death…"

"I'm sorry, Kingsley. You must've felt very alone all these years, especially during the holidays." She smiles warmly at me, understanding the loneliness of not having close family. Christmases have been hell. I try to go somewhere tropical to avoid the holiday every year. Palm trees and women strolling the beaches in barely-there bikinis help me forget what time of year it really is.

"What can one do?" I shrug because I know there isn't a fucking thing I can do to change things. "I still can't believe you know Oliver, I mean Ollie. I suppose you two did belong to the same social circles."

"Our mothers were friends when we were growing up." There is a troubled look in her eyes, as if the memory of their friendship is painful.

"Hmm. They were friends? Does that mean they aren't any longer?" Kathryn moves back up onto the pillows. Now I know I've hit the nail on the head.

"After my father's death, my mother and Ollie's quit being friends. Their friendship is irreparable." She gives nothing away with her brief comment. Only the bare facts, and it feels like the tables are turned and I'm talking to myself.

"I can see you like talking about the Thorpe's as much as I do." She smiles weakly at me, but it's a smile at least. "Maybe we've had enough talking for the night. I'm beat."

The truth is, my mind is more exhausted than my body. Emotionally, I'm completely spent. Kathryn moves over next to me and lays her head on my pillow. She turns her back to me and I fold my arm around her waist, pulling her flush against me.

"I'm tired, too. I can't remember the last time I've gone to bed this early. But we need our sleep, since I have hours and hours of Tantra planned for tomorrow."

"Damn, how am I supposed to sleep now that my mind is thinking about you as my sexy Tantra teacher?" I bury my head in her hair. The scent rushes to my lungs. Between smelling her perfume and the talk of Tantra, my cock gets rock hard and I push against her ass. The mention of her planned sexcapades causes a Pavlovian reaction; one I have no control over, an involuntary response around this vixen.

She moves her hips back against my erection. I respond by pushing forward into the softness of her ass, finding that my erection fits nicely between her. Her teasing stops after a few more pushes and pulls, when she flips herself around to face me and wraps her skilled fingers around my erection. Slowly stroking up and down, I groan loudly as she increases the speed of her hand's movement. Fuck, her touch is so good.

"Make love to me, Kingsley." Her voice is faint but needy. Even in the shadowy darkness, I can see the desire in her eyes.

"Lie back for me, beautiful." My voice is gravelly and rough as I anticipate the feel of sinking deep into her.

She responds immediately to my request and rolls onto her back, a raven-haired goddess waiting for me.

Reaching for the foil pack on the nightstand where I left it, I smile to myself because I didn't think sex was in the cards tonight after all we've discussed. I should've known better, though. No matter our mood, the sexual pull between us is too strong to ignore.

After rolling the condom on, I sit back on my knees. Kathryn has her legs slightly spread, watching as I prepare myself for her. I swallow hard when I see her fingers begin pulling at her nipples.

"Damn, those are mine," I practically growl as I fall forward between her legs and take one erect nipple into my mouth. She whimpers softly with need. Kathryn grabs hold of my hair, tightly pulling her fingers through it. The sensations I feel are driving me wild with need. I've never wanted to be with any woman like I do her.

I spread her legs farther with my hand and run my fingertips up her thighs. Feeling her shiver at my touch, I grasp my cock, and I begin to rub myself around her sex. Even under the condom, she feels slick and wet, and I feel no resistance as I brush myself against her.

I give a full lunge with my hips and she cries out when I push fully inside her. I close my eyes briefly to stay in control, as the feel of her around me is almost more than I can take. I'm falling deep and hard for this woman.

As she gyrates her hips beneath me, I ravish her with kisses. She returns my fervor and we imitate the circling of hips with our tongues. A hot and slow cadence of passion builds as I make love to her. I pull and twist one nipple with my fingers. When I give it a little pinch, she responds by pushing her hips firm against mine. Taking my cues from her actions, I drag my lips down her throat and to the other nipple.

"God, Kingsley." She moans and presses my head harder against her breast as I continue my onslaught

I'm getting close to coming and feel her legs starting to shake. Every time I've brought her to climax, her legs always react to the build-up first. It's been her trademark response signaling an impending orgasm.

"Look at me, Kathryn." I've pulled my mouth from her nipple and gaze down into her eyes. I slide my hand down, between us and find her clit. I work my fingers against her, watching the desire in her eyes to gauge how close she is to coming. The second I feel her tightening around my cock, I plunge deep and fast into her. She arches up into me and scratches her nails desperately against my back.

We release together, looking into each other's eyes. Watching her surrender to the pleasures I give her is so fucking powerful. I had no idea sex could be like this. In this moment I feel as if Kathryn and I are truly one.

I drop down and rest my elbows at her sides, keeping most of my weight from falling on her.

Once I catch my breath, I bring my lips to her ears.

"Thanks, beautiful," I murmur while kissing a trail from her ear to her throat. Finally, her breathing becomes slow and even, and I know she's drifting off to sleep.

While holding her I realize I've never wanted a woman to be mine before. Only mine. But I've never met a woman like Kathryn, either. My feelings for her are foreign and unrecognizable. Somewhere in the back of my mind, I wonder if I might be falling in love with her.

Chapter 22

A faint buzzing sound awakens me from my sleep. I rise from the bed to find the source and see our clothes in a pile on the floor by my bed. I discover my phone still in the pocket of my pants and illuminate the screen to see several missed calls and texts. The battery is low again. I shake my head realizing this beautiful woman totally distracts me and makes me forget the simplest parts of my daily routine.

However, her distraction has had a positive effect on me. I had another peaceful night of sleep. She may be the cure for my ten long years of insomnia.

Then again, I recall being awakened by a pair of sweet, hot hands rubbing all over my body last night. I smile remembering our nocturnal lovemaking and Kathryn's definite preference for being on top. I preferred it, too, because that position lets my hands be free to roam over her perfect body.

I glance over at Kathryn sleeping quietly in my bed. Her hair is a mess of black curls, and the sheets cover up to her hips as she lies on her back. Her full breasts are on display for me. She looks like an erotic Sleeping Beauty waiting to be awoken by her prince's kiss. I'd love to stay and kiss her, too, but I'll be late to see Tom if I don't start getting ready.

Deciding to let her sleep as long as possible, I take a quick and lonely shower. I throw on a pair of casual black pants, followed with a light gray cashmere sweater. It's still early enough in the spring to need something more than just a shirt to keep me warm.

When I finish getting ready, I head to the kitchen to make coffee for Kathryn and myself. I don't know how she likes hers prepared, so I put some cream and sugar in little containers and place them and our coffee cups on a tray to take them back to my bedroom.

Before I deliver her coffee, I tap on the door of the butler's bedroom off the kitchen to check in with Goliath. I need to confirm with him that I'll be leaving in a few minutes to head to my office.

"Come in." I hear Goliath's gruff voice calling to me from behind the door. After opening it, I see him sitting at a desk, fully ready for the day, dressed in all black, and analyzing three CCTV feeds in front of him.

"Good morning, Hayes. I'll be ready to leave in about ten minutes, maybe less. Eddie sent me a text stating he'll be here shortly. Did you receive one from him, as well?"

"I did and also one from Peters. Nothing new to report here. I've been watching the surveillance camera we set up in front of the building to make sure the area's secure when we're ready to leave."

I feel like this entire security thing is overkill, especially since all the leads trace Simon to being in Canada. But I'll put up with it all for now.

"All right, we'll meet you in the front foyer. Say in five to eight minutes." He nods and returns back to the screens in front of him. What a damn boring job. I'm thankful he is dedicated; I'd be going nuts in his shoes.

I stop back in the kitchen and pick up the breakfast tray with our coffee. When I enter my bedroom, it's like déjà vu, because the bed is empty and Kathryn's nowhere in sight. I set the tray on the smooth sheets and hear water running in the bathroom.

The door to the bathroom is ajar, and I peek through to see Kathryn reflected in one of the mirrors over the sink. She's bent over the sink, splashing water on her face. I step into the room and hand her a towel. She looks up and smiles brightly at me. What a sight to see in the morning.

"Thanks," she says, taking the towel from my hand.

"You're welcome." Patting it against her face, she quickly finishes and turns to me, naked from head to toe. What a lucky fucker I am to have a woman who is so carefree with her body.

"Good morning, beautiful."

I peruse her and watch her nipples harden. It's a heady feeling knowing my inspection can turn her on. I pull her into my arms; my hands run the length of her back, ending at her lovely ass. She brings her arms tightly around me and lays her head on my chest.

"I wish we had a little more time this morning." She has to feel my erection pressing against her and know the meaning behind my words. "But I need to meet Tom at the office in a few minutes."

She pulls her head away from my chest and looks up at me. I run my fingers over her soft cheek, fresh from just being washed.

"It's okay. I have a few errands to run. What time will you be done? Remember we have a Tantra date," she says as I raise my eyebrows at her and smirk.

"You think I'd forget that?" I press my erection against her. "Believe me when I say this, I can't fucking wait. I should be done by noon or sooner."

She reaches between us and palms me over the zipper of my pants. The pressure makes me groan and I throw my head back.

"You're going to kill me, beautiful." My voice is tight as my need for her courses through me. It's taking everything I have to keep from placing her on the bathroom counter and fucking her brains out.

"I better quit touching you. I know boys hate a prick tease." She bats her eyes at me.

"How many times have I been buried inside of you?" I raise my brows in a challenge. She gives a coy shrug at my question. "Exactly, there's been no teasing."

"Oh, Kingsley." She laughs and walks back into the bedroom. I follow behind, watching her sweet little ass sashay in front of me.

"Hey, any chance you might call me Adam one of these days? It's just four simple letters. I'm starting to think you're just being stubborn." Kathryn stops to scoop up her clothes and begins to put them on. Clothes should be a crime with a body like hers.

"I'm not stubborn, just careful." She winks. "We haven't even known each other a week. Seeing a woman for seven days will be an all-time record for you, wouldn't it?"

As usual I throw my hands up in surrender as she stands before me fully dressed and ready to leave. But I think she might be missing an important article of clothing.

"Commando?" I say when I see her panties still on the floor.

She stuffs them in her purse and answers my question with that one swift move. She smiles wickedly and walks toward me.

"I'd prefer to leave you knowing I didn't have anything underneath my dress."

"I think it's official. You're going to slowly kill me with sex."

"Oh, I'll make it worth dying for." She winks and runs a finger down my chest, stopping just below my belt.

"You like torturing me. Don't you?" My voice is unsteady and gravelly. She gives me a quick nod while biting her lip. Yes, it will be worth dying for.

We join Goliath in the foyer and head down to meet Eddie, who's waiting for us in front of my building. Kathryn and I are holding hands in the elevator, but we don't give Hayes quite the PDA scene we did last night.

The walk through The Pierre's lobby is uneventful. A few hotel quests are checking out at the desk, but the area is calm for a Saturday morning. We approach the double glass doors, skipping the revolving ones.

Through the glass, I see Eddie has the SUV. For some reason, knowing it's back from the being impounded by the police makes me feel that things in my life can return to normal. Time will tell, and I don't want to get my hopes up yet.

"I think you better come back to my place for Tantra. I don't know if I'm allowed to go out yet." I feel like a grounded teenager only able to go to work or be at home. "Is that okay?"

"Sure, don't worry about it. Remember, Tantra doesn't use any outside equipment. I'll just bring the body oils, and we can put your mattress on the floor."

I hold her hand tighter as I think of us rubbing some exotic smelling oil all over each other.

"Body oils?" She silently replies to my question by curling her lip up at me in a sexy smirk, and I know then that she is truly going to kill me.

Eddie stands by the limo with his hand on the open door, signaling it's time for me to say goodbye to Kathryn. Standing close to the back wheel, I pull Kathryn's body flush with mine and kiss her passionately. Out of the corner of my eye, I see Hayes backing up a foot or two to give us a little space.

Suddenly the beautiful woman I'm fervently kissing in my arms is gone. My arms are now empty. I open my eyes, and in a flash of movements I see a blonde man dressed in black, wrapping his arm around her as he brings a pistol up to her temple.

"What the fuck? Let go of her!" I scream at the man until I feel the muscles straining in my neck. Starting to lurch forward to get her away from this man, I stop dead in my tracks, because I know who the fuck has her.

Simon.

The fucker bleached his hair and is wearing sunglasses. I've known him since we were eighteen, so he can't hide from me behind the disguise.

"Simon, let her go!" I yell again, pleading. Kathryn looks at me in complete terror. I mouth the words, it will be okay, and hold up my hands as if I'm trying to reach out to her. Hayes stands next to me, but his gun remains concealed.

"Shut the fuck up, Adam. Or I'll shoot her. Not that you would even care. She's just another screw to you, I'm sure."

"No, she's not. She means the world to me."

"Well, isn't that something. It's time for you to listen to me." He presses the gun harder against Kathryn's temple. I'm physically ill but need to think. Keep a cool head. Try to find a way to get him to release her.

"Last summer, the woman I loved was one of your whores, Adam. You fucked her and don't even remember her, do you?

When I told you her name there was no recognition on your fucking face. None at all."

Simon is starting to pay less attention to Kathryn as he unloads his anger at me. I'm his true target, and she's just his pawn. I keep glancing back and forth between them, wanting to let Kathryn know that somehow it's all going to be okay. I'll make sure of it.

"Well, she sure as fuck remembers you. Wanted you desperately. So desperately that she used me to see you again. You. The man who fucks every woman in the city. Women drop to their knees at a snap of your finger. And finally I found someone who I thought wanted me. But. She. Wanted. You. So now I'm going to take something of yours." Simon finishes his tirade and focuses on the gun at Kathryn's head.

I hear Hayes yelling, but I have no time to wait. Instead I need to act and save Kathryn. A police sedan pulls up to the sidewalk with sirens blaring. Simon looks to his right, and in that split second I run full force straight into him.

Grabbing the arm holding the gun as I hit him, I pull it away so it's no longer pointing at Kathryn. Simon loosens his grip on her as I continue to struggle with him. Kathryn falls onto the ground as I scream for her to move away. Out of the corner of my eye, I see her scooting toward the limo.

As I'm fighting to get the gun out of Simon's hand, I feel one of his fingers moving against the trigger. An earsplitting blast is followed simultaneously by an inhuman pain in my side.

I cry out while falling to the ground. My shaking hands find the gritty sidewalk, and my arms try to hold me up. In front of me, Simon is raging and pointing his gun around in the air. I glance over my shoulder to check on Kathryn. I see her eyes wide in shock and her mouth forms a perfect "O" in a silent scream.

Simon moves closer to me. All I can do is try to block him from Kathryn and hold my hand out in front of me. A vain attempt to keep him at bay.

"Drop the gun," Hayes shouts the orders at Simon, but instead of complying Simon aims the pistol right at my head. I close my eyes waiting for the gun to fire off. Instead I hear a gunshot but oddly feel nothing hit me. My eyes snap open and see Simon lying in front of me with a bullet hole between his eyes. His sunglasses must've flown off because his lifeless eyes are staring right at me.

Hayes gets to me first and kneels down at my side. He pulls up my blood-soaked sweater and inspects my injury. Everything he's doing hurts like hell.

"You're going to be all right, Mr. Kingsley. Had two tours in Iraq and this isn't bad. More than a graze, but you'll be okay." Hayes places his jacket under my head for support.

"Thanks for… what you did," I say, gritting through the pain.

Kathryn appears above me as I lie on the sidewalk; tears are streaming down her soft cheeks.

"Beautiful, you're okay?" My voice is barely audible. She smiles weakly through her tears and gently caresses my cheek.

"You saved my life, Adam."

Finally, she says the one word I've longed to hear. My name. Adam.

To be continued…

For the Reader

Thank you for taking a chance on an independent author. I truly appreciate you choosing to buy and read my debut novel.

I'd love to hear from you too. Perhaps leave a review on Amazon, or a comment on my web site or Facebook page.
www.livmorris.com or http://www.facebook.com/livingwrite

You can also connect with me on twitter. It's a favorite of mine.
http://twitter.com/Living_Write

All the best,
Liv

Adam's Fall

The #2 book in the Touch of Tantra series
Due for release January 2014

About the Author

Liv Morris resides in Manhattan with her first and hopefully last husband. After relocating eleven times during his corporate career, she qualifies as a professional mover. Learning to bloom where she's planted, Liv brings her moving and life experiences to her writing.

Liv received a degree in communication from the University of Maryland. She has published five short stories in the Love in the City series. Her debut novel, Adam's Apple, is due for release this summer.

To learn more, visit: www.livmorris.com.

Other books available by Liv Morris

Love in the City Short Story Series

Magic at Macy's

Perfect Strangers

The Panty Dropper

The Love Handles Club

Drunk and Disorderly

Love in the City (The Complete Collection) Boxed Set

November 2013

The Touch of Tantra Series

Adam's Apple (Touch of Tantra #1)

July 2013

Temptation (Touch of Tantra #1.5)

December 2013

Adam's Fall (Touch of Tantra #2)

January 2014

Made in the USA
San Bernardino, CA
19 March 2014